D1168683

SISTER LIGHT, SISTER DARK

SISTER LIGHT, SISTER DARK

JANE YOLEN

TOR

A TOM DOHERTY ASSOCIATES BOOK
NEW YORK

For Jessica
who mothered the book
and for
Patty, Ann, Shulamith, Zane, and Kara
who nursed it along the way

Special thanks to Joyce Rankin, who
helped me write down the music of the Dales

SISTER LIGHT, SISTER DARK

A TOR BOOK
Published by Tom Doherty Associates, Inc.
49 West 24 Street
New York, NY 10010

Library of Congress Cataloging-in-Publication Data

Yolen, Jane.
    Sister Light, Sister Dark / Jane Yolen.—1st ed.
        p.   cm.
    "A TOR book."
    ISBN 0-312-93091-7
    I. Title.
PS3575.043S57 1988
813'.54—dc19   88-12177

First edition: October 1988
0 9 8 7 6 5 4 3 2 1

PROPHECY & EXEGESIS

And the prophet says a white babe with black eyes shall be born unto a virgin in the winter of the year. The ox in the field, the hound at the hearth, the bear in the cave, the cat in the tree, all, all shall bow before her, singing, "Holy, holy, holiest of sisters, who is both black and white, both dark and light, your coming is the beginning and it is the end." Three times shall her mother die and three times shall she be orphaned and she shall be set apart that all shall know her. So begins the Garunian prophecy about the magical birth of the White Babe, layering in all kinds of folkloric absurdities and gnomic utterings to explain away the rise of a female warrior queen. These "hero birth" tales emerge long after the fact, and it is no coincidence that one tale resembles another. (Cf., the birth of Alta's *Anna*, or *the white one*, motif #275f in Hyatt's *Folklore Motif Index of the Dales*.) This one points to the birth of White Jenna, the Amazonian queen of the Dark Riding, a figure of some staying power in the myth sequences out of the early Garunian period during and after the infamous Gender Wars.

BOOK ONE

THE WHITE BABE

THE MYTH:

Then Great Alta plaited the left side of her hair, the golden
side, and let it fall into the sinkhole of night. And there she drew
up the queen of shadows and set her upon the earth. Next she
plaited the right side of her hair, the dark side, and with it she
caught the queen of light. And she set her next to the black queen.

"And you two shall be sisters," quoth Great Alta. "You shall
be as images in a glass, the one reflecting the other. As I have
bound you in my hair, so it shall be."

Then she twined her living braids around and about them
and they were as one.

THE LEGEND:

It happened in the town of Slipskin on a day far into the
winter's rind that a strange and wonderful child was born. As her

mother, who was but a girl herself, knelt between the piles of skins, straddling the shallow hole in the earth floor, the birth cord descended between her legs like a rope. The child emerged, feet first, climbing down the cord. When her tiny toes touched the ground, she bent down and cut the cord with her teeth, saluted the astonished midwife, and walked out the door.

The midwife fainted dead away, but when she came to and discovered the child gone and the mother dead of blood-loss, she told her eldest daughter what had happened. At first they thought to hide what had occurred. But miracles have a way of announcing themselves. The daughter told a sister who told a friend and, in that way, the story was uncovered.

The tale of that rare birthing is still recounted in Slipskin —now called New Moulting—to this very day. They say the child was the White Babe, Jenna, Sister Light of the Dark Riding, the Anna.

THE STORY:

It was an ordinary birth until the very end and then the child hurtled screaming from the womb, the cord wrapped around her tiny hands. The village midwife echoed the baby's scream. Although she had attended many births, and some near miraculous with babes born covered with cauls or twins bound together with a mantling of skin, the midwife had never heard anything like this. Quickly she made the sign of the Goddess with her right hand, thumb and forefinger curved and touching, and cried out, "Great Alta, save us."

At the name, the babe was quiet.

The midwife sighed and picked up the child from the birth hide stretched over the hole scraped in the floor. "She is a girl," the midwife said, "the Goddess' own. Blessed be." She turned to the new mother and only then realized that she spoke to a corpse.

Well, what was the midwife to do then but cut the cord and

tend the living first. The dead mother would wait for her washing and the mourning her man would make over her, with the patience of eternity. But so as not to have the haunt follow her down the rest of her days, the midwife spoke a quick prayer as she went about the first lessons of the newborn:

> *In the name of the cave,*
> *The dark grave,*
> *And all who swing twixt*
> *Light and light,*
> *Great Alta,*
> *Take this woman*
> *Into your sight.*
> *Wrap her in your hair*
> *And, cradled there,*
> *Let her be a babe again,*
> *Forever.*

"And that should satisfy her," the midwife mumbled to herself, knowing that to be a babe again, to be cradled against the breast of the eternal Alta, was the goal of all life. She had faith the quick prayer would shrive the poor dead woman at least until the candles could be lit, one for each year of her life and an extra for her shadow-soul, at the bedfoot. Meanwhile, there was the child, blessedly a girl, and blessedly alive. In these past years of hard living it was not always so. But the man was lucky. He had only to grieve for one.

Once cleansed of the birthblood, the midwife saw the babe was fair-skinned with a fine covering of white hair on her head and tiny arms. Her body was unblemished and her dark eyes looked as if they could already see, following the midwife's finger left and right, up and down. And if that were not miracle enough, the child's little hand locked upon the midwife's finger with a hold that could not be broken, not even when a suck was made for her using a linen cloth twisted about and dipped in goat's milk. Even then she hung on, though she pulled on the makeshift teat with long, rhythmic sighs.

When the child's father came back from the fields and could be torn from his dead wife's side long enough to touch the babe, she was still holding the midwife's finger.

"She's a fighter," said the midwife, offering the bundle to his arms.

He would not take her. It was all he could do to care. The white babe was a poor, mewling exchange for his lusty redheaded wife. He touched the child's head gently, where beneath the fragile shield of skin the pulse beat, and said, "Then if you think her a fighter, give her to the warrior women in the mountains to foster. I cannot bide her while I grieve for her mother. She is the sole cause of my loss. I cannot love where loss is so great." He said it quietly and without apparent anger, for he was ever a quiet, gentle man, but the midwife heard the rock beneath the quiet tone. It was the kind of rock against which a child would bruise herself again and again to no avail.

She said then what she thought right. "The mountain tribes will take her and love her as you cannot. They are known for their mothering. And I swear they will bring her to a stranger destiny than her tiny gripping hand and her early sight have already foretold."

If he remarked her words, the man did not respond, his shoulders already set in the grief he would carry with him to his own grave, and that—though he knew it not—soon enough, for as they said often in Slipskin, *The heart is not a knee that can bend.*

So the midwife took the child and left. She paused only long enough to cry out the village diggers and two women to bathe and shroud the corpse before it set badly in the rigor of death. She told them of the child's miraculous birth, the wonder of it still imprinted on her face.

Because she was known to be a stubborn woman with a mind set in a single direction—like a needle in water pointing north—none of them gainsaid her going to the mountain clans. They did not know she was more frightened than even she herself knew, frightened of both the child and the trip. One part of her hoped the villagers would stop her. But the other part, the stubborn part, would have gone whatever they said, and perhaps they guessed it and saved their breath for telling her story afterward. For as it was said in Slipskin, *Telling a tale is better than living it.*

And so the midwife turned toward the mountains where she had never been before, trusting Great Alta's guardians to track her before she was gone too far, and clutching the child to her breast like an amulet.

It was luck that an early spring melt had cleared most of the paths to the mountain foot or the midwife would never have gotten even that far. She was a woman of the towns, her duties bringing her from house to house like a scavenger. She knew nothing of the forest perils or the great tan-colored cats that roamed the rockslides. With the babe swaddled and wrapped to her breast, she had started out bravely enough and managed surprisingly well, getting to the mountain foot without a scratch or slip. Many a strong hunting man had not done as well that year. And perhaps it was true, as the villagers said, that *Fish are not the best authority on water.*

She sheltered the first night among the twisted roots of a blasted tree, giving the child suck from a milk crock with a linen teat dipped in. Herself, she ate cheese and brown bread and stayed warm with half a skin of sweet wine she carried. She ate unsparingly, for she thought she had but a single overnight to go before she reached the holds of the mountain clans. And she was sure the women of the mountains—whom she had long desired to visit, that longing compounded of envy and fear—would give her plenty of food and drink and gold to sustain her when they saw what it was she carried to them. She was a townswoman in her thinking, always trade for trade. She did not understand the mountains or the people who lived there; she did not know that they would feed her independent of all else but her need and that they had little use for gold so never kept it.

The second day was bright and pearly. Clouds lined only the

horizon. She chose to walk along the bank of a swift-flowing stream because it seemed easier than breaking a new trail. If she had noticed the scat and could have read it, she would have known this was a favorite run of mountain cats, for trout were plentiful in the stream, and foolish, especially in the evening in the presence of bugs. But she was a woman of the town and she could read print only, a minor learning, and so she never heard the cat on her trail or noticed its scratchy warnings on the trees.

That second night she stashed the babe in a high crotch of a tree, believing it quite safe there, and walked down to the stream to bathe in the moonlight. Being a townswoman and a midwife, she valued cleanliness above all other things.

It was while she was bent over, dipping her hair in the cold water of the stream and muttering aloud about how long the trip was taking, that the cat struck. Swiftly, silently, surely. She never felt more than a moment of pain. But at her death the child cried out, a high, thin wailing. The cat, startled, dropped its prey and looked about uneasily.

An arrow took it in the eye, its death more painful than the midwife's. It whimpered and trembled for several moments before one of the hunters cut its throat in pity.

The babe in the tree cried out again and the entire wood seemed to still at the sound.

"What was that?" asked the heavier of the two hunters, the one who had cut the cat's throat. They were both kneeling over the dead woman, seeking in vain for a pulse.

"Perhaps the lion had cubs and they are hungry?"

"Do not be foolish, Marjo; this early in spring?"

The thinner hunter shrugged her shoulders.

The child, uncomfortable in its makeshift cradle, cried out again.

The hunters stood.

"That is no lion cub," said Marjo.

"But cub nonetheless," said her companion.

They went to the tree as unerringly as woodsense could lead them and found the babe.

"Alta's Hairs!" said the first hunter. She took the child from the tree, unwrapped it, and gazed at its smooth, fair-skinned body.

Marjo nodded. "A girl, Selna."

"Bless you," whispered Selna, but whether she spoke to Marjo or to the dead midwife or to the ears of Alta, high and far away, was not clear.

They buried the midwife and it was a long and arduous task, for the ground was still part frozen. Then they skinned the cat and wrapped the babe in its warm skin. The child settled into her new wrapping and fell asleep at once.

"She was meant for us," said Selna. "She does not even wrinkle her nose at the cat smell."

"She is too young to wrinkle her nose."

Selna ignored the remark and gazed at the child. "It is true, then, what the villagers say: *When a dead tree falls, it carries with it a live one.*"

"You speak too often with another's mouth," said Marjo. "And a village mouth at that."

"And you speak with mine."

They were silent after that, neither saying a word as they trotted along the familiar paths toward the mountains and home.

They expected no grand reception at their return and got none, though their coming had been remarked by many hidden watchers. They signaled their secret names with careful hand signs at every appointed place, and the guardians of each of those turnings melted back into the forest or the seemingly impenetrable rock face without a sound.

What messages, what bits of news were passed to them as they traveled through the night, came to them in the form of birdsong or the howling fall of a wolf's call, where bird and wolf were not. It told them they were welcome and recognized and one particular cry told them to bring their bundle at once to the Great Hall. They understood, though no words, no human words, were exchanged.

But before they reached the hall, the moon slipped down behind the western mountains and Marjo bade farewell to her companion and disappeared.

Hefting the child in its cat cloak, Selna whispered, "Till evening, then." But she said it so softly, the child in her arms did not even stir.

THE SONG:

Lullaby to the Cat's Babe

Hush little mountain cat,
Sleep in your den,
I'll sing of your mother
Who cradled Fair Jen.

I'll sing of your mother
Who covered Jen's skin.
Flesh of your flesh
Did sweet Jenna lay in.

Sleep, little catkin,
Perchance you shall dream
Of rabbit and pheasant
And trout in the stream.

But Jenna will dream
Of the dark and the light.
Your mother will shelter her
From the cold night.

THE STORY:

There were cradles scattered around the Great Hall, some of oak with the grain running like rivers to the sea, and some of white pine, so soft the marks of a baby's nails could be seen, like runes, on the headboards. But for some reason Selna did not put the child in any of them. She kept it on her breast when she showed it in the Great Hall and all the rest of the day, hoping the steady beat of her heart would comfort it.

It was not unusual for a new fosterling to be kept, swaddled, at one breast or another. The women of Alta's-hame shared the care of them, though Selna had never before shown any interest in fostering. The stink of the babes and their high, cranky crying had always put her off. But this one was different. She smelled not of sour milk and spittle but of mountain cat, moonshine, and blackthorn, that being the tree she had been wedged in when the cat had struck her mother. She had cried only twice, each time at a death, which Selna thought an omen. Surely the child must be hungry or fearful or cold. Selna was ready to put her away at the first sign of fretting. But the babe had stared at her with eyes the color of a spring night, as if reading her very soul. And so Selna had kept her heart to heart far into the morning. By then everyone had noticed and commented, so that she could not—for fear of being shamed—let her small burden go. Physical abuse had never bothered Selna. Indeed she was proud of her ability to withstand the worst punishments. She was always in the forefront of any battle line, she was the last to the fire, the first into a cold stream. But she never could stand the tauntings of the women in her Hame.

By midmorning, though, the child was hungry and let her know with small pipings, like a chick in the henyard. She fed the babe as best she could with one of the Eastern bottles so prized by the kitcheners. Both she and the babe were thoroughly splattered in the process, and so Selna took the child down to the baths, heated the water well below her usual steaming, and holding the naked child against her own bare shoulder, plunged in.

At the water's touch, the child cooed contentedly and fell asleep. Selna sat on the third step of the bath, so that only their heads showed above the water. She stayed until her fingers had wrinkled and the water began to grow chill and her hand around the child cramped. Then she got out reluctantly, dried the sleeping babe, and wrapped toweling around herself for the long walk back to her room. This time there were no comments, even though she passed many of her holdmates. Whether she willed it or not, the child was hers.

THE HISTORY:

The women of the mountain warrior clans did not take fostering lightly. Once a child was chosen by her foster mother, the woman had full charge of the child's care. A kitchener's child grew up amongst the great pots; took her first steps on the tiled kitchen floor; ate, napped, and slept out her childhood sicknesses in a special children's nook in the kitchen.

So, too, a child chosen for rearing by one of the warrior/huntresses was carried about in a special pack wherever her foster mother went. Lowentrout finds evidence of this in the famous Baryard Tapestries (his essay "Pack-Children of the Western Holds," Nature and History, *Vol. 39, is especially interesting). There is a leathern pack unearthed from the famous gravemound at Arrundale, and preliminary examination leads to speculation that it may be one of the Amazonian child-carriers. (For more about this dig, see Sigel and Salmon's video "Graverobbing Among the Dales.") Such burdens did not hamper the women warriors either in battle or on the hunt, according to Lowentrout, and textual evidence supports his claim. The three scrolls ascribed to the Great Archive of G'run Far Shooter graphically depict the battles in which the mountain clans took part. One in particular speaks of "the double heads of the Amazons" and, in another place, "the precious burden carried by (them)." And most striking, "She fought, all the ways her breast to the foe for as not to expose the one at her back." Vargo argues that the word "at" simply refers to another fighter, since fighting back-to-back was a familiar style in sword-battle. She further states that if a pack-child had been meant, the word "on" rather than "at" would have been used. However, Doyle, whose seminal work on Alta-linguistics has just been published, points out that in the old tongue* on/at/upon *and* by *were used interchangeably.*

THE STORY:

"You will have to name her, you know," Marjo said that night, lying on the far side of the bed. The lantern hanging above them cast shadows on the wall and floor.

Selna looked at the child sleeping between them. She touched the soft cheek with a tentative finger. "If I name her, she really is mine forever."

"Forever is longer than either one of us shall last," said Marjo, her finger stroking the child's other cheek.

"A child is a kind of immortality," Selna murmured. "A link forged. A bond. Even if she is not of my blood."

"She will be," Marjo said. "If you claim her."

"How can I not—now?" Selna sat up and Marjo followed suit. "She looks to me first, whoever holds her. She trusts me. When I brought her into the kitchen at dinner and everyone wanted to touch her, all the while her tiny head swiveled around to see me."

"You are being sentimental," said Marjo with a laugh. "Newborns cannot swivel their heads. They cannot even see."

"She can. Jenna can."

"So—you have already named her," Marjo said. "And without waiting for my approval."

"You are my sister, not my keeper," Selna answered testily. At the sharpness in her voice, the child stirred between them. Selna smiled a lopsided apology. "Besides," she said, "Jenna is just her baby name. I want to name her Jo-an-enna in full."

"*Jo* for lover, *an* for white, *enna* for tree. That makes sense, for she was found in a tree and her hair—what there is of it—is white. I presume that *Jo* is because you love her, though I wonder at how quickly such a thing came about. You usually do not *love* so quickly. It is usually your hatred that is quickly aroused."

"Do not be an idiot. *Jo* is for you, Marjo," Selna said, "and well you know it." She reached out to touch her companion across the child.

Marjo's hand met hers halfway and they both smiled.

The child between them cooed.

In the morning Selna took Jenna to the infirmarer, Kadreen, who checked the babe from the crown of her head to the soles of her feet.

"A strong one," said Kadreen. She did not smile, but then she rarely did. It was said she had stitched too many wounds and set too many bones to find life amusing enough for a smile. But Selna knew that even as a young woman, before she was long in her calling, Kadreen had not found much to smile at. Perhaps, Selna thought, the calling had found her *because* of that.

"Her fingers grip surprisingly well for a newborn. And she can follow the movement of my hand. That is rare. I clapped my hands to test her hearing and she startled at once. She will be a good companion for you in the woods."

Selna nodded.

"Make sure you feed her at the same time and she will sleep through the night within the first moon's change."

"She slept through the night last night," Selna said.

"She will not again."

But despite the infirmarer's warning, Jenna did sleep soundly through that night and the next. And though Selna tried to feed her on the schedule dictated by Kadreen's long experience with infants, she was always too busy to do so. Yet the babe seemed to thrive on the erratic meals and, in the woods, strapped to Selna's breast or back, she was as quiet as any seasoned hunter.

Selna boasted of her fosterling at every opportunity until everyone but Marjo grew weary of it.

"You are in danger of becoming a bore," said Donya, the head kitchener, when Selna dropped off a fine roebuck and seven rabbits after a two-day hunt. "She is a fine babe, no doubt. Strong and quite pleasant to look upon. But she is not Great Alta. She does not walk across the Lake of Sighs or ride the summer rainbow or leap between the drops of falling rain."

"I did not say she was the Goddess," mumbled Selna. The child at her breast laughed delightedly as she tickled it under the chin with one of the rabbit's feet. Then she looked at the kitchener squarely and roared. "And I am *not* a bore."

"I did not say you were. I said you were in danger of becoming one," said Donya calmly. "Ask anyone."

Selna glared around the kitchen, but the girls all dropped their eyes and suddenly the room was quiet of voices. All that could be heard was the *snick-snack* of kitchen knives at work. Donya's young ones knew better than to tangle with one of the warriors. Selna, especially, was known for her hot temper, though she, unlike some of them, seldom bore a lasting grudge. Still, not a one of them envied her fosterling that temper when it roared.

Selna shook her head, still angry, and turned back to Donya. "I shall want the rabbit skins," she said. "They will make a soft lining for the pack. Jenna has fine skin."

"Jenna has a baby's skin," said Donya evenly, ignoring Selna's scowl. "And of course you shall have the fur. I will also save you the deerskin. It should make a fine pair of leggings and many mocs."

Selna smiled suddenly. "She will need many mocs."

"But not right away," Donya said, with a laugh.

There was a titter around the room as her own fosterlings enjoyed the joke.

"What do you mean?" The anger was back in Selna's voice.

Donya set down the heavy crockery bowl and wooden

spoon, wiped her hands on her apron, and held out her arms. Reluctantly Selna recognized the signal and unstrapped the babe, handing her over to Donya.

Donya smiled and rocked the babe in her arms. "This is an infant, Selna. A babe. Look around at my own maids. Seven of them. And once they were each this size. They walked at a year, only one sooner. Do not expect too much from your child and she will grow in your love. When her moon time comes, she will not turn from you. When she reads from the *Book of Light* and calls her own sister into this world, she will not forsake you. But if you push her too much, you will push her away. A child is not yours to own but yours to raise. She may not be what you will have her be, but she will be what she has to be. Remember what they say, that *Wood may remain twenty years in the water, but it is still not a fish.*"

"Who is becoming the bore now?" asked Selna in a weary voice. She took Jenna, who was still smiling, back from the kitchener and went from the room.

That night there was a full moon and all the dark sisters were called forth. In the great open amphitheater the circle of women and their children was complete.

Selna stood in the circle's center below the altar, which was flanked by three rowan trees. Marjo was by her side. For the first time in almost a year there was a new fosterling to celebrate, though two of the gardeners and one warrior had each borne a babe. But those infants had already had their consecration to the Goddess. It was Jenna's turn now.

The priestess sat silently on the backless throne atop the rock altar, her own dark sister throned beside her. Black hair braided with tiny white flowers, lips stained red with the juice of berries, they waited until the crowd of worshippers quieted. Then they leaned forward, hands on knees, and stared down at Selna and Marjo, but only the priestess herself spoke.

"Who bears the child?"

"Mother, I do," said Selna, raising Jenna to eye level. For

her the word "mother" had a double meaning, for the priestess had been her own foster mother, who had grieved sorely when Selna had chosen to follow the warrior way.

"And I," said Marjo.

They stepped together up onto the first altar rise.

"And who bore the child?" the priestess asked.

"Mother, a woman of the town," said Selna.

"She died in the woods," Marjo added.

They mounted the second step.

"And who now bleeds for the child?" the priestess asked.

"She shall have my blood," said Selna.

"And mine." Marjo's voice was a quiet echo.

They reached the third step and the priestess and her dark sister rose. The priestess took the silent babe from Selna's hands, turned, and placed the child upon the throne. Marjo and Selna were beside her in one fluid movement.

Then the priestess dropped to her knees before the child. She took her long black braid, and wound it about the child's waist. Her sister, on the other side of the throne, did the same. As soon as they were done, Selna and Marjo knelt and offered their hands, wrists up.

Taking a silver pin from a box mounted in the arm of the throne, the priestess pierced Selna's wrist where the blue vein branched. At the same time, her sister with an identical pin did the same for Marjo. They held the warriors' wrists together so that the blood flowed each to each.

Next the priestess turned and pricked Jenna lightly, above the navel, signaling to Selna and Marjo silently with her free hand. They bent over and placed their wrists side by side on the baby's belly so that their blood mingled.

Then the priestess and her sister drew their twined braids over the steady hands.

"Blood to blood," the priestess intoned. "Life to life."

The entire congregation of Alta's-hame repeated the words, a rolling echo in the clearing.

"What is the child's name?"

Selna could not keep from smiling. "Jo-an-enna," she said.

The priestess spelled out the name and then, in the old tongue, gave the child her secret name that only the four of them—and Jenna in her time—would know. "Annuanna," she said. "The white birch, the goddess tree, the tree of everlasting light."

"Annuanna," they whispered to one another and the child.

Then the priestess and her sister unwrapped their hair and stood. Holding their hands over the two kneelers and the babe, both priestess and sister spoke the final prayer.

> She who holds us
> in her hand,
> She who molds us
> in this land,
> She who drives
> away the night,
> She who wrote
> the Book of Light,
> *In her name,*
> *Blessed be.*

The assembled women came in perfectly on the responses. When they were done, Selna and Marjo stood together, Selna holding out the infant so that all could see. At the great cheer that arose below them, Jenna woke up, startled, and began to cry. Selna did not comfort her, though the priestess looked sharply at her. A warrior had to learn young that crying brought no comfort.

Back inside, after the magnificent feast that followed, the baby was handed around the table for all to see. She began in the priestess' arms and was handed over to the plump arms of Donya, who dandled her expertly but "as routinely as a bit of mutton just off the spit," Selna commented testily to Marjo. Donya handed the child to the leaner arms of the warriors. They chucked and clucked at Jenna's chin, and one dark sister threw her up into the air. She screamed with delight, but Selna pushed aside the circle of companions angrily to catch the child on her downward flight.

"What kind of a misbegotten son-of-a-son are you?" she cried out. "What if the light had failed? Whose arms would have caught her then?"

The dark sister Sammor shrugged her shoulders and laughed. "This late mothering has made mush of your brains, Selna. We are *inside*. There are no clouds to hide the moon. The lights of Alta's-hame never fail."

Selna tucked Jenna under one arm and raised the other to strike Sammor, but her hand was caught from behind.

"Selna, she is right and you are wrong in this. The babe is safe," Marjo said. "Come. Drink a toast with us all to forget and forgive, and then we will play at the Wands." They brought their arms down together.

But Selna's anger did not abate, which was unusual, and she sat outside the circle of sisters when they threw the wands around the ring in the complicated patterns that trained them for sword-handling.

With Selna out, Marjo could not play either, and she sat across from her sister and sulked as the game went on. It became more and more complex as a second, then a third, and finally a fourth set of wands was introduced into the circle. The flexible willows flipped end over end in the air, passing from woman to woman, from hand to hand, and soon the dining hall was quiet except for the *slip-slap* of the wands as they hit palm after palm after palm.

"The lights!" someone shouted, and a cheer went up from the watchers around the ring. Sammor's sister Amalda nodded and two of the kitcheners, new enough to the sisterhood that they stuck together as close as shadows, rose to stand by the torches that illuminated the circle.

The game went on without stopping, the wands slipping even more quickly through the air. Not a hand had missed since the throws began. The whizzing of the wands as they passed one another was punctuated by the slapping of palms.

Then without warning both torches were doused in the

water buckets and the dark sisters in the circle disappeared. The circle was halved and there was a clatter of wands hitting the floor. Only Marjo, who sat beyond the range of the two doused torches, and the dark sisters of the watchers, who stood far from the game, remained, for the lights from the kitchen shone upon them.

Amalda's voice counted out those who had lost their wands. "Domina, Catrona, Marna." Then she turned and nodded for two new torches to be brought.

The relighted circle arranged itself as dark sisters appeared again. The losers—Domina, Catrona, and Marna and their dark halves—went into the kitchen for something to drink. Playing at the wands was thirsty work. But Selna stood, the child at her breast, and spoke so loudly no one could miss it.

"It has been a tiring day, sweet Jenna, and time we were both in bed. I will put out the light tonight."

There was a gasp heard around the circle. To put out the light was to send your sister back into the darkness. To announce it so was an affront.

Marjo's mouth grew tighter, but she said nothing as she stood with Selna and followed her out of the room. But Sammor spoke to their departing backs.

"Remember, Selna, that it is said, *If your mouth turns into a knife, it will cut off your lips.*" She did not expect an answer and, indeed, got none.

"You shamed me," Marjo said softly when they reached their room. "You have never done such a thing before. Selna, what is wrong?"

"Nothing is wrong," Selna answered, arranging the baby in her cot, smoothing the blanket and touching the child's white hair with a finger. She began to hum an old cradle song. "Look! She is already asleep."

"I mean, what is wrong between *us?*" Marjo bent over the cot and stared at the sleeping child. "She *is* a sweetling."

"There, you see? Nothing is wrong between *us.* We both love her."

"How can you love her after so short a time? She is nothing but a bit of flesh and coos. Later she shall be someone to love—strong or weak, bright-eyed or sad, handy with her hands or her mouth. But now she is only—" Marjo's voice stopped abruptly in mid-sentence, for Selna had blown out the large candle over the bed.

"There is nothing wrong between us now, sister," Selna whispered into the black room.

She lay down on the bed, conscious of Marjo's empty half, for her sister could always be counted on to talk and laugh and come up with a quick answer before they slept. Then she turned over and, holding her breath, listened a moment for the baby's breathing. When she was sure the child was safe, she let out the air with a loud percussive sigh and fell asleep.

THE HISTORY:

The "game of wands" has come down to us in a highly suspect form. It is played today only by girl children in the Upper Dales, where the chorus, sung in modal tuning by watchers (usually boys) standing outside the circle, goes:

> *Round and round and round the ring*
> *The willow sword we now do fling.*

The concentric circles of players sit on the ground facing one another, wands in hand. Once made of willow (which no longer grows in the Upper Dales, though evidence of a different flora-culture proves willows may have been plentiful a thousand years ago), the wands today are manufactured of a plastine that is both flexible and strong. At a drum signal, the wands are passed from hand to hand in a clockwise manner for seven beats, then returned for seven beats. Next the wands are flipped between the circles in preset partnerships for seven more beats. Finally, to the accompaniment of the choral singing of the watchers, and an ever-rapidly increasing pattern beat out on the drum, the wands are flipped across the circle, first to the partner and back, then to the person directly to the partner's right. The wands must be caught in the sword hand, which gives left-handed players a decided disadvantage in the game. As soon as a player drops a wand, she is "out."

Lowentrout points to the famous "insert piece" of the Baryard Tapestries, which had been found in the vault of the Eastern potentate Achmed Mubarek thirty years ago, as proof positive that the "game of wands" played by warriors in the mountain clans and the nursery circle game are one and the same. While it is true that the "insert piece" (which has been repaired inexpertly by many Eastern hands—some say as many as thirty times, as evidenced by the different colored threads) shows concentric circles of women warriors, they are holding swords, not wands. One of the so-called players is lying on her back, sword in her breast, obviously dead. She is ignored by the other players. Cowan argues forcibly that the "insert piece" has been too mangled over the years to be plain in its correspondences, but that it is more likely a picture of a specific form of execution, as the "insert piece" occurs in that section of the tapestry which deals with traitors and spies. Perhaps the true meaning of the "insert piece" will never be known, but Magon's shrill argument that the inner circle consisted of the "dark sisters" or "shadow sisters," who could be seen by the light of the moon or the heavy tallow candles (still popular in the Upper and Lower Dales) and that the outer circle was that of the "light sisters" harkens back to the last century, when the Luxophists sought to resurrect the Book of Light practices. Those practices had been banned for at least seven generations and the Book of Light has been so thoroughly discredited by Duane's brilliant "Das Volk lichtet nicht" I need not reiterate her arguments here.

Some confusion over the intricately engraved silver rings found in the Arrundale gravemound still exists. Sigel and Salmon call them "wand holders," giving credence to Magon's shaky thesis, but there is even more evidence that these artifacts are napkin rings or possibly pack cups for long trips, and that is convincingly argued in Cowan's "Rings of the Clans" in Nature and History, Vol. 51.

THE STORY:

Selna's shameful behavior became the talk of the Hame. Though sisters had quarreled before, little fiery arguments that sent a moment of heat and light and then died down without even embers of memory, what Selna did was unheard of. Even the priestess' records mentioned nothing like it, and the Hame had seventeen generations listed and eight great tapestries as well.

Selna stayed in the bright sunlight with her child during the day and at night, babe bound fast to her breast or back, avoided the well-lighted rooms of the Hame. Once or twice, when it was absolutely unavoidable and Selna had to come into a torchlit room, Marjo crept behind her, a thin, attenuated figure. Gone was the dark sister's robust laughter, her hearty ringing tones.

"Selna," she would cry to her sister's back with a voice like a single strand of sigh, "what is wrong between us?" It was a ghost's voice, hollow and dying. "Selna . . ."

Once, in the kitchen begging some milk for the babe, Selna turned for a moment when Marjo called. She put her hands over the child's ears as if to block out the sound of her sister's voice, though it was so low by now it could scarcely be heard. Behind her, Donya and her own sister Doey and two of the older girls watched in horror. They saw in Marjo's wasting figure their own slow death.

Marjo's eyes, the color of bruises, wept black tears. "Sister, why do you do this? I would share the child with you. I have no wish to stand between."

But Selna turned slowly and deliberately away from the pleading figure, back toward the kitchen's light. When she noticed Donya and Doey and the two girls standing there, stricken, she bowed her head and hunched her shoulders up as if expecting a blow. Then she turned and went back without the milk into the darkest part of the hall.

On the thirteenth day of her shame, the priestess banished her from the Hame.

"My daughter," the priestess said, her voice heavy, "you have brought this upon yourself. We cannot stop what you do to your own dark sister. Once you accepted the teachings of the *Book of Light,* we could instruct you no more. What falls between the two of you is your own concern. But the Hame is shattered. We cannot continue to watch what you do. So you must leave us and finish out what you have so ill begun alone."

"Alone?" Selna asked. For the first time her voice quivered. She had not been alone for as long as she could remember. She clutched baby Jenna to her.

"You have thrust your own dark sister from you," said the priestess. "You have shamed us all. The child stays here."

"No!" Selna cried, turning. By her side, the gray shadow that was Marjo turned, too. But they ran into six sturdy warriors who pinned them against the wall and took the babe, despite Selna's screams and pleading.

They took Selna out into the bright day, which meant she would be truly alone at the start of her journey, with only the clothes she wore. Her bow, sword, and gutting knife they threw after her, tied in a heavy bag that took her near an hour to unknot. They said nothing to her, not even a word of farewell, for so the priestess had instructed them.

She left the Hame by day, but she returned that night, a shadow among shadows, and stole away the child.

There were no guards by the infant's cot. Selna knew there would be none. The women of the Hame would be sure she would never return, so shamed and low had they left her. They would trust in the guards of the outer gates. But Selna was a warrior, the best of them, and often she and Marjo had played among the secret passageways. So silently, Selna stole back in, more quietly even than a shadow. She doused three lights along the hallways before Marjo's pale voice could alert the sleepers.

Jenna awoke and recognized her foster mother's smell. Giving a satisfied sound, she fell asleep again. It was that small wisp of sound that confirmed Selna's determination. She raced down the secret ways and was at the forest's edge again before it was dawn.

As she slipped along the old paths where the rocks were worn smooth by the passage of so many feet, the birds heralded her arrival. She found the large boulder off to the side of the path where she had left her weapons. Shamed as she was, she would still not have raised her sword or bow against her Hame mates. Leaning back against the rock, into a niche that seemed to exactly fit her body, she slipped her tunic down to her waist. Now that she was truly the child's mother, she could nurse it as well. She gave the baby her breast. For a few moments Jenna sucked eagerly, but when no milk came, she turned her head to the side and wailed.

"Hush!" Selna said sharply, taking the child's face between her fingers and squeezing. "A warrior must be silent."

But the baby, hungry and frightened, cried even more.

Selna shook the infant roughly, unaware that tears were coursing down her own cheeks. Startled, the child stopped crying. Then Selna stood up and looked around, making sure no one had been alerted by the child's cries. When she heard nothing, she sat back down, leaned against the rock, and slept, the baby in her arms.

But Jenna did not sleep. Restless and hungry, she caught at dust motes in the rays of the sun that filtered through the canopy of aspen and birch. At last she put her tiny hand into her mouth and sucked noisily.

It was hours before Selna awoke, and when she did the sun was already high overhead and a fox was puzzling on the edge of the small clearing, its sharp little muzzle poking into the undergrowth. At Selna's waking, it looked up, ears stiff with warning, then turned abruptly and disappeared into the shadows.

Selna stretched and looked at the babe sleeping on her lap. She smiled, touching Jenna's white hair. In the sunlight she could see the infant's pink scalp under the fine hair and the beating of the pulse beneath the shield of skin.

"You are mine," she whispered fiercely. "I shall care for you. I shall protect you. I shall feed you. I—and no others."

At her voice, Jenna awoke and her cry was cranky and thin.

"You are hungry. So am I," Selna said quietly. "I shall find us both something to eat."

She pulled up her tunic and bound the child to her back, slipping the ribbands under her own arms, tight enough so that the child was safe, loose enough so that they both could move. Holding her bow and sword in her left hand, she slipped the gutting knife into its sheath over her right shoulder where she could reach it for a fast throw. Then she began loping down the forest paths.

She was lucky. She found tracks of a small rabbit, stalked it easily, and brought it down with a light arrow at the first try. Fearing to make a large fire still so close to the Hame, she nevertheless knew better than to eat a rabbit raw. So she dug a deep hole and made a small fire there, enough to at least sear the meat. She chewed it, then spit the juices into Jenna's mouth. After the second try, the babe did not refuse the offering and sucked it up eagerly, mouth to mouth.

"As soon as I can, I will find you milk," Selna promised, wiping the baby's mouth and then tickling her under the chin. "I will hire out to guard one of the small border towns. Or I will find the High King's army. They like Alta's warriors. They will not refuse me."

Jenna smiled her response, her little hands waving about in the air. Selna kissed her on the brow, feeling the brush of the child's white hair under her nose, as soft as the wing of a butterfly. Then she bound the baby on her back again.

"We have many more miles to go tonight before I will feel safe," Selna said. She did not add that she wanted to stay the night in the forest because the full moon was due and she could not bear to speak to her pale shadow and explain all that she had done.

THE LEGEND:

In the dark forest near Altashame there is a clearing. Under a stand of white birch grows a red-tipped iris. The people who live in Selkirk, on the west side of the forest, say that three ghosts may be seen on the second moon of each year. One is a warrior woman, a dark necklace at her throat. The second is her shadowy twin. And the third is a snow-white bird that flies above them crying with a child's voice. At dawn the two women strike each other with their swords. Where their blood falls the iris springs up, as white as the bird, as red as the blood. "Snow-iris," the folk of the East call the flower. "Cold Heart," say the folk from the South. "But "Sister's Blood" is the Selkirk name, and the people of that town leave the flowers alone. Though the juice from the iris heart binds up a woman in her time of troubles and gives her relief from flashes of heat, the Selkirk folk will not touch so much as a leaf of the flower, and they will not go into the clearing after dark.

THE STORY:

At the edge of a small clearing, a short run to the outskirts of the town of Seldenkirk, Selna rested. Leaning against a small oak which protected her from the bright full moon, she caught her breath and dropped both bow and sword. Her breathing was so labored at first, she did not hear the noise and then, when she heard it, it was already too late. Strong, callused hands grabbed her from behind and twisted a knife point into the hollow below her chin.

She stopped herself from crying out in pain, and then the knife slipped down and carved a circle of blood like a necklace around her throat.

"These be the only jewels an Alta-slut should own," came the gruff voice behind her. "You be mighty far from your own, my girl."

She fell to her knees, trying to twist and protect the child at her back, and the movement frightened the man, who jammed the knife deep in her throat. She tried to scream but no sound came out.

The man laughed raggedly and ripped her tunic down the front, exposing her breasts and belly. "Built like a boy," he said disgustedly. "Your kind be good only dying or dead." He grabbed her by one leg and pulled her out from the forest onto the softer grass of the moonlit clearing. Then he tried to turn her from her side onto her back.

She could not scream, though she could still fight him. But another woman screamed from behind, a strange gurgling.

Startled, he looked over his shoulder, saw a twin of the first woman, her own throat banded by a black line of blood. Turning back, he realized his mistake, for Selna had managed to get her hand on her knife. With the last remaining strength in her arm, she threw the knife at his face. It hit him cleanly between the eyes. But Selna did not see it, for she had already rolled over on her stomach and died, her fingertips touching Marjo's.

The man tried to get to his feet, managed only to his knees, then fell on top of Selna, the handle of the knife between his eyes coming to rest in baby Jenna's hand. She held on to it and cried.

They were found in the morning by a shepherd who always took his flock to that clearing, where the spring grass was sweetest. He arrived just before sunrise and thought he saw three dead folk by the clearing's edge. When he got to them, pushing his way through his reluctant sheep, he saw that there were only two: a woman, her throat cut, and a man, a gutting knife between his eyes. A silent infant was holding on to the bloody knife handle as if she herself had set it on its deadly path.

The shepherd ran all the way back to Seldenkirk, forgetting his sheep, who bleated around the ghastly remains. When he returned, with six strong ploughboys and the portly high sheriff, only the man lay there, on his back, in a circle of sheep. The dead woman, the babe, the knife, and one of the shepherd's nursing ewes were gone.

THE BALLAD:

The Ballad of the Selden Babe

Do not go down, ye maidens all,
Who wear the golden gown,
Do not go to the clearing
At the edge of Seldentown,
For wicked are the men who wait
To bring young maidens down.

A maiden went to Seldentown,
A maid no more was she,
Her hair hung loose about her neck,
Her gown about her knee,
A babe was slung upon her back,
A bonny babe was he.

She went into the clearing wild,
She went too far from town,
A man came up behind her
And he cut her neck aroun',
A man came up behind her
And he pushed that fair maid down.

"And will ye have your way wi' me,
   Or will ye cut me dead,
Or do ye hope to take from me
   My long-lost maidenhead?
Why have ye brought me far from town
   Upon this grass-green bed?"

He never spoke a single word,
   Nor gave to her his name,
Nor whence and where his parentage,
   Nor from which town he came,
He only thought to bring her low
   And heap her high wi' shame.

But as he set about his plan
   And went about his work,
The babe upon the maiden's back
   Had touched her hidden dirk,
And from its sheath had taken it
   All in the clearing's mirk.

And one and two, the tiny hands
   Did fell the evil man,
Who all upon his mother had
   Commenced the wicked plan.
God grant us all such bonny babes
   And a good and long life span.

THE STORY:

The priestess called off the banishment, for four of the hunters had found Selna's body hand in hand with Marjo. The hunters had melted quickly back into the forest when the shepherd had appeared, waited out his discovery, then taken Selna, the babe, and the ewe back to the Hame.

"Our sisters are once more with us," the priestess said, and she made Alta's mark—the circle and the crux—on Selna's forehead when she met the hunters with their sad burden at the great gate. "Bring her in. The child also. She now belongs to us all. No one of us shall mother her alone."

"The prophecy, Mother," Amalda cried out, and many echoed her. "Is this the child spoke of?"

The priestess shook her head. "The *Book* speaks of a thrice-orphaned babe and this sweetling has lost but two mothers, her first mother and Selna."

"But, Mother," Amalda continued, "was not Marjo her mother as well?"

The priestess' mouth grew tight. "We may not help a prophecy along, sister. Remember that it is written that *Miracles come to the unsuspecting.* I have spoken. The child will not have one mother here at Alta's-hame hereafter but a multitude." She twisted her long braid through her fingers.

The women murmured amongst themselves, but at last they agreed she was right. So they set Selna's corpse into the withy burial basket and brought her into the infirmarer's room. There they washed and dressed her body, brushed her hair until it shone, then twined the top withes of the basket closed.

It took six of them, one at each corner of the basket and two at head and foot, to carry the burden up Holy Hill to the great mazed cave, Alta's Rock, where the bodies of generations of sisters lay wrapped and preserved, under blazing torches.

Though they went up to Alta's Rock at noon, they waited until night for the ceremony, eating sparingly of the fruits they had brought with them. They spoke quietly of Selna's life, of her hunting skills and her fearlessness, her quick temper and her quicker smile. And they spoke as often of Marjo, not the pale shadow, but the hearty, laughing companion.

Kadreen remarked that it was Alta's luck that had led them to find Selna's body.

"No, sister, it was the skill of my sisters and me. We trailed her through several nights, and if she had not been out of her mind, we would never have picked up her trail, for she was the best of us," said Amalda.

Kadreen shook her head and placed her hand on Amalda's shoulder. "I mean, sister, that it was Alta's gracious gift that we have her body with us at Holy Hill, for how many of our own lie far away in unmarked graves?"

When the moon rose, the group on the Hill was almost doubled, the children alone without dark sisters.

Marjo's body appeared in its own basket by Selna's side, the withy latticework as finely done as her sister's.

Then the priestess, her voice ragged with sorrow, began. "For our sisters who are united even in death," she said, then breaking a moment out of the ritual whispered to the two corpses, "There is nothing wrong between you now."

Donya drew a loud, groaning breath, and the two kitchen maids burst into tears.

The priestess sang the first of the seven praises, with the others quickly joining in, singing the parts they had known from childhood.

In the name of Alta's cave,
The dark and lonely grave . . .

When the seventh was done, and only the last lovely echo lingered in the air, they picked up the baskets and carried Selna and Marjo into the cave.

Donya and her dark sister were the last, Donya carrying the white-haired babe, who was so full of ewe's milk she slept peacefully on the kitchener's ample breast.

THE MYTH:

Then Great Alta said, "There shall be one of you, my only daughter, who shall be thrice born and thrice orphaned. She shall lie by a dead mother's side three times yet shall herself live. She shall be queen above all things yet queen she will not be. She shall carry a babe for each mother, yet mother them not. The three shall be as one and begin the world anew. So I say and so shall it be."

And then Great Alta picked out of the light a weeping child as white as snow, as red as blood, as black as night, and suckled her until the child was still.

TWO

THE BOOK OF LIGHT

THE MYTH:

And when Great Alta spoke, her words were slivers of glass. Where the sun struck them, then were her words like shafts of the purest light. Where fell the tears of her daughters, then were the words rainbows. But each time Great Alta's words were spoken, they reflected back the mind of the listener, shape for shape, shadow for shadow, light for light.

THE LEGEND:

There was once a great teacher who came into the Dales from the East with the rising sun. The teacher's words were so fine, those who heard them said they were like the purest crystal, giving off a high, sweet ringing when touched.

The teacher lived among the people of the Dales for a year and a day, and then disappeared into the West with the setting sun. No one could say for certain afterward whether the teacher had been a man or a woman, short or tall, fair-skinned or dark. But all the words that the teacher had spoken at moonrise—for the teacher was mute except at the full moon—were gathered up by disciples in the Dales and set down in a book. The Dalites were surprised how small the book was when it was done, and how light, and so it was called the Book of Light.

THE STORY:

Jenna was seven years old when she first touched the *Book of Light*. She stood with the three other girls her age in a straight line, or at least as straight as Marna, the teacher, and Zo, her dark sister, could make them. Selinda always fidgeted. And Alna, who had trouble breathing in the spring, wheezed her way through the ceremony. Only Marga—called Pynt after the small measure —and Jenna were still.

The priestess gave the line of girls a smile, but there was no warmth in that smile, only a formal lifting of the lips. It looked to Jenna like one of the wolves in the forest near Seldenkirk when frightened off its prey. She had seen a pack once. The priestess' dark sister gave the same smile, though it seemed infinitely more welcoming.

Jenna turned slightly so that she could look only straight upon that second smile, but she watched the priestess out of the side of her eye, the way she looked at things in the woods. Alta knew she had tried to please the Mother. But there seemed to be no pleasing her.

Overhead, the full spring moon illumined the stone altar. From the rowans came a rustling of new leaves as a small wind puzzled through the treetops. For a moment a rag of cloud covered the moon, and the priestess' dark sister disappeared from her altar-top throne. No one moved until the cloud passed by and the moon called them out again, all the dark ones. Then there was a quiet, contented sigh from the eighty mouths in the amphitheater.

The priestess lifted her head slightly to check out the skies. There were no other clouds in sight, and so she began. Opening the great leather-bound book on her lap, her pointing finger with its sharpened nail underlining each syllable on the page, she read aloud.

Jenna could not take her eyes off that nail. No one else was allowed such a hand, nor would want one. Nails such as a priestess had would crack and break in the kitchen or at the forge, would get in the way of a bowstring or knife. Jenna surreptitiously flexed her own hand, wondering what it would feel like to have fingernails like that. She decided against it.

The priestess' voice, clear and low, filled the spaces between the girls.

"And the child of seven summers, and the child of seven autumns, and the child of seven winters, and the child of seven springs shall come to the altar and choose her own way. And when she has chosen, she shall follow that path for seven more years, never wavering in her mind or heart. And thus shall the Chosen Way become the True Way."

The priestess looked up from the book where the letters seemed to take the moonlight and fling it back at her, causing little sparks to dance across the bib of her robe.

"Do you, my children, choose your own way?" she asked.

Her dark sister looked up at the same time, waiting for their answers.

"We do," the four girls answered as they had practiced, only Selinda came in late, for, as usual, she was dreaming about something else and had to be nudged from behind by Marna and Zo.

Then one by one the girls walked up the stairs to touch the book on the priestess' lap, Selinda first, for she was the oldest by nine months, and Jenna last. Touch the book, make the vow, name the choice. It was all so simple and not so simple. Jenna shuddered.

She knew that Selinda would go with her own mother and

work the gardens. There she could stare off into space without harm, going into what Marna and Zo called her "green dreams."

Alna, also born to a gardener, would choose the kitchen, where she wheezed less and where she would—it was thought —put a bit of weight on her thin bones. She was not happy about the choice, Jenna knew, for she really wanted to stay with her mother and her mother's dark sister, who babied and spoiled her, holding her through the rough nights when she labored between breath and breath. But every one of the sisters agreed that Alna needed to be as far from the bursting seeds and floating autumn weed silks as possible. The infirmarer, Kadreen, had warned again and again that one day the space between breaths would grow too long and Alna could die out in the garden. It was that warning that had, at last, decided them all. All except Alna, who had cried every night the past month, thinking about her coming exile, so she had told Jenna. But being an obedient child, she would say what had to be said at the Choosing.

Black-haired Pynt, a warrior's womb child, would choose the hunter/warrior path despite being so small and fine-boned, her father's legacy. If they tried to change Pynt's mind, Jenna knew she would fight them. Pynt would never waver, not for a moment. Loyalty coursed like blood through her veins.

And what of herself? Mothered by all but fostered by none, Jenna had already tried out many different paths. The gardens made her restless with their even rows. The kitchen was worse —everything in its place. She had even spent months by the priestess' side, which caused her to bite her nails to the quick, sure evidence that it would be the wrong choice. The fact was, she was happiest out in the forest or when playing warriors' games such as the wands, though only a few times did the women let a child into their circle. And then she and Pynt had been matched as light sister and dark. It was as if Jenna could see better in the woods than in the confines of the Hame. And next year, once she had chosen, she would be taught the bow and knife.

Jenna watched as first mousy Selinda, then wheezy Alna, and then strong-minded Pynt mounted the three steps to the altar where the priestess and her dark twin sat on their backless thrones.

One by one, the girls placed their right hand on the *Book*, their left touching the four places that were Alta's own: head, left breast, navel, groin. Then they recited the words of the oath after the priestess, speaking to her of their choices. What was said became so, so powerful were the words now: Selinda to the garden, Alna to the kitchen, Pynt to the hunt.

When Pynt came down the stairs, with a big grin on her face, she patted Jenna's hand. "Her breath is sour," she whispered.

After that Jenna found it difficult to take the first step seriously. Her mouth would not stay set in the thin line she had practiced. But once she set foot on the second step, it was different. It brought her closer to her choice. By the time she reached the third step, she found she was trembling. Not with fear of the priestess or awe of the *Book*, but with a kind of eagerness, like the young kit fox Amalda had rescued and trained, when it was in the presence of the hens. Even when he was not hungry, he trembled with anticipation. *That* was how Jenna felt.

Putting her hand on the *Book of Light*, she was surprised at how cold it was. The letters were raised up and she could feel them impress themselves on her palm. She touched her forehead with her left hand and it felt cool and dry. Then she put her hand over her heart, comforted to feel it beating steadily beneath her fingertips. Quickly she completed the rest of the ritual.

The priestess spoke, and her breath was not so much sour as alien, smelling of age and dignity and the trappings of state.

"You must say the words after me, Jo-an-enna, daughter of us all."

"I will, Mother Alta," Jenna whispered, her voice cracking suddenly.

"I am a child of seven springs . . ." began the priestess.

"I am a child of seven springs," Jenna repeated.

"I choose and I am chosen."

Jenna drew in a deep breath. "I choose and I am chosen."

The priestess smiled. Jenna saw that it was not such a distant smile after all, but a sad smile and not much practiced.

"The path I choose is . . ."

"The path I choose is . . ." Jenna said.

The priestess nodded, her face oddly expectant.

Jenna took another breath, deeper than the first. So many ways lay open to her at this moment. She closed her eyes to savor it, then opened them and was surprised by the predatory look in the priestess' face. Jenna turned slightly and spoke to the dark sister, more loudly than she had meant. "A warrior. A huntress. A keeper of the wood." She sighed, glad to be done with it.

The priestess did not speak for a moment. She looked almost angry. Then she and her dark sister leaned forward and embraced Jenna, whispering in Jenna's ears, "Well chosen, warrior." There was no warmth in it.

As Jenna walked back down the steps, she heard again the echo of the second thing the priestess alone had whispered in her ear. She wondered if the others had been told the same. Somehow she doubted they had, for the priestess had added, trembling strangely, "Alta's own chosen child."

The lessons began in earnest the next morning. It was not that the woods-days had been a time of play before, but the formal teaching—question and answer, memory tests, and the Game —could begin only after the Choosing.

"This is thimbleflower," said Pynt's mother Amalda, kneeling beside a dull green plant. "Soon it will have flowers that look like little purple bells."

"Why is it not called bellflower?" murmured Jenna, but Amalda only smiled.

"Pretty!" said Pynt, putting out her hand to stroke a leaf.

Amalda slapped it away, and when Pynt looked offended, said, "Remember, child, *Spilled water is better than a broken jar.* Do not touch something unless you know what it can do to you. There are thistles that prick, briars that snag, nettles that sting at the touch. Then there are the subtler plants whose poisons reveal themselves only long after."

Pynt put her smarting hand to her mouth.

At Amalda's signal, both girls knelt down next to her, Jenna

close and Pynt, still offended, a little way off. Then her own sunny
nature overcame her resentment, and she crowded next to Jenna.

"Smell these first," Amalda said, pointing to the leaf of the
thimbleflower.

They leaned over and sniffed. There was a slight, sharp odor.

"If I let you taste the leaves," Pynt's mother said, "you
would spit them out quickly." She shuddered deliberately, and the
girls imitated her, Pynt with a broad smile on her face. "But
should you swell up with water that will not release itself, should
your heart beat too quickly and loudly and Kadreen fears for it,
then she would make a tea of the leaves and you would soon be
relieved. Only . . ." And she held a hand up in warning. The girls
knew that sign well. It meant they must be silent and listen. "Only
beware of this *pretty* plant. In small doses it is a help to one in
distress, but too strong a brew, made with a wicked intent, and the
drinker dies."

Jenna shivered and Pynt nodded.

"Mark this place well," said Amalda. "For we do not pick the
leaves until the flower is full out. But Kadreen will be pleased that
we have found her a dell full of thimbleflower."

The girls looked around.

"Jenna, how have you marked it?"

Jenna thought. "By the big white tree with the two branches
in the trunk."

"Good. Pynt?"

"It was the third turning, A-ma. And to the right." In her
excitement, Pynt had reverted to her baby name for her mother.

Amalda smiled. "Fine! You both have good eyes. But that is
not all that is necessary in the woods. Come." She stood up and
strode down the path.

The girls followed after, skipping hand in hand.

The second lesson came close upon the first, for not another
turn further and Amalda held up her hand. Immediately the girls
were silent, stopped in their tracks. Amalda's chin went up and the
girls imitated her. She touched her right ear with her hand and
they listened intently. At first they heard nothing but the wind

through the trees. Then there came a strange, loud creaking, followed by a high chittering.

Amalda pointed to a fallen tree. They went over to it silently and stared.

"What beast?" Amalda asked at last.

Pynt shrugged.

"Hare?" Jenna guessed.

"Look, child. Listen. Your ears are as important as your eyes. Did you hear that squeaky scolding? It sounded like this." Lifting her head, she made a high noise with her tongue against the roof of her mouth.

The girls laughed in delighted admiration and then Amalda showed them how to make the sound. They each tried and Pynt got it right first.

"*That* is the sound squirrel makes," said Amalda.

"I know that!" said Jenna, surprised, for now that the name was spoken, she found that she had, indeed, known it.

"Me, too!" said Pynt.

"So we know squirrel watches us and scolds us for entering her domain." Amalda nodded and looked around.

The girls did the same.

"Therefore we look for signs to tell us where squirrel especially likes to come, her favorite places." She pointed again to the fallen tree. "Stumps are often such a spot."

They looked carefully at the stump. Around the base was a small midden heap of cone scales and nut shellings.

"Squirrel eats here," said Amalda. "She has left these signs for us but she does not know it. See now if you can find her little digging places, for she loves to bury things."

They scattered, as silently as two seven-year-olds can, and soon each came upon the small dead-end diggings. Jenna's held a buried acorn but Pynt's only the acorn caps. Amalda praised them for their finds. Afterward she showed them the slight scratches on the trees where the squirrels had chased one another up and over their favorite routes, leaving a few tiny patches of squirrel hair caught in the trunk. Deftly Amalda picked out the hair and tucked it into her leather pouch.

"Sada and Lina will find a use for these with their weavers," she said.

The girls scrambled over several more trees, each coming up with handfuls of more hair. Jenna found a tree marked with larger scratches.

"Squirrel?" she asked.

Amalda patted her on the head. "Sharp-eyed girl," she said, "but that is no squirrel."

Pynt shook her head, her dark curls bouncing. "Too big," she said wisely. "Too deep."

Together Pynt and Jenna whispered, "Fox?" and Jenna added by herself, "Coon?"

Amalda smiled. "Mountain cat," she said.

With that the lesson ended, for they all knew the danger, and though Amalda had seen no recent scat and doubted the cat was even in the area, she thought *caution* a fine moral to teach the girls, and led them back home.

At the noon table, piled high with fresh, twisted loaves of bread and steaming mugs of squirrel stew, Amalda could not help but show the girls off.

"Tell the sisters what you learned today," she said.

"That thimbleflowers can be good," said Pynt.

"Or bad," Jenna added.

"For your heart or . . ." Pynt stopped, unable to remember more.

"Or your water," Jenna said, and then wondered at the chuckle that ran around the table.

"And squirrels sound like this." Pynt made the sound and was rewarded with applause. She smiled, delighted, for she and Jenna had practiced the squirrel call all the way home.

Jenna clapped, too, and then, when the noise had died down, she spoke out, eager to win her share of the praise. "We found the mark of a mountain cat." When there was no applause, she added, "A mountain cat killed my first mother."

There was a sudden silence at the table. The priestess looked over at Amalda from her place at the head. "Who has told the child this . . . this tale?"

"Mother, not I," Amalda said quickly.

"Nor I."

"Nor I."

Swiftly the denials ran around the table.

The priestess stood, her voice deep with anger and authority. "This child belongs to all of us. There is no first mother. There is no second mother. Am I understood?" She waited for their complete silence, took it for approval, spun on her heel, and left.

No one spoke for many minutes after, though the children continued to eat noisily, their spoons loud against the mugs.

"What does all that mean?" asked Donya, peering in from the kitchen doorway.

"It means age is wearing away her senses," muttered Catrona, wiping wine from her mouth with the back of her hand. "She feels heat even on the coldest days. She looks into mirrors and sees her mother's face."

Domina added, "She cannot get a child to choose *her* way, even after so many springtimes of trying. We will have to send to another Hame when *she* dies."

Jenna was the only child not eating, staring at her plate and feeling first hot, then cold on her cheeks. She had wanted attention when she said what she said, but not this kind. She scuffed her sandal against the chair leg. The slight sound, which only she heard, comforted her.

"Hush!" said Amalda, her hand on Domina's arm for emphasis.

"She is right, Domina, Catrona," said Kadreen in her flat, unsmiling way. She nodded her head toward the table where the gardeners sat, meaning—they all knew—that what was spoken here would find its way soon enough into the ears of the priestess herself. The workers of the field always served the one who blessed their crops; they were hers unquestioningly. Not that Kadreen cared. She took no sides in any disputes, just set the bones and stitched the wounds, but she was not above a warning now and again. "And you, Catrona, remember that when the villagers say *There is no medicine to cure hatred*, they are right. I have warned you about these passions. Just a month past and your stomach was bad again and you were abed with the bloody flux. Drink goat's milk as I told you, instead of that rough grape swill, and practice your *latani* breathing for calm. I do not want you back soon."

Catrona snorted through her nose and turned her attention back to her food, pointedly pushing the soup and wine aside and attacking the bread with gusto, smearing it liberally with honey from the pot.

Jenna gulped in a deep breath. "I did not mean anything," she said in a piercing child's voice. "What did I say? Why is everyone so mad?"

Amalda struck her on top of the head lightly with a pair of foodsticks. "Not your fault, child," she said. "Sometimes grown sisters speak before they think."

"Speak for yourself, Amalda," muttered Catrona. She pushed the bread aside, shoved her chair back, and stood up. "I meant exactly what I said. Besides, the child has a right to know . . ."

"There is nothing to know," said Kadreen.

Catrona snorted again and left.

"Know what?" asked Pynt. She was answered with a sharper tapping on the head than Jenna had received.

Jenna said nothing but stood up. Without even asking to be excused, she walked to the door. Then, turning, she spoke. "I *will* know. And if none of you will tell me, I will ask Mother Alta myself."

"That one . . ." Donya said later to her maids in the kitchen, "she will one day tackle the Goddess Great Alta herself, mark my words." But they did not mark them, for Donya tended to ramble and make such pronouncements all the time.

Jenna went directly to the priestess' rooms, though as she came closer, she could feel her heart pounding madly. She wondered if Kadreen would have to give her a draught of thimbleflower potion for it. She worried that if the potion were too strong, she would die. To die just as she had chosen her way. It would be terribly sad. All the wondering and worrying disguised how quickly she was walking, and she came to the priestess' room rather faster than she had planned.

The door was open and Mother Alta was sitting behind a great loom at which she was working on a tapestry of the Hame, one of those endless priestess tasks that Jenna had found so boring. *Snip-snap* went her fingernails against the shuttle; *click-clack* went the shuttle across the threads from side to side. Mother Alta must have seen movement from the corner of her eye. She looked up. "Come in, Jo-an-enna," she said.

There was no help for it. Jenna went in.

"Have you come to ask my forgiveness?" She smiled but the smile did not reach her eyes.

"I have come to ask why you say my first mother was *not* killed by a cat when all the others say it." Jenna could not help fiddling with her right braid and the leather thong binding it. "They say she was killed trying to save me."

"Who are *they?*" the priestess asked, her voice low and carefully uninflected. Her right hand moved over the left, turning and turning her great agate ring. Jenna could not take her eyes off the ring.

"Which others, Jo-an-enna?" Mother Alta asked again.

Jenna looked up and tried to smile. "I have heard that story ever since I can remember," she said. "But is it not peculiar, Mother, I do not remember exactly *who* told me first." She caught her breath because that was not really a lie. She could remember Amalda saying it. And Domina. Even Catrona. And the girls repeating it. But she did not want them to be in trouble. Especially not Amalda, whom she often pretended was her mother as much as Pynt's. She secretly called her "A-ma" at night, into her pillow. "And there is a song about it, too."

"Do not believe songs," said the priestess, her hands having left the ring to play with the great chain of metal half-moons and moonstones around her neck. "Next you will believe the ravings of village priests and the puns of itinerant rhymesters."

"Then what should I believe?" Jenna asked. "*Who* should I believe?"

"Believe me. Believe the *Book of Light.* Soon enough you shall know it. And believe that Great Alta hears all." Her finger with its long, glittering nail pointed to the ceiling for emphasis.

"Did she hear that I had a mother killed by a cat?" Jenna asked, appalled that her tongue spoke what her mind had made up, without waiting for her to judge it.

"Be gone, child, you tire me." The priestess waved the back of her hand at Jenna.

Relieved, Jenna left.

No sooner had the child gone out the door than Mother Alta rose, pushing aside the heavy loom. She went over to the great polished mirror standing in its ornate wooden frame. Often she spoke to it as she would to her own dark sister, when she needed counsel in the day, for indeed the two images were near the same, the only difference being in the color and the fact that the mirror did not talk back. *Sometimes,* Mother Alta thought wearily, *I prefer the glass's silence to the answers I receive from my dark twin.*

"Do you remember the man in the town," she whispered, "the Slipskin farmer? He had rough hands and a rougher tongue. We were younger then by seven years, but older by far than he. He did not know it, though. How could he, used as he was to the coarse women of his coarse town." She smiled wryly at the memory and the image smiled back.

"We surprised him, sister, when we took off our cloaks. And we surprised him with our silken skins. And we surprised him out of the story of his only child, the one who had, all unknowing, killed her mother and the midwife who took her into the mountains and never returned. He will remember our passion as a dream, for we came to him secretly at midnight. And all the others we questioned knew but one of us, disguised in the day, and she an old, old crone." This time she did not smile, and the image stared back at her in silence.

"His story—it had to be true. No man cries in the arms of a woman lest the story he tell be true. We were the first who had come to warm his bed since his wife's death. His wounds though nine months old were fresh. And so there *were* three: mother, midwife, fosterer. Three in one. And dead, all dead."

She bit her lower lip. The eyes in the mirror, as green as her own, stared back at her.

"Oh, Great Alta, speak to me. It is one of thy priestesses begging." She held up her hands and the mark of Alta, incised in blue, stood out vividly on her palms. "Here am I, Mother to thy children, ruling them in this small Hame in thy name. I have neither helper nor child but my dark sister, no one to speak to but thee. Oh, Great Alta, who is sower and reaper, who is in the beginning and in the end, hear me." She touched herself: head, left breast, navel, and groin. "Have I done right, Great One? Have I done wrong? This child is thrice orphaned, as it says in the prophecy. But there have been rumors of others before her. One came from the Hame near Calla's Ford, and one so long ago fostered in the Hame near Nill. But they proved themselves just girls after all.

"Then what is this child, this Annuanna? She is marked with hair the color of new snow, and of such the prophecy speaks. But she laughs and cries like any child. She is quick-tongued and quick-footed, but no better at the games than her foster sister Marga. Many times have I given her the choice of following me as thine own, a priestess to lead thy children. But she chose instead the woods and the hunt and other such follies. How can this be the child we seek?

"Oh, Great Alta, I know thou speakest to me in the sun that rises and in the moon that shapes itself anew each month. I know thy voice echoes in the pattering of rain and the rising up of the dew. So it is written, and so I believe. But I need a clearer sign before I unfold this wonder to all of them. Not just the piqued mouthings of jealous women, not just the guilty, tearful confidences of an unhappy man. And not just my own trembling heart. A true sign.

"The burden, Great One, is so hard to bear. I am so very lonely. I grow old before my time with this secret. Look here. And here." She pulled aside her gown to show how flaccid her breasts had become. She touched the loosening skin under her chin. Tears began to well up in her eyes and she knelt before the mirror, sighing.

"And one thing more, Great Alta, though thou knowest it already. Yet still I must confess it aloud to thee. The greatest fear of all. If I am not thy priestess, I am nothing. It is all my life. I need a promise, Great One, a promise if she—Annuanna, Jo-an-enna, Jenna—is the one of whom it is written, the light sister thrice born and thrice orphaned, the one who will be queen over all and change what we know. And the promise I beg is that if it is she, then I will still serve thee as I have. That the place at the head of the table will still be mine. That I shall still sit on the throne under the moon and call thy name that the sisters might hear me and pray. Promise me that, Great Alta, and I shall reveal her."

The mirror image's face flushed suddenly and the priestess put her hand up to her cheeks, which burned fiercely beneath her fingers. Other than the fire in her face, there was no sign.

She stood up heavily. "I must think upon this more." Turning, she went out the other door, the hidden door, behind the heavy patched tapestry upon which the forms of sisters light and dark played at wands.

THE HISTORY:

There is, of course, no extant copy of the Book of Light, *the great text of the moon-centered Mother Goddess worshippers. Though presumably each Hame or community of Altites had a hand-*

lettered and illuminated copy of the Book. *Such volumes disappeared during the Gender Wars, either—if the Sigel and Salmon dig logs are accurate—into underground chambers especially constructed against such eventualities or—if one is to trust Vargo's reconstruction of the priestess codes—into ritual fires.*

However, the meat of the Book's *history and its gnomic teachings can be plucked from the rich stew of folk life in the towns that still flourish near the ancient Hame sites. Buss and Bee's monumental work,* So Speak the Folk, *gives strong support to the idea that the Alta Hames (or Alta's Shames, as the priests of the Lower Dales still call them) were in fact merely extensions of the towns and cities which bordered their lands, in effect suburban satellites, at least as far as their speech patterns and folk beliefs are concerned.*

Of course, the story of Alta worship is intelligible only in the light of early Garunian history. The G'runs, an ancient, well-connected noble family from the Continent, had come to the Isles in the invasions of the 800s. Worshippers of a male trinity of gods—Hargo, god of fire, Vendre, god of water, and Lord Cres, the brutal god of the dead—they settled along the seacoasts. Slowly they infiltrated into the upper councils of the semimatriarchal civilization they found there. Trying at first to undermine it, they in fact later compromised and accepted a matrilineal succession only after the devastating Gender Wars wrecked both the ancient Hame sites and the famous palace of G'run Far Shooter.

The religion the Garunians were trying to supplant was anathema to the first invaders because of its emphasis on a white-haired goddess who seeded herself without the aid of a male consort. It was a religion that had grown up in part because of the overflow of women following much earlier, devastating wars of succession which had been fought some four hundred years before. Because of the created imbalance between the sexes that followed the civil strife, it had become the custom to expose unwanted, superfluous girl babies on the hillsides. However, in the late 600s, a female reputedly of great height and with long, flowing white

*hair (possibly an albino, though more probably an old woman)
named Alta wandered the countryside speaking out against the
brutal custom and gathering what live children she could find. She
fashioned carts linked together to trundle the rescued babes
behind her. Slowly this Alta was joined by like-minded women
who were either unmarried (there were many spinsters, the
so-called unclaimed treasures, because of the ratio of men to
women), widows, or multiple wives in polygamous marriages.
(Especially in the Lower Dales such radical couplings
had been tolerated, though only the children of the first wife
might inherit.) Thus was the first of seventeen Hames estab-
lished, as havens for the discarded children and extra women.
This reconstruction, first set forth by the late Professor Davis
Temple of Hofbreeder University in his now-classic Alta-
Natives, is so thoroughly accepted that I need not comment
further.*

*The communities of foster mothers, needing some religious
underpinnings, developed the worship of a White Goddess called
Great Alta. The genius and genuine goodness of the original Alta
was rewarded in this fashion. Over the years, the real Alta and a
subsequent itinerant preacher whose name has been given vari-
ously as Gennra, Hendra, Hanna, Anna, and The Dark One
have merged into the figure of a goddess whose hair is both light
and dark, a strange hermaphroditic creature who has babies
without recourse to a male consort. The religion borrowed many
aspects of the surrounding patriarchal tribes and, later, even took
on some of the Garunian worship. (For example, the custom of
cave burials, a later addition, was patterned after the G'runs, who
came originally from a small valley between cave-riddled mountains where land for cultivation was too prime to be turned over
to the dead. Earlier Altite burials were in great mounds.)*

*Just as the white-haired Alta had been a savior for many a
girl child left to die upon a hillside, rumors of a second savior
arose. The rumors became belief, set down—if we are again to
believe Vargo—in the Book of Light itself. This savior was to be
the child of a dead mother; the easy psychological substitution*

—dead child to dead mother—is the most basic of folk shifts. Not one dead mother, in fact, but three, that magical number. It is a belief still encapsulated in some of the folk songs and sayings in the Upper Dales.

THE SONG:

Alta's Song

I am a babe, an only babe,
Fire and water and all,
Who in my mother's womb was made,
Great Alta take my soul.

But from that mother I was torn,
Fire and water and all,
And to a hillside I was borne,
Great Alta take my soul.

And on that hillside was I laid,
Fire and water and all,
And taken up all by a maid,
Great Alta take my soul.

And one and two and three we rode,
Fire and water and all,
Till others took the heavy load,
Great Alta take my soul.

Let all good women hark to me,
Fire and water and all,
For fostering shall set thee free,
Great Alta take my soul.

THE STORY:

"What did she say? What did you say?" Pynt asked breathlessly, twisting her fingers in her dark curls. She was sitting on the floor of their shared room by the window. The room tended toward darkness, as did all the rooms in the Hame, so the girls always played close to the narrow slits of windows, winter and summer. "Did she hit you?"

Jenna thought about what to say. She almost wished Mother Alta *had* hit her. Amalda had a quick hand and both girls had had recent willow whippings, Pynt for her quick mouth and Jenna for supporting her. But they were not long or hard whippings and besides, such punishment was always followed swiftly by hugs and tears and kisses. If the priestess had acted so, Jenna might not have stayed beyond the door, quiet as a wood mouse, listening. Was she the babe who had, all unknowing, killed her mother not once but three times? The thought had so frightened her, she had not stayed to hear more but run away to hide, down in the cellar, where the great casks of dark red wine were kept. In the dark she had breathed first very fast, with the sobs threatening to burst out of her chest, because if she were that child, then all her hoping for A-ma to be her mother, all her pretending, was just that: a game. And then she had slowed her breathing down and forced herself to stand dry-eyed. She would find Pynt and ask her.

Only now, standing over Pynt, she knew this was too heavy a burden to share. "She asked who had told me such a thing and I said that I could not remember who had told me first." She slumped to the floor next to Pynt.

"A-ma was first," said Pynt. "I remember. It was like a story. We were both sleeping in the big bed, a special treat, between A-ma and Sammor, and . . ."

"Maybe not," said Jenna, relieved to be past the hardest part. "Maybe I heard it first from Catrona. Or Donya. She talks too much, she probably . . ."

". . . said it three times over." Pynt laughed. It was a common joke at the Hame, even among the children.

"I heard Domina say something about it. And something about my second mother, too. They were friends." Was this treading too close to the treacherous ground? Jenna felt her fingers start to twitch, but Pynt seemed not to notice.

Pynt put her elbows on her knees and rested her chin in her hands. "Not Kadreen, though. You would not have heard it from her."

They both shook their heads wisely. Kadreen never gossiped or gave information freely.

"I *like* Kadreen," said Jenna, "even though she is a Solitary. Even though she never smiles." Solitaries, women without dark sisters, were rare at the Hames, and Jenna felt very much as she suspected a Solitary felt, alone and without the comfort of a companion who knew your every thought.

"I saw her smile once. It was when Alna stopped breathing and then started again with those funny coughs and the bubbles coming out of her mouth. When we were in the garden hunting down the rabbit. Well, the pretend rabbit. Children's games! And you ran to get Kadreen because you are the fastest, and she put her ear down on Alna's chest and thumped it."

"And Alna had a black mark as big as a fist for seven days."

"Eight—and she loved to show it off."

"Kadreen did not smile then."

"Did."

"Did not."

"Did. And anyway, A-ma gave me these." Pynt reached behind her back and brought up two new corn dolls in one hand and a pair of reed backpacks in the other. "She and Sammor made them for us to celebrate the Choosing."

"Ooh, they are nicer than Alna's."

"Much nicer," agreed Pynt.

"And the packs have the Hame sign on them." Jenna pointed to the sign in the circle.

"Now," Pynt said, "we can be truly truly sisters, just the way you like to play it, sharing everything. You take the light pack and the light doll and I will take the dark."

Jenna took the pack guiltily, remembering how little she had actually shared with Pynt, remembering how Mother Alta had looked, standing in front of the great framed mirror, and speaking the words which had so frightened her. She remembered and wondered if she and Pynt could ever be *truly truly* sisters again.

Then the dolls proved much more interesting than her own black thoughts and she put the babe in the pack, the pack on her back, and played at light sister and dark with Pynt for an hour or more, until the ringing bell recalled them to their lessons.

"This afternoon," Catrona informed them, "I shall instruct you in the Game of the Eye-Mind."

The girls grinned and Pynt elbowed Jenna playfully. They had both heard of the Game. The older girls talked of it secretly at the table sometimes. But none of them had ever really explained it, for it was one of the Mysteries reserved for *after* the Choosing.

Pynt looked around quickly as if to see if anyone was noticing them. There were three older girls in the warrior yard, but they were busy with their own things: red-headed Mina aiming at the arrow target and hitting it regularly with comfortable *thumps*, and Varsa and Little Domina having at each other with wicker swords to the accompaniment of Big Domina's shouted corrections.

"Pynt, watch me!" Catrona said, her voice not at all sharp, but laughing. "I know there is much to see here, but you must learn to focus."

"What of the *eye's corner?* Amalda said . . ." Jenna hesitated.

"You get ahead of me, child," said Catrona. She pulled lightly on one of Jenna's braids, not enough to hurt but enough to get Jenna's full attention. "First you learn to focus and then diffuse."

"What is *diffuse?*" asked Pynt.

Catrona laughed again. "It means to be able to see many things at once. But first you must *listen*, Marga." She stopped laughing abruptly.

They listened.

Catrona turned to the table by her side, a small wooden table, much scarred around the legs. It was covered by an old cloth which disguised a number of strange lumps and bumps on the top.

"First, what do you see here?" Catrona asked, gesturing them to the tabletop.

"A table with an old cloth," said Pynt, quickly adding, "And a ragged old cloth."

"A cloth covering many things," said Jenna.

"You are both correct. But remember this—caution in the woods and in battle is the greatest virtue. Often what *seems* is not what *is*." She whisked away the cloth and they saw that the table was a solid carved representation of a mountaintop with peaks and valleys. "This we use to teach the way through the mountain range in which our Hame is nestled. *And* to plan our stratagems."

Pynt clapped her hands together, delightedly, while Jenna bent over closer to run her finger thoughtfully over the ridges and trails.

"Now what do you see here?" Catrona asked, guiding them over to the alcove where a second table covered with a similar cloth stood. There were even more ridges and peaks under this cloth.

"Another mountain," said Pynt, eager as always to be first with the answer.

"Caution, with caution," reminded Catrona.

Jenna shook her head. "It does not look like a mountain to me. The peaks are not as high. There are round places, as round as . . . as an . . ."

"An apple!" Pynt interjected.

"Let us see," said Catrona. She took the cloth away by lifting it up from the middle. On the table was a strange assortment of objects.

"Oh!" said Pynt. "You fooled me!" She looked up at Catrona, grinning.

"Look back, child. *Focus.*"

Pynt looked back just as Catrona dropped the cloth back onto the tabletop, covering it completely.

"Now comes the Game," said Catrona. "We will start with Marga. Since you so love being first, you shall name an object on the table. Then Jenna. Then Marga again. On and on until you can remember no more. The one who remembers the most gets a sweet."

Pynt clapped her hands, for she loved sweets. "A spoon. There was a spoon," she said.

Jenna nodded. "And it *was* an apple, the round thing."

"And a pair of foodsticks," Pynt said.

"One only," said Jenna.

"One," agreed Catrona.

"A card of some kind," said Pynt.

"A buckle, like A-ma—Amalda's," said Jenna.

"I did not see that," Pynt said, turning to look at Jenna, who shrugged.

"It was there," Catrona said. "Go on, Marga."

Pynt's forehead made wavy lines as she concentrated. She put her fist into her cheek and thought. Then she smiled. "There were *two* apples!"

"Good girl!" Catrona smiled.

"On a plate," said Jenna.

"Two plates?" Pynt asked uncertainly.

"You are lucky," Catrona answered.

"A knife," said Jenna.

Pynt thought for a good long while and at last shrugged. "There was nothing else," she said.

"Jenna?" Catrona turned and looked directly at Jenna, who was pulling on her braids. Jenna knew there had been more objects and could name them, but she also knew how much Pynt wanted to win the sweet. How much Pynt *needed* to win the sweet. Then she sighed. "A bowl of water. A pin. Some thread."

"Thread?" Catrona shook her head. "No thread, Jenna."

"Yes, thread," Jenna said. "And two or maybe three pebbles or berries. And . . . and that is all I can remember."

Catrona smiled. "Five berries, two of them black and three red. And you both neglected to mention the piece of tapestry with the wand players or the ribband or the writing stick, tapestry needle and—the sweet! But for all that you forgot, you remembered quite a good bit. I am very proud of the two of you for your first time at the Game." She pulled away the cloth. "Now look closely again."

It was Pynt who pointed first. "Look, Catrona, there is Jenna's thread!"

Lying next to the tapestry piece, but far enough away from it to be read as a single item, was a long dark thread.

Catrona laughed out loud. "Sharp eyes indeed, Jo-an-enna! And I am getting foolish and careless in my old age. Fine teacher I am. Such a miss might mean my doom in the woods or in the midst of battle."

The girls nodded sagely back at her as she picked up the sweet and solemnly handed it to Jenna.

"We will play again and again until you remember *all* that you see. Tomorrow we will play with different objects under the cloth. By the time this Game is done, you will be able to name everything the first time and there will be more than thirty things to name. But it is not just a Game, my children. The point of it is this—you must look at everything twice—once with your outer eye and once with the eye of your mind. That is why it is called the Eye-Mind Game. You must learn to resee everything, to recall it as clearly the second time as the first."

"Do we do the same thing in the woods?" asked Pynt.

Jenna had not asked the question because she already knew the answer. Of course they must do the same thing in the woods. And in the Hame and in the towns. Everywhere. What a foolish thing to ask. She was surprised at Pynt.

But Catrona did not seem surprised. "The same," she said calmly. "What *good* girls!" She put a hand on the shoulders of each and pushed them closer to the table. "Now look again."

They crowded close and stared intently at the tabletop, Pynt's mouth moving in a strange litany as she reminded herself the names of each object there. Jenna stared with such intensity she trembled.

In the evening, the four new Choosers met in their room and sat on Jenna's bed. They each had much to share.

Pynt bubbled through a recitation of the Game and how Jenna had shared the sweet with her.

"Though she really won it," Pynt finished. "But tomorrow I will win. I think I have found the secret." She rocked her new doll in her arms as she spoke.

"You always have a secret way, Pynt," said Selinda. "And it almost never works."

"Does."

"Does not."

"Does."

"Tell us about the kitchen, Alna," said Jenna. Suddenly she could not stand the argument. What did it matter if Pynt sometimes tried to find secret ways or that they seldom worked?

Alna said in her whispery voice, "I never knew there was so much to learn in a *kitchen*. I got to help cut up things. In the garden they never let me use a knife. And I did not hurt myself once. It smells good in there, too, but . . ." She sighed and did not finish.

"You would not have liked the gardens today anyway," Selinda said quickly. "All we did was weed. Weed! I have done that ever since I can remember. How was it different to have chosen? I should have gone to the kitchen. Or the woods. Or to the weavers. Or . . ."

"I like weeding," Alna whispered.

"You do *not*," said Pynt. "You used to complain about it all the time."

"Did not."

"Did."

"Did not."

Amalda came into the room. "It is time to get into bed, little ones," she said. "You must be like the birds. As high as they fly, they always return to earth." She gave them each a hug before leaving, and Jenna squeezed back extra hard.

Minutes later Selinda's womb mother came in and stayed only a moment, tucking in Selinda and giving each of the other girls a nod. And then, because it was past dark, and Jenna had gotten out of bed again and lit all the lanterns, Alna's mother and dark sister both came in. They gave each girl a touch but they fussed nervously and—to Jenna's mind—endlessly over Alna despite her reassurances to them that she felt fine.

At last Marna and Zo came in and, to everyone's delight, they carried their tembalas with them. Marna's instrument had a sweet sound. Zo's was lower and complementary, just like their voices.

"Sing 'Come, Ye Women,' " begged Pynt.

"And the 'Ballad of Ringer's Forge,' " Alna whispered.

" 'Derry Down.' Sing 'Derry Down,' " Selinda said, bouncing on her bed.

Jenna alone was silent as she unbraided her white hair, which was crinkled from its long plaiting.

"And do you not have a favorite also, Jo-an-enna?" asked Marna softly, watching Jenna's swift hands.

Jenna was slow in answering, but at last very seriously said, "Is there a new song we can hear? One just for this first day after the Choosing?" She wanted this day to be as special as it was supposed to be, not just a strange, hollow feeling under her breastbone where all the little squabbles with Pynt and the odd sense of distance from the other girls were growing. She wanted to be close to them, and ordinary again; she wanted to wash away the memory of Mother Alta before her great mirror. "Something we have never heard before."

"Of course, Jenna. I will sing something I learned last year when we had that mission visit from the singer from Calla's Ford Hame. Theirs is such a large Hame, some seven hundred members, one can be *just* a singer there."

"Would you want to be *just* a singer, dear Marna?" asked Pynt.

It was Zo who answered. "In a large Hame, our small talent would scarcely be recognized," she said.

"Besides, this is our Hame," said Marna. "We would be no place else."

"But you were someplace else once," said Jenna thoughtfully. She wondered if she would feel different, more ordinary, scarcely recognized someplace else.

"Of course I was, Jenna. When I went on my year mission before the final Choosing, before calling my sister from the dark, just as you shall. But for all the Hames I visited and all the sisters there who would have had me stay, I came back here, to Selden Hame, though it is the smallest of them all."

"Why?" asked Pynt.

"Yes—why?" the other three echoed.

"Because it is *our* Hame," Marna and Zo said together.

"Now, enough questions," Marna said, "or there will be no time for even one song."

They snuggled down in their beds.

"First I will sing the new song. It is called 'Alta's Song.' And then I will sing the others. Afterward, you must all go right to sleep. You are no longer my little ones, you know, and there will be much for you to do come morning."

She began the first song. By the end of the third, the girls were all asleep except for Jenna, but Marna and Zo did not notice and they tiptoed out of the room.

The fire in the Great Hall's hearth crackled merrily and two hounds dozing nearby scrabbled on the stones with their claws as they chased after rabbits in their dreams. The room smelled comfortably of rushes and woodsmoke and of the bowls of dried rose petals and verbena.

When Marna and Zo entered, they saw that all the big chairs near the fire were taken already and the three older girls lay on their stomachs on the rug by the hearth.

"Over here," called Amalda.

They turned and saw that two places at the large round table off to the side of the hearth had been reserved for them.

"How are the Choosers?" asked Amalda intently.

"Are they still excited?" Her dark sister Sammor seemed more relaxed.

"They are quiet for now. We sang them four songs—well, three, actually. They fell asleep before the fourth. Poor little mites, the day had quite exhausted them and I promised them more work for the morrow." Marna sat down heavily in the chair.

"We miss those little imps already," said Zo as soon as she, too, was seated.

Catrona smiled. "This is not such a great Hame that you will not see them every day."

"But they have been our special charges for the last seven years," Marna said. "And I feel them growing away from us already."

Domina sniffed. "You say that every spring at Choosing."

"Not *every* spring. We have not had a Choosing since Varsa, and that three years ago. And now four at once. It is very hard."

Alna's mother looked across the table at her. "It is harder on Glon and me. They have taken our baby from the gardens. To be a kitchener. Under Donya. Feh."

"What do you mean by *they?*" Catrona flared. "You were as worried as we were that she might someday stop breathing out in that weedy trap of yours."

"Weedy? What do you mean? Our garden is as clean of weeds as any you will find in a larger Hame. Weeds indeed!" Alinda started to stand and Glon, next to her, reached out to steady her. They sat down together, but Alinda still trembled with anger.

"She just meant it was hard," said Glon to Catrona. "Forgive her. We are both out of sorts today."

Catrona snorted and looked away.

"The first day after a Choosing is always difficult," said Kadreen, coming to sit at the table's head. "And we say the same thing every time. Are we children to have such short memories? Come, sisters, look at one another and smile. This feeling will pass." She looked around the table and though she herself did not smile, soon the rest were returned to their normal happy moods. "Now are we all here?"

"Donya and Doey are late, as usual," said Domina.

"We must wait, then. This concerns the new Choosers and so everyone who is involved with them must be here." Kadreen folded her hands on top of the table, lacing the blunt, squared-off fingers loosely. "Marna, Zo, why not give us a song while we wait? Something—something bright."

They needed no more prompting, but picked up the tembalas and with an almost imperceptible nod between them to establish the beat, started plucking a quick-step dance that involved a melody which seemed to leap from one instrument to the other. It lightened the mood around the table considerably. They were just reaching the finale, with four strums alternating on the drone strings, when Donya and her dark sister Doey bustled in, wiping their hands on their stained aprons, eager to offer full excuses for being late.

Kadreen signaled them to sit with a wave of her hands, so that the dying strum of the tembalas was accompanied by the scraping of chair legs against the wooden floor.

"As you all know, we must talk now of the future for our new Choosers. These girls *are* our future. First, though, we must know from Marna what to expect. What do they know and how fast do they learn?"

Marna and Zo nodded. "What I say now is not new to you. Over the years I have consulted with the mothers and with you, Kadreen, when there was illness. But telling it again to all may bring out some other truths, hidden even from Zo and me.

"All four are bright, quick learners and have their first letters already. Jenna can read sentences and will soon begin on the first of the *Little Books*, though it is Alna who loves the tales the best."

Alinda nodded complacently. "We always told her stories to calm her when her breath would not come easily."

Marna smiled and continued. "Selinda is a dreamy sort and she needs much recalling to her tasks."

Selinda's womb mother laughed. "Takes after her father. Three boys I had after but a week with their fathers. But Selinda's needed so much recalling to his work, I was with him three months."

They all laughed with her.

Marna waited out their laughter. "Pynt—Marga, as I suppose she should be called now, though I shall always think of her as Pynt—is the very quickest at most things—"

Zo interrupted. "But she forgets caution much of the time. We fear that very quickness will lead her into trouble."

Nodding, Marna added, "We do."

"It has already." Catrona shifted in her chair and leaned forward, over the table. "She did not get the sweet she wanted at her first try at the Game."

Marna laughed at that and Zo explained. "She got the sweet anyway. And the larger half at that. Jenna shared it with her."

Kadreen unlaced her fingers, speaking slowly. "They are like shadow sisters, Jenna and Pynt. It will go harder on them when they have their own dark twins, will it not?" She asked it carefully, aware that as a Solitary she had little right to speak of such things. She had come to the Hame as a full adult, choosing to live apart from the busy towns where she had learned her craft, arriving much too late in life to be introduced to the Hame Mysteries or to learn to call up a sister from Alta's eternal dark. "I mean, they shall have to wrench themselves when . . ."

"That is almost seven years from now, Kadreen. And you know what childhood friendships are," said Marna.

"No," Kadreen muttered under her breath.

"We could consider it if they still hold fast together when it is time for the mission," suggested Domina.

"The *Book* speaks of loyalties," reminded Kadreen. "This much I know. And Mother Alta has asked me to warn all of you about encouraging their special friendship overmuch. Jenna's needs cannot be met by one friend alone. She must be loyal equally to all in the Hame. Not just one teacher, not just one mother, not just one friend. Mother Alta has made that quite clear." She said the words as if they left a sour taste in her mouth.

"She is a *child*, Kadreen," Amalda said. "I would have taken her long ago as my own, had the Mother allowed it."

The others nodded.

"Perhaps she is more than that," Kadreen muttered, but she did not say more.

THE HISTORY:

Another game that has a tangled ancient history is the popular "I-Mine" of the Lower Dales, which Lowentrout, in one of his brilliant but eccentric leaps of scholarship, has dubbed "a classic Alta warrior training pattern game." (See his Letter to the Editor, Games Magazine, Vol. 544.) His evidence, which is extremely shaky, rests on Vargo's highly suspect linguistic shift thesis and interpretations of the priestess codes, rather than the more laborious but detailed archaeological work such as Cowan's and Temple's.

The game as it is played today is a board-and-counter game, the board consisting of 64 contiguous squares of 32 light and 32 dark. There are an equal number of counters with inscribed faces, 32 with light backs and 32 dark.

The inscriptions are paired, so that there are 32 of each color. They include: a knife, crossed sticks, ribbons tied in a bow, a flower, a circle (presumably representing a stone, since it is called so), an apple, a bowl, a spoon, a threaded pin, grapes (or berries; both names are given), a triangle, a square, a crescent moon, a sun, a crown, a bow, an arrow, a dog, a cow, a bird, a hand, a foot, a rainbow, a wavy line which is called "river" by the players, a tree, a cat, a cart, a house, a fish, a mask, a chair, and a sign which is designated "Alta" and is, in fact, the sign for female that is as ancient as any in the Dales.

The point of the game is to capture the opponent's counters. The play begins with all the counters turned inscription-side down and shuffled, then set onto the squares in a haphazard manner called "scuffling," though light-backed counters go on the light squares, dark on dark. Play begins with each player turning over two counters. (They may be two of his own or one of each player's.) Then those counters are returned to their face-down positions.

Now the memory part of the game begins, for each player, in turn, turns over two counters, one of each color. If the inscriptions match, he keeps or "captures" them both. As the player turns over the counters, he says—on turning over his own—"I," and if he suspects a pair, as he turns over his opponent's, "Mine." If he suspects (or remembers) they are not paired, he says "Thine." If he should say "I-Mine" to an unmatched pair, he loses a turn. If he says "I-Thine" to a matched pair, he does not win or keep the pair (which are called "suites") and his opponent then has a free opportunity to turn up the two. That's the game at its simplest. But in tournament and adult play, certain inscriptions are also paired. If those paired signs—hand/foot, fish/river, bow/arrow, flower/grapes—are uncovered by the player right after one another, they count as two "suites," rather than one. If the moon suite is uncovered on the very first play, the player gets an extra turn. If the Alta pair is uncovered last, it counts as three. So the game is both a game of memory and of strategy.

If Lowentrout is correct, then another piece of the puzzle of the Dales has been found. But if—as is likelier—this is a later game phenomenon with no early antecedents among the Altites but rather (as A. Baum writes) "a Continental import" (see his naive but striking piece "Point, Counter, Point in the Dales," Games, Vol. 543), then we must search even further for evidence of Altism in the Isles.

THE STORY:

Jenna marked the years after her Choosing by certain accomplishments. By the rind of the first year, she had read all the children's books, the *Books of Little Lights*, at least once through and had learned the Game completely. She played at the Game out-of-doors with Pynt and at night before they went to sleep, until the two of them could remember everything set before them and the colors and counts and placements besides.

The second year Jenna mastered the bow and the throwing knife and was allowed to camp out overnight with just Pynt and Little Domina, who was that year to call out her dark sister, having come home from her mission. Little Domina taught them a new game, one she had learned in another Hame, that of telling frightening stories of girls who had called out demons and ogres from the dark instead of their sisters. The first time she had terrified both Jenna and Pynt, especially as they thought they heard a cat scratching nearby. The second time only Pynt was frightened, and then but a little. The third time Jenna figured out a trick they could play on Little Domina, which had to do with a rope and a blanket and an old tembala with only its top three strings. It so frightened the older girl that she refused to camp with them again, saying that she had much studying to do before her Night of Sisterhood. But Jenna and Pynt knew better. They had to settle for Varsa, who was not as much fun, being stolid, unimaginative, and—so Pynt said—"slightly dim."

Jenna called the third year the year of the Sword and the Ford. She had learned to handle both the short broadsword and the double-edged blade, using the smaller versions made for a child's hand. When she complained that she was almost as tall as Varsa, Catrona, laughing, had put a large sword in her hand. Jenna was able to lift it, but that was all. Catrona had thought she would be content with just the knowledge that an adult sword was as yet beyond her. But Jenna had sworn to herself that she would handle one easily by the year's last turning. She practiced with pieces of wood, heavier and heavier, not even realizing herself that she was growing at a pace far faster than Pynt or Alna or Selinda could maintain. When Catrona had solemnly placed a big sword in her hand on the very last day of the year, Jenna was surprised how light it felt, lighter than any of the pieces of wood she had used and smaller to grip. It sang through the air as she paced it through the seven positions of thrust and the eight of parry.

That was the same day the Selden River overflowed its banks, something that happened only once every hundred years, and a runner from the town came to beg the Hame's assistance in digging a channel to contain the angry waters. All the warriors and the girls went with him, plus Kadreen, for the town of Selden had but an herbwife and she near eighty-five. Mother Alta sent as many of the others as might be spared, though she had been firm about sending too many. They had done what they could, but seven farmers died anyway, out in the fields trying to save their flocks. The town itself was water up to the rooftrees of the houses. When the Altites tried to return up the mountain, the one bridge had been washed away and they had to ford the still-furious river, going across by holding on to a line which Catrona had begun with a well-placed arrow fired across the flood. Jenna and Pynt admired the strength of her arm and aim. Neither of them was fond of the icy water, but they were among the first across. The Sword and the Ford.

The fourth year they began their instruction in the *Book*.

Jenna could feel an itch between her toes. She ignored it. She could see Selinda settling herself more comfortably and hear Alna's rough breathing and feel Pynt's knee touching her own. But she drew herself in and away from them, focusing only on Mother Alta.

The priestess sat whey-faced and stony-eyed in her high-backed chair. She looked small, even shrunken with age. Yet when she opened the *Book* on her lap, she seemed to swell visibly, as if the very act of turning the *Book*'s pages filled her with an awesome power.

Jenna and the others sat cross-legged on the floor before her. They no longer wore their work clothes. Gone were the rough warrior skins, the smudged smocks of the kitchen, the gardener's dirty-kneed pants. Now they dressed alike in their worship clothes: the white and green of young Choosers, with the full sleeves, the belled pants tied at the ankle, their heads covered with scarves as was the custom of girls in the presence of the open *Book*. They were all shining with recent scrubbings and even Selinda's fingernails were clean for once. Jenna noticed them out of the corner of her eye.

Mother Alta cleared her throat, which brought complete attention to her. Then she began with a series of hand signs, mysterious in their meanings but clearly potent. She spoke in a high, nasal voice.

"In the beginning of your lives is the *Book of Light*," she said. "And in the end." Her fingers continued to weave a descant to her words.

The girls nodded, Selinda a half beat behind.

Tap-tap-tap went Mother Alta's great pointing nail on the page. "It is here that all knowledge can be found." *Tap-tap*. The fingers began to dance in the air again. "And here all wisdom set out." *Tap-tap-tap*. "And so we begin, my children. And so we begin."

The girls nodded in rhythm to her words.

"Now you must close your eyes. Yes, that is it. Selinda, you, too. Good. Good. Bring in the dark that I may teach you to breathe. For it is breath that is behind words. And words that are the shapers of knowledge. And knowledge that is the base of understanding. And understanding, the link between sister and sister."

And love? thought Jenna, closing her eyes tightly. *What about love?* But she did not say it aloud.

"This is how you must breathe when you hear the *Book* and . . ." Mother Alta paused as if to gather them in more thoroughly. "And when you call your sister from the dark."

It was as if, instead of breathing, at her words they all

stopped, for the room was completely silent now except for the faint echo of her voice.

So. We are here, Jenna thought. *At last.*

Into the silence Mother Alta's nasal voice began again, a voice of instruction that had little warmth or inflection in it. "The body's breath comes and goes without conscious thought, yet there is an art to breathing that will make your every thought larger, your every gift greater, your every moment longer. Without this breath—which I will teach you—your dark sister cannot breathe. She will be condemned to a life of eternal darkness, eternal ignorance, eternal loneliness. Yet no one but the followers of Great Alta knows these things. And if you should ever speak of them to others, you shall die the Death of a Thousand Arrows." Her voice sharpened at the last.

Jenna had heard of that death and could easily imagine the pain, though whether it was a real death or a story death, she could not guess.

Mother Alta stopped speaking and, as if on a signal, all four girls caught their breath and opened their eyes. Alna gave three quick little involuntary coughs.

THE PARABLE:

Once five beasts quarreled over what was most important to life: the eyes, the ears, the teeth, the mind, or the breath.

"Let us test this ourselves," said Cat. And as he was the strongest, they all agreed.

So Tortoise took out his eyes and without them he was blind. He could not see sunrise or sunset. He could not see the seven layers of color in his pond. But still he could hear and he could eat and he could think. So the beasts decided that eyes were of little importance.

Next Hare gave away his ears. And without them he could not hear the breaking of twigs near his home or the wind through the briars. He looked very strange. But still he could see and think and was not without the ability to eat well. So there was that for ears.

Then Wolf pulled out all his teeth. It certainly made eating difficult, but he managed. He was a great deal thinner, but he could see and hear and with his sharp mind he devised other ways of eating. So much for teeth.

So Spider gave away his mind. It was such a little mind, anyway, said Cat, and besides, he was no stupider than he had been before. Flies, being even more stupid, still came to his webs, though the webs themselves were very strange, and no longer very beautiful.

And so Cat laughed. "We have proved, dear friends, that the eye, the ear, the teeth, and the mind are of but little importance, as I always suspected. The important one is breath."

"That is yet to be proved," the other beasts said together.

So Cat himself had to give away his breath.

After a while, when it was clear to the others that he was quite dead, they buried him. And that is how five beasts proved completely that it is breath that is the most important thing in life, for, indeed, without it there is no life.

THE STORY:

"It is said in the *Book* that we breathe over twenty thousand times in a single day. Half the time we breathe in and half the time out. Imagine, my children, doing something that many times a day and not ever giving it thought." Mother Alta smiled at them, her serpent smile, all lips and no teeth.

The girls smiled back, except for Jenna, who wondered if she would ever be able to breathe again so comfortably unaware. Twenty thousand. The number was beyond her calculations.

"So—say with me:

The breath of life,
The power of life,
The wind of life
It flows from me to thee,
Always the breath."

Dutifully they repeated her words, one phrase at a time, until they could say the entire thing without stumbling. Then she had them repeat it over and over until it was a chant filling the entire room. Ten times, twenty times, a hundred times they repeated it, until at last she silenced them with a wave of her right hand.

"Each morning when you come to me, we will recite that together one hundred times. And then we will breathe—yes, my children, *breathe*—together. We will make my breath yours, and your breath mine. We will do this for a whole year's turning, for the *Book* says, 'And the light sister and the dark sister they shall have one breath.' We will do this over and over until it is as natural to you as life itself."

Jenna thought about the sisters she had seen quarreling and the sisters whom she had seen laughing and crying at different times. But before she could wonder further, Mother Alta's voice recalled her to her task.

"Repeat with me again," said Mother Alta.

And the breathing began.

That night in their room, before the mothers came in, Selinda began talking excitedly. Jenna had never seen her so enthusiastic about anything before.

"I have seen it!" she said, her hands moving in a dreamy, rhythmic accompaniment to her words. "I watched at dinner. Amalda and Sammor, breath for breath they were, though neither of them was watching the other. *Breath for breath*."

"I saw, too," Pynt said, running her fingers through her dark curls. "But I was watching Marna and Zo."

"I sat between Alinda and Glon by the fire," said Alna. "And I could feel them. Like one bellows, in and out together.

Funny not to have noticed it before. I made myself breathe with them and I felt such power. *Well, I did!"* she added in case anyone dared question her.

Jenna said nothing. She, too, had found herself watching the sisters at dinner, though she had observed each pair in turn. But she had also kept an eye on Kadreen as well. It had seemed to her that the Solitary's breathing shifted from one pair of sisters to another whenever she sat close, as if, without thinking, she were drawn into their twinned breath. When Jenna had tried to observe her own patterns, she found that the very act of observation changed the way she breathed. It was simply not possible to be both observer and observed.

Tired by the excitement of the day, the other girls fell asleep quickly. Alna drifted off first, then Pynt, then Selinda, shifting and turning in her bed. Long after, Jenna lay awake, testing her own breathing and matching it to the sleepers' until she could slip easily from one to the next with scarcely any effort at all.

The rest of the year, far into the winter's rind, they learned about breath from Mother Alta. Every morning began with their hundred chantings and the breathing exercises. They learned the difference between nose breathing (*altai*) and mouth breathing (*alani*), between chest breathing (*lanai*) and the breath that comes from lower down (*latani*). They learned how to overcome the faintness that came with rapid breath. They learned how to breathe standing, sitting, lying down, walking, and even running. They learned how the proper breathing could send them into a strange dream state even while awake. Jenna practiced the different breaths whenever she could—Cat breath, which gave great running power for short distances; Wolf breath, which gave the runner the ability to go over many miles; Spider breath for climbing; Tortoise breath for deep sleep; and Hare breath to help in leaping. She found that she could outlast Pynt in every contest of strength and running.

"You are getting better and I am getting worse," Pynt said after they had run several miles, stopping to rest by a cross-path. Her chest heaved.

"I am bigger than you," Jenna answered. Unlike Pynt, she was scarcely out of breath.

"*You* are a giant, but that is not what I mean," Pynt said. The sweat at her brow and neck had turned her curls into damp tendrils.

"I use *altai* and you use *alani* when running, and you have never practiced Wolf breath," said Jenna. "And that is why you are puffing like one of Donya's kettles on boil and I am not." She crossed her arms in front of her, letting the careful, long breaths out through her nose until her head hummed. She had come to love the feeling.

"I do use *altai*," said Pynt, "but not after the first mile. And Wolf does not help. It is all just words anyway. Besides, *altai* is really for calling up a dark sister, and we have years more to go before we do that. The only dark sister you can call up now is me." She fanned herself with her hands.

"Why would I want to call you up?" teased Jenna. "You just pop up whenever and wherever you want to. Usually behind me. You are not a dark sister, you are a shadow. That is what they call you, you know! *Jenna's little shadow.*"

"Little, maybe," said Pynt, "but that is because my father was small and yours—whoever he was—was a monster. But I am not your shadow."

"No?"

"No! I cannot keep up with you. What kind of shadow is that?"

"What is it they say in the Dales? *Does the rabbit keep up with the cat?*"

"I do not know if they say it in the Dales. I have never been in the Dales, except for the flood, and then all that was being said there was *Hold this. Bail that. Hurry up.*"

"And *Help!!!*"

They laughed together.

"But Donya says it . . ." Pynt hesitated.

"All the time!" They spoke the three words together and began laughing in earnest, so uncontrollably that Pynt stumbled back against a tree and a small rabbit was startled out of the tangled underbrush and leaped away down the path.

"There, cat, see if you can catch up to that one," said Pynt.

At Pynt's dare, Jenna bounded away into the brush after the rabbit and Pynt heard her noisy trampling for many minutes. When Jenna returned, her white braid was peppered with tiny briars, there was a fresh, triangular tear in her leggings, and a long scratch on the back of her right hand. But she held the quivering rabbit in her arms.

"I do not believe it," said Pynt. "How did you get her? She is not shot?"

"My hand is quick where breath is long," Jenna said, speaking in a high, nasal voice and waggling her fingers in imitation of the priestess. "She is yours, little shadow." She handed the trembling rabbit to Pynt.

"But she is only a baby," said Pynt, taking the rabbit from Jenna and stroking its velvety ears. "Did you hurt her?"

"Hurt *her*? Look at me," said Jenna, thrusting her right hand in Pynt's face. "That scratch is from her hind nails."

"Poor, frightened rabbit," said Pynt, pointedly ignoring Jenna.

"Put her down now."

"I am keeping her."

"Let her go," said Jenna. "If you bring her home, Donya will want her for the stew tonight."

"She is mine," said Pynt.

"She is yours," agreed Jenna, "but that is not an argument to convince Donya. Or Doey."

Pynt nodded. "You know, Alna is beginning to sound just like them. Chattering and pompous."

"I know," Jenna said. "I think I liked her better before, full of coughs and fears."

Pynt let the rabbit go and they trotted back up the path to the Hame.

In the heat of the baths, the scratch on Jenna's hand looked inflamed and Pynt examined it worriedly.

"Should you show that to Kadreen?" she asked.

"And what would I say of it? That it is a scar gotten on my shadow's behalf? It is nothing. We have both had worse." She splashed water at Pynt, who ducked under and pulled Jenna by the legs until her head went under as well. Spluttering, they both emerged from the steaming bath and let the cooler air dry them.

"We will have time before dinner . . ." Pynt began, letting the sentence trail off.

"And you would like to help with the babes," said Jenna. "*Again.*" But she nodded her head and followed after Pynt to the Great Hall, where there were three infants in the cradles, all fast asleep, and two younglings, the latest a two-year-old just newly fostered at the Hame.

At dinner Jenna sat with Amalda and Sammor, leaving Pynt to play with the little ones and help feed them. Jenna's patience with the younglings lasted only until the first bit of food was flung. She preferred the company of adults.

"Mother Alta says that the dark sisters dwelt in ignorance and loneliness until we called them forth," Jenna said. "Is that true, Sammor?"

Sammor's black eyes grew wary. "That is what the *Book* says," she said carefully, looking at Amalda.

"I did not ask what the *Book* says," Jenna was quick to point out. "We hear the *Book* every day." She imitated Mother Alta's high, nasal tones. "*The dark sisters dwelt in ig-no-rance.*" She elongated each syllable.

Sammor looked down at her food.

Jenna persisted. "But when I ask questions of Mother Alta, she reads me another passage in the *Book*. I think it tells only some of the truth. I want to know more."

"Jenna!" exclaimed Amalda, slapping her hand quickly on Jenna's wrist.

Sammor's hand touched her other wrist, but lightly, more as a prelude to speech.

"Wait, let me explain," said Jenna. "Some things Mother

Alta teaches us I can see and feel and make true. Like the breathing. When I do it right, I *am* the better for it. But when I talk to the dark sisters, they do not seem to be ignorant. And I have heard Catrona weep with loneliness, though she has a dark sister. And Kadreen seems to savor being a Solitary. So the *Book* does not explain everything. Mother Alta answers no questions beyond what is written."

Sammor breathed deeply. "The *Book* tells all the truth, Jo-an-enna, but it is how we hear it that makes the difference."

"So . . ." Jenna waited.

Sammor and Amalda breathed together several times, slowly, before Sammor continued. "If darkness is ignorance, then I dwelt in ignorance before I saw the light. If to lack knowledge is ignorance, then indeed I was a fool. If to be sisterless is to be lonely, then I was truly alone. But I did not know I was ignorant or lonely before I came here at A-ma's behest. I simply *was*."

"Was what?" asked Jenna.

"I was myself in the dark but without any understanding of my condition."

Jenna thought a minute. "But Kadreen is solitary and she is not lonely."

Sammor smiled. "There are many kinds of knowledge, child, and Kadreen has but one. There are many ways to be alone and not all are lonely."

"There are also many ways of being together, and for some that is as bad as being alone," Amalda said.

"You talk in riddles," Jenna said. "Riddles are for children. I am not a child anymore." She looked across the table, past the sisters sitting there, to the little table where Pynt was spooning food into two-year-old Kara, Donya's latest fosterling. The child was laughing as she tried to eat, and both she and Pynt were covered with porridge. "Do all loneliness and all jealousy and all anger end when your sister is called forth?"

"So it tells us in the *Book*," Amalda said.

Behind Jenna, Sammor snorted. "Do not try to fool this one, A-ma, this child who is not a child. She heard Donya curse out Doey this evening for a sauce slightly burned. She sees Nevara still mooning after Marna. She has heard of Selna . . ."

"Sammor, shut up!" Amalda's voice was hard.

"What about Selna?" Jenna turned to Sammor, whose mouth was in a thin line. When she turned back to Amalda, her mouth was the same. "And why does everyone always shut up when I ask about Selna? She was *my* mother, after all. My *second* mother. My fosterer. And no one will talk to me about her." Her voice was low so that it reached only the two of them.

They were silent.

"Never mind, then. I shall ask Mother Alta in the morning."

Amalda and Sammor stood as one, and each held out a hand to Jenna.

"Come, Jenna, come outside," whispered Amalda. "The moon is full and we can walk the paths, all three of us together. Do not ask Mother Alta anything. She will just hurt you with her silence. She will try to break you with obedience to the *Book.* We will tell you what you want to know."

Outside there was a small breeze puzzling through the far trees. The Hame walkways were of a dark stone flecked with something shiny that reflected the moonlight. As the three of them paced by the great walls, the moon was occasionally hidden by thready clouds. Each time Sammor would disappear for a moment, reappearing with the cleared moon.

"There is a story, Jo-an-enna, of the thrice-orphaned child," said Amalda.

"I have heard that tale ever since I was little." Jenna spoke impatiently. "What does my life have to do with stories?"

"There are some who think *you* could be that child," said Sammor a moment before the moon was once again cloud-hidden. Her voice trailed off. One minute her hand held firmly to Jenna's, the next it was gone.

Jenna waited until Sammor reappeared. "That is not I. I have had but two mothers. One dead in the forest and one—I do not know where or how. No one will tell me."

Amalda said softly, "If I had had my way, you *would* have had three mothers, for I would have fostered you."

"Whether you have the name, I always called you that in my mind, A-ma," Jenna said.

"You have called her that in your sleep as well," said Sammor. "And the one time you were sick with the Little Pox. But it was the fever speaking or the dream."

"You see, I have no third mother and besides, you are alive and shall remain so for some time, Alta willing." She held her hand up in the goddess sign, thumb and forefinger touching in a circle. "So, you see, I can *not* be the One spoken of."

They placed their arms around her and spoke as one. "But Mother Alta fears you are and has ordered that no one foster you in truth."

"And my mother Selna?"

"Dead," said Sammor.

"Dead saving you," said Amalda, and she told Jenna all of the tale save the last, about the knife in the babe's hand, though why she left it out she could not have said, but Sammor, too, was careful not to add it.

Jenna listened intently, pacing her breath to theirs. When they were done with the story, she shook her head. "None of that makes me the One, the Anna. Why, then, did she force this orphaning on me? It is not fair. I shall hate Mother Alta forever. She was afraid of a nursery tale. But for me it is my life."

"She did what she thought was right for you and for the Hame," Sammor said, stroking Jenna's white hair on one side while Amalda stroked it on the other.

"She did what she wanted to and for her own reasons," Jenna said, remembering the time she had watched the priestess speak to her mirror. "And a priestess who cares more for words than for her children is . . ." She could not finish, her anger hot and hard.

"That is not true, child, and I forbid you to say it again," said Amalda.

"I will not say it again because *you* forbid it, A-ma. But I cannot promise I will not think it. And I am glad my mission year comes soon, for I want to be away from her stale breath and bleak eyes."

"Jenna!" Amalda and Sammor said together, their shock evident.

Sammor added quickly, "There will be other Mother Altas in the Hames you visit."

"Other Mother Altas?" It was Jenna's turn to be shocked.

"Child, you really are very young," said Amalda, holding her hand. "We may be a small Hame, but in shape we are like them all. There are warriors and kitcheners and gardeners and teachers. And each Hame is headed by a priestess with the blue Goddess sign burned into her palms. Surely you understood that."

"But not like ours," said Jenna, a pleading in her voice. "Not a hard, uncaring woman with a serpent's smile. Please." She turned to Sammor, but the moon had gone suddenly behind a great cloud and Sammor was no longer there.

"*We* may be different—each hunter, each gardener," said Amalda, chuckling. "But, my darling Jenna, I have found that priestesses tend to be the same." She stroked Jenna's cheek. "Though I have never been able to figure out if they start out that way or simply grow into it. However, sweetling, it is time for bed, and besides . . ." She looked up at the sky. ". . . with the moon so well hidden, we will not be able to include Sammor in our conversation out here. Inside, where the lanterns bring her forth, we can say our good-nights. She will be furious with me if we stay out here. She hates to miss anything."

They turned and walked quickly up the stone stairs and into the hall. At the first trembling lantern light, Sammor returned.

Jenna stopped and held out a hand to each of them. "I shall miss you both with all my heart when I am off on mission. But I shall have Pynt with me. And Selinda, who, for all her dreaming, is a good friend. And Alna."

"That you will, child," said Sammor. "Not all are that lucky."

"We will visit as many of the other Hames as we can. A year is a long time. And when we return there will be other young ones for Mother Alta to trouble. I will be old enough then to call my dark sister out, and there is nothing in the tale that says the thrice-orphaned child has a twin! Besides, look at me—do I look like a queen?" She laughed.

"A queen and not a queen," reminded Sammor.

But Jenna's laugh was so infectious that both Amalda and Sammor joined her and, still laughing, they walked toward the girls' room.

Standing in front of Mother Alta's great mirror, each girl in turn raised her hands and stared into her own face intently.

"Lock eyes. Then breathe," Mother Alta instructed. "*Altai* first. Good, good. *Alani*. Breathe. Slower, slower."

Her voice became the only sound, the silvered twin the only sight. In those moments, Jenna could almost feel her own dark sister calling in a far-off voice, low, musical, with a hint of hidden laughter. Only she could not quite make it out. The words were like water over stone. She concentrated so hard trying to hear, it took a hand on her shoulder to recall her to the room.

"Enough, child, you are trembling. It is Marga's turn."

Reluctantly Jenna moved away and the movement of her mirrored self was what finally broke the spell. Pynt stepped in front of her with a broad grin that was reflected back.

So the pattern of the fifth year was set. Breathing exercises, mirror exercises, and then a reading from the *Book* with long, weighty explications from Mother Alta. Selinda mostly dozed through the history lessons, with her eyes wide open. But Jenna could tell from the glossy blue of her eyes that she was fast asleep. Alna and Pynt often had trouble sitting through the endless lectures, poking each other and occasionally breaking out into fits of giggles, for which they were rewarded with a bleak stare by the priestess. But Jenna was fascinated by it all, though why she could not say. She took it in and argued it out, though when she spoke out loud, she was silenced by Mother Alta's short responses that were not, after all, answers but merely simple restatements of the things she had just said. So Jenna's arguments soon became silent ones, the more unanswerable because of it.

THE HISTORY:

In the Museum of the Lower Dales is the remainder of a large standing mirror whose antiquity is without question. The ornate, carved wood frame has been dated at two thousand years, and is in fact of a type of laburnum not seen in those parts for centuries. Riddled with wormholes and fire-scorched, it is the one whole wood piece discovered in the Arrundale dig. It was not directly in the gravemound but buried separately some hundred meters distant. Wrapped in a waxy shroud and contained in a large iron casket, the mirror is notably unmarred from its long interment.

We know this was a mirror because large fragments of coated glass were found embedded in the shroud. Obviously of sophisticated make, the shards had beveled edges and a backing of an amalgam of mercury and tin, which indicates a glass-making craftsmanship unknown in the Dales but popular in the major cities of the Isles as early as the G'runian period.

What, then, was such a mirror used for and why its elaborate burial? There have been two likely theses put forth by Cowan and Temple, and a third, rather shaky mystical suggestion by the indefatigable mytho-culturist, Magon. Cowan, reminding us that artwork was practically unknown in the Hames save for the great tapestries and the carvings on the mirror, argues the provocative idea that handsomely framed mirrors in which living figures were artfully framed were—in fact—the artwork of the Alta sororities. Lacking the skill to draw or sculpt, they saw the human figure as reflected in the mirror as the highest form of art. The burial, Cowan further asserts, suggests that this particular piece was the property of the ruler of the Hame; perhaps only her image was allowed to be reflected in the glass. It is a fascinating theory set down with wit and style in Cowan's essay "Orbis Pictus: The Mirrored World of the Hames," Art 99. What is especially intriguing about Cowan's thesis is that it flies in the face of all other anthropological work with primitive artless cultures, none of which feature mirrors, great or small, in their tribal homes.

Professor Temple, on the other hand, stakes out the more conventional ground in the chapter "Vanities" in his book Alta-Natives. He suggests that the Hames, being places of women, would naturally be filled with mirrors. He offers no explanation, however, for the peculiar burial of the piece. Though his later work has been pilloried by feminist dialecticians, it is the very sensibleness of his thesis that recommends it.

Off in the stratosphere once again is Magon, who tries to prove (in "The Twinned Universe," monograph, Pasden University Press, #417) that the great mirror found in the Arrundale dig was part of a ritual or patterning device in which young girls learned to call up their dark sisters. Leaving aside the flimsiness of the dark-sister thesis for the moment, we find the monograph offers no real proof that the mirror had any but the most mundane of uses. Magon cites the odd carvings on the frame, but except for the fact that each carving has a mirror image on the opposite side—a perfect symmetry that reflects its use as a mirror frame and nothing more (if I may be forgiven the little joke)—there is little else to back up his wild thesis.

THE STORY:

Mother Alta touched the Goddess sign at the right side of the mirror frame and sighed. Now that the four girls were gone, the room was quiet again. She had come to treasure more and more the quiet aftermath, the echoing silence of her rooms when no one else was there. Yet this very evening the rooms would be filled again—with Varsa, her foster mother, and the rest of the adult sisters. Varsa would be saying her final vows, calling her sister from the dark. That is, if she could remember all the words and could concentrate long enough. It was always hardest on the slower girls, and Varsa was none too bright. And if, as had happened before, the dark sister did not emerge on the Night of Sisterhood, despite Varsa's years of training and the vocal encouragement of the others, there would be tears and recriminations and the great sobbing gasps of a disappointed child. Even with the assurance that the dark sister would eventually appear (and Mother Alta knew of no instances when one did *not*), the girl's hopes were so entwined with the ceremony it was always a terrible blow.

She signed again. She was definitely not looking forward to the evening. Putting a hand on each side of the mirror, she drew herself so close to it, her breath fogged the glass. For a moment her image looked younger. She closed her eyes and spoke aloud as if the mirror twin could hear her.

"Is she the One? Is it Annuanna, Jo-an-enna who is the White Goddess returned? How can she not be?" Mother Alta opened her eyes and wiped the fog away with the long, loose sleeve of her robe. The mirror's green eyes stared back at her. She noticed new lines etched across the image's forehead and frowned at it, adding yet another line. "The child runs farther, dives deeper, moves faster than any child her age. She asks questions I cannot answer. I *dare not* answer. Yet there is no one in Selden Hame who does not love her. Excepting me. Oh, Great Alta, except me. I fear her. I fear what she may, all unwitting, do to us.

"Oh, Alta, speak to me, thou who dancest between the raindrops and canst walk on the back of the lightning." She held her hands up to the mirror, so that the blue on her palms was repeated. How new the mark looked, how old her hands. "If she *is* the One, how do I tell her? If she is not, have I done wrong in keeping her apart? She *must* remain apart, else she taints them all." Her voice ended in a pleading whisper.

The room was silent and Mother Alta leaned both palms against the mirror. Then she drew back. The moist shadow of each hand shimmered on the surface.

"You do not answer your servant, Great Alta. Do you not

care? If only you would give me a sign. *Any* sign. Without it the decisions are mine alone."

She turned abruptly from the mirror and left the room just as the prints of her hands faded from the glass.

Mother Alta's room was crowded with sisters, light and dark, the only singleton being Varsa. Kadreen, as a Solitary, could not take part in the ceremony and, of course, the younger girls were not present.

The little fires in the lanterns blew about merrily and in the hearth there was a great blaze. Shadows danced across the ceiling and floor in profusion. Because the fresh rushes on the floor had been mixed with dried rose petals, the room was sweet with the smells of past springs.

Varsa, her hair crowned with fresh woodflowers, stood with her back to the hearth as if the fire could warm her. But Mother Alta knew she was cold and afraid, even though the flush of excitement stained her cheeks. She was naked, as naked as her sister would come from the dark the first time. *If she comes at all*, the priestess thought warily.

Mother Alta and her dark sister walked over to Varsa holding their right hands up in blessing. Varsa bowed her head. When the blessing was done, they removed Varsa's crown of flowers and threw it into the hearth. The fire consumed it eagerly, giving back another sweet smell. In past days, the girls' garments had been stripped from them in front of the fire and thrown into the flames as well. But that was in the days of great plenty. In a small, poor Hame, there were many economies to be made, even at the time of ceremony. Mother Alta had made that particular change ten years before, to only a small amount of grumbling from the sisters.

The priestess and her dark sister held out their right hands and Varsa took them eagerly, her own hands sweaty and cold. They led her to the mirror, between the rows of white-clad sisters, each holding a single red blossom. In the silence, their steps through the crackling rushes seemed as loud as thunderclaps. Varsa could not stop shivering.

Slowly Mother Alta and her sister turned Varsa around three

times in front of the mirror, and at each turn the watching women murmured, "For your birth. For your blood. For your death." Then the priestesses stopped the spinning girl, keeping their hands on her shoulders lest she fall. Often a nervous girl ate little for days before the ceremony, and fainting was common. But Varsa, though she trembled, did not faint. She stared at her image in the glass and raised her hands, her fear blotching her small breasts and the flush creeping down her neck from her cheeks. She closed her eyes, slowed her breathing, and opened her eyes again.

From behind her, Mother Alta and her twin intoned:

> *Dark to light*
> *Day to night*
> *Hear my plea,*
> *Thee to me.*

Varsa turned her palms toward her breasts and made a slow, beckoning motion, reciting the chant along with the two priestesses. Over and over and over she called, till first the dark priestess, then Mother Alta, dropped away and only Varsa's soft importunings could be heard.

The room was tense with anticipation as the sisters all breathed in Varsa's rhythm.

A slight mist began to form on the mirror, veiling Varsa's image, clothing it in a mantle of moisture. Varsa caught her breath at the sight, swallowed hard, and missed a beat of the chant. As she stopped, the mist faded slowly, first at the edges and then contracting inward to a white, snowy spot over the heart.

Varsa kept up the chant for another few minutes, but her eyes were brimmed with tears and she knew with the others that it was no good. Once the mist began to break up, all hope of the sister emerging that night was gone.

Mother Alta and her sister touched Varsa on the back, below the shoulder blades, whispering, "It is over for tonight, child."

Varsa lowered her arms slowly and then, suddenly, put her

hands up to her face and wept aloud. Her shoulders shook, and though the priestesses whispered to her to stop, she could not. Her mother and her mother's dark sister came over and draped a green cloak around her shoulders and led her away.

Mother Alta turned to the others. "It happens," she said. "Never mind. She will call her sister another night, without the extra burden of the ceremony. It will be as good in the end."

Nodding and arguing among themselves, the women left the room to go to the kitchen, where a feast awaited. They would eat well, whatever the night's outcome.

But Catrona and her dark sister Katri waited. "It is never as good," Catrona said fiercely to Mother Alta.

Katri nodded, adding, "The bond is not the same."

Catrona touched her on the arm. "Remember Selna . . ."

"You, Catrona, you, Katri—you are never to say this to Varsa. Not ever." Mother Alta's hands were clenched. "The child has a right to believe in her sister. *You shall not say other.*"

Catrona and Katri turned and walked silently out of the room.

Varsa was still weeping in the morning, her eyes raw-looking, her nails bitten to the quick.

Jenna and Pynt sat on either side of her at the table, stroking her hands.

Pynt murmured, "But you will call her eventually. She will come. No one who calls has ever gone without."

Varsa snuffled and swiped at her nose with the back of her hand. "It is the worst thing that can happen. All those people staring and then my sister not coming. Nothing worse could ever happen in my whole life."

"Of course something worse could happen," said Pynt cheerfully. "You tell her, Jenna. Of course something worse could happen."

Jenna made a face at Pynt. "Some help you are," she mouthed.

"Well, tell her, Jenna," Pynt said.

Jenna thought a minute. "You could be without a mother. Or without friends," she said. "Or you could be Hameless. Why—you could live in a town and never even know about sisters. *Those* would be worse."

Varsa stood up, pulling her hands angrily from theirs. "What do you know? You have not even tried yet. Nothing could be worse." She walked away through the arch.

"Let her go, Jenna," said Pynt as Jenna started up after her. "She is right, you know. Nothing *could* be worse."

"Oh, there you go being stupid, Pynt. There is a lot worse. But she *is* right about something. We cannot know how she feels. Not yet."

"Well, I know one thing," Pynt said, "I am not going to make a mistake. I am going to get my sister the first time."

Selinda, sitting across the table, shook her head. "Why such a fuss? She will get her sister eventually." She spooned more porridge into her mouth.

But in fact it was Alna who understood best. "Right now it hurts her more than anything and of course she cannot think otherwise. And nothing we say will console her. I was the same when I had to choose the kitchen. And now—well—I cannot think of a better place to be." She smiled in satisfaction and cleared the table.

As soon as Alna left the room, Selinda spoke up. "How can she say that? She knows that being in the fields and gardens is the *best*. She, of all people . . . How can she say it?"

Pynt put her hand on Selinda's but Jenna laughed. "What is it they say? *Words are merely interrupted breath.* That is how she says it. By interrupting her breathing. Easy, quite easy, Selinda."

Selinda got up and walked away without speaking.

Pynt slid close to Jenna and whispered urgently, "You do not suppose we were the cause of her failure?"

"Because we watched from behind the door?" Jenna asked. "No one saw. No one heard. And we will know the ceremony ourselves in time. We hurt nothing."

"But suppose . . ." Pynt let the sentence hang.

"Varsa is slow and afraid of too many around her. That is what caused it. Not two extra pairs of eyes and ears. You saw her; you heard how she hesitated the moment she saw the mist." Jenna shook her head slowly. "She will find her sister. And soon."

"I know what happened last night to Varsa has affected us all. It happens, sometimes, that a girl does not call out her sister during the Night of Sisterhood. It does not happen often, but it does happen."

Jenna elbowed Pynt meaningfully.

"But you shall see," said Mother Alta. "All will be for the best." She raised her hands and held them in Alta's blessing over the girls.

They bowed their heads and closed their eyes.

"Sometimes Great Alta, she who runs across the surface of the rivers, who hides her glory in a single leaf, sometimes she tests us and we are too small to see the pattern. All we feel is the pain. But there *is* a pattern and that you must believe."

Selinda made a small, comfortable sound and Alna nodded her head, as if remembering her Night of Choosing. Pynt poked a tentative finger into Jenna's leg but Jenna ignored her, thinking, *There is something more. I feel it. She is saying something more.* For some reason she felt chilled and there was a strange emptiness in her stomach, though they had just come from the meal.

Mother Alta spoke the words of Alta's grace, the girls following in response. "Great Alta, who holds us . . ."

The girls answered, "In thy care."

"Great Alta, who enfolds us . . ."

"In thy bounteous hair."

"Great Alta, who knows us . . ."

"As thy only kin."

"Great Alta, who shows us . . ."

"How to call the twin."

"Great Alta, give us grace."

The girls repeated, "Great Alta, give us grace." Then they looked up at Mother Alta and began to breathe in her rhythm.

After they had chanted the hundredfold breathing prayer and had worked for an hour, each in turn, in front of the great mirror, Mother Alta had them sit once more on the floor in front of her. She took the *Book* from its ornate wood stand and opened it to the place marked off with a gold ribband.

"It says in the *Book* that *Before a child becomes a woman she shall greet the sisters of her faith in every Hame, for a child who knows not of the world chooses out of ignorance and fear, just as the dark sisters before they came into the light.*" She looked up from the *Book*, smiling her smile of little warmth. "And what does this mean, my children?"

Jenna sat still. She no longer answered immediately, even though she knew the expected response, for the priestess always became angry when she spoke first. Now she held her counsel, reserving the last place to speak, summing up when the others were done, adding to it and refining.

"It means our mission," said Alna, clearing her throat halfway through the short sentence, a sure sign of spring.

Selinda, elbowed by Alna, added, "We go to every Hame in turn."

"Or at least as many as we can get to in the year," added Pynt.

Mother Alta nodded. "And Jo-an-enna—have you nothing to add?"

Jenna nodded back, holding on to her right braid as she spoke as a reminder to herself not to be sharp. "It is true, Mother, that we go from Hame to Hame, but not just to visit and play. We must go with open eyes and ears, mind and heart. We go to learn, to compare, to think, and to . . . to . . ."

"To grow!" interrupted Pynt.

"Very good, Marga," said Mother Alta. "And it is that growth the Mother of each Hame must be concerned with. Sometimes growth comes when all the girls go together and . . ."

Jenna felt the cold return. She pulled on her braid until it hurt in order to keep herself from shivering.

Mother Alta drew in a deep breath and instinctively the girls breathed in with her, all except Jenna. "And sometimes the growth comes when they are apart. It is my judgment therefore, as your guide and as the Mother of this Hame, that you will do best separated during your mission year. Marga, Selinda, and Alna, you will begin by going to Calla's Ford. But you, Jo-an-enna . . ."

"No!" Jenna said, the word exploding from her. Startled, the other girls moved away from her anger. "Girls are never separated in their mission year if there be more than one girl ready."

"Nowhere does it say that in the *Book*," Mother Alta said slowly, carefully, as if speaking to a very young child. "All the rest is mere custom and laziness, subject to change *at the discretion of the Mother of the Hame*." She opened the *Book* to another page, one not marked by the ribband, but obviously often consulted, for the pages stayed open without any pressure from her hands. "Here, child, read this aloud."

Jenna stood and read the sentence underlined by Mother Alta's long nail. Her lips moved but no sound came out.

"Aloud, Jo-an-enna!" commanded the priestess.

Jenna's voice was strong as she read, betraying neither her anger nor her sorrow. *"The Mother's wisdom is in all things. If it is cold, she shall light the fire. If it is hot, she shall let air into the room. But all she does, she does for the good of her children."* Jenna sat back down.

"You see, my child," said Mother Alta, a smile starting in her mouth and ending up, for the first time, in her eyes, "you will do as I say, for I am the Mother and I know what is best for you, Jo-an-enna, and what is best for the others. They are like little flowers and you the tree. They cannot grow in the shade you cast."

Pynt's hand crept into Jenna's and squeezed, but Jenna did not respond. She willed the tears *not* to start in her eyes. She willed her heart to stop pounding so wildly. Slowly she brought her breath under control and stared at Mother Alta, thinking, *I will not forgive you this, not ever.*

Mother Alta raised her hands over the girls, and Selinda, Alna, and Pynt obediently bowed their heads to receive her final words. But Jenna stared up at her, dark eyes into green, and had the blessing of Great Alta flung into her upturned face.

They packed the next week, on a morning so filled with the trillings of birdsong, Jenna's heart ached. She had been silent about the priestess' ruling, but everyone else at the Hame was abuzz with it. The girls, especially, had been inconsolable and Pynt had cried herself to sleep every night. But Jenna nursed her sorrow to herself, thinking that way she would not double anyone else's, not realizing that her silence was more troubling to the sisters than any tears might have been.

Only once during the week did she refer to it. She pulled Amalda aside as the girls and their mothers went on the traditional walk around the Hame for departing missioners.

"Am I a tree shading everyone?" she asked Amalda. "A-ma, does nothing grow around me?"

Amalda smiled and pulled Jenna into the circle of her arms. Then she turned her around and pointed to a great chestnut by the path. "Look under that," Amalda said.

Jenna looked. By the roots of the tree grew white trillium and clumps of violets, all nodding in the breeze.

"Your friends are hardy little plants," said Amalda. Then she laughed. "And you are not yet a mighty tree. Another few years, perhaps." But she hugged Jenna fiercely and they walked in silence the rest of the way around the Hame.

Jenna remembered that silence as she packed, putting her best leggings at the bottom and her nightdress in the middle. She reserved the top space for the food she would get from Donya, and for her corn doll. She picked up the doll and was preparing to put it in the pack when Pynt stopped her.

"No," said Pynt. "Give me your doll, the light sister, and I will give you mine. Then we will not really be parted."

Her earnestness convinced Jenna, who traded dolls solemnly. Pynt stroked the cornsilk hair before setting Jenna's doll in her own pack.

Selinda gave Jenna a moon snail shell which had been a

present from her mother on the day of her Choosing, and Alna gave her a posy of dried flowers.

"From the garden. I've always kept it by my pillow," she said shyly, as if it were a secret, though they had all known of it.

Jenna cut a lock of her hair for each of them and, as she set the white curl in her friends' palms, said quietly, "It is only a year. One year. And then we will be back here, together again."

She had meant it to sound brave and jaunty, but Alna turned away, and Selinda gave her a quick hug and ran from the room. Only Pynt stayed, staring down at the bone-white curl resting in her hand.

Down in the warrior yard, Catrona waited for them by the tabletop map. She stared at each of them in turn, noting Alna's reddened eyes, Selinda's pale complexion, the determined look on Pynt's face. Only Jenna seemed calm.

Folding her arms, Catrona said briskly, "Let us go over the way again. And then you must be off. Remember—*The sun moves slowly, but it crosses the land*. You must not waste the best part of the day. The trip is long enough as it is."

The girls moved closer to the table.

"Now show me the way," said Catrona.

Pynt started forward.

"Not you, Marga. You know the woods so well, I would have Selinda or Alna show me. *Just in case*."

Alna's hand flew rapidly along the route, first west away from the sun, down the path toward the town of Slipskin, and along the river. At the mountain's foot she hesitated for a moment and Selinda's hand pushed hers off toward the south.

"And that," Catrona interrupted, "Jenna, is where you leave them. You must take the more northerly journey to Nill's Hame. Your markers are what?"

Jenna moved closer to the map, tracing the path with a steady hand. "The river has two paths. I go around toward the Old Hanging Man, the mountain with the high cliff shaped like a man's face, till I come to the Sea of Bells, the lily field."

"Good. And you others?"

"We go with our back to the Old Man, our faces toward the twin peaks of Alta's Breast," Pynt said.

They recited the rest of the route in like fashion, several times through, so that Catrona was finally assured. Then she gave them each a hug, reserving the final embrace for Jenna.

All the women of Selden Hame waited at the great gates. Even the outer guards had been alerted and had come in from their posts. They stood in silence while the girls knelt before the priestess for their final blessing.

"Hand to guide them," Mother Alta intoned. "Heart to shield them. Hold them in thy hair forevermore."

"Evermore," the watching women echoed.

Jenna lifted her face and stared at the priestess, but Mother Alta was already looking down the road.

The girls hoisted their packs and started off to the accompanying ululation of the watchers. The eerie quavering sounds followed them around the first three turns of the trail, but long after the sounds had died away, the girls were silent, thinking only of the path.

THREE

SISTER LIGHT, SISTER DARK

THE MYTH:

Then Great Alta shall touch her only daughter with a wand of light and the child will fall away from her down to Earth. Wherever the child steps, there will spring up flowers like bells that shall ring hosannas to her name. "O child of light," the bells will peal, "O little sister, O white daughter, O queen who is to come."

THE LEGEND:

Once a shepherdess from Neverston went up the flank of the Old Man to tend her flock. But it was her first time up the mountain and darkness still stained his granite cheeks. The girl was young and afraid. Fearing to lose her way, she put a handful of white pebbles in her apron pocket and at every step she placed a pebble on a green leaf to mark her path.

All day she watched her ewes and lambs eating the sweet spring grass that was the Old Man's beard, and prayed for guidance for a safe return.

While the shepherdess and her flock remained on the high mountain, the pebbles slowly took root and became tiny white bells.

When it was evening and the sun had set behind the Old Man's head, the shepherdess led her flock safely home, following the sound of the tinkling bells. Or at least that is what they say in Neverston, where "lamb-bells," or Lilies of the Old Man's Valley, grow in great profusion.

THE STORY:

It had been cooler along the water than at the Hame and the girls had stopped at the confluence of the two rivers to eat their noon meal and wash off some of the trail dirt. It was there they said their farewells to Jenna. Selinda and Alna had wept without restraint, but Pynt had laughed oddly and winked at Jenna. Shrugging slightly, Jenna winked back, but as she trudged up the twisting northern path alone, she was still puzzling over Pynt's odd behavior.

As she walked, Jenna swung her head from side to side as Amalda and Catrona had taught her. Just because she was thinking did not mean that her ears and eyes should be unaware. As Amalda was fond of saying, *You must set the trap before the rat passes, not after.*

She noted a pair of squirrels chasing each other through the treetops, the scat of a large mountain cat, and deer tracks. An owl pellet below a tree contained the skull of a wood mouse. There would be much to eat if she needed it, though she still had plenty in her pack. But she checked everything as a cook might check the larder.

Stopping for a moment to listen to the trillings of a wood

thrush, Jenna smiled. She had been worried about being alone, but though she missed Selinda and Alna and especially Pynt, she realized with a kind of surprised elation that she did not *feel* alone. This puzzled her. She wanted to hold on to her anger, as if anger alone could make her strong enough, so she repeated as if it were a prayer, "I will never forgive her. I will hate Mother Alta forever." But the words seemed hollow. Spoken aloud in the joyous cacophony of the forest, the litany of hate had no power. She shook her head.

"I *am* the woods," she whispered. Then she said, more loudly, "The woods are in *me!*" She laughed, not because the thought was humorous but because it was true, and because Mother Alta, all unknowing, had sent her out to her true destiny.

"Or . . ." she said, hesitantly, "*did* she know?"

There was no answer from the woods, at least none that she could understand, so she put her fingers to her mouth and whistled like a thrush. It returned her call instantly.

Sunset came earlier than Jenna expected because she was still in the deep woods and in the massive shadow of the Old Man's western flank. She had hoped to come upon the white lily field by dark, having gotten the impression from Catrona that she should spend the first night there. But they had wasted so much time with their good-byes, and then she had not pushed herself along the trail, dawdling and enjoying her freedom. Now she would have to camp in the woods rather than the field.

In the gathering dark, she picked a tree with a high crotch, for the cat scat had been fresh. Not wanting to take chances with a cat in her face at night, she decided to sleep high up in the tree. It would not be comfortable, but she had been trained how to do it. And, as Catrona often said, *Better the cat under your heel than at your throat!*

She made a small fire below the tree and ringed it with stones. It would be only a small protection, none at all if the cat were really interested. But it might scare off one that was only mildly curious.

Then she climbed the tree and stashed her pack several feet

above her head. She balanced her unsheathed sword in a branch just above the fork she had chosen to sleep in. That way she would be able to get to it quickly. Her knife she kept by her side.

The tree was smooth, not nubbly like the first tree she and Pynt had ever tried to sleep in. She chuckled to herself, remembering the uncomfortable bark. Both she and Pynt had had the print of that bark impressed on their backs. They had joked about it in the morning. Suddenly she missed Pynt unbearably, so she stretched up, took down the pack, and removed the doll from it. She held the doll tightly in her arms and imagined she could smell Pynt's hands on its skirt. Her eyes grew misty at the thought, so she looked up at the stars through the interlacing of limbs, and tried to name the patterns, as if naming them would keep away her tears.

"The Huntress," she whispered into the dark. "The Great Hound." She sighed. "Alta's Braid."

The sound of river water washing over stone lulled her quickly and she was asleep before the count was done, one hand slipping off her lap to dangle in the air.

In the morning, Jenna woke up before the sun had found the valley, cramped and with a tingling sensation in the dangling hand. But that disappeared as soon as she used it. The cramp in her right leg took longer to go away. She descended the tree with the sword, climbed back up for her pack, then stretched lazily before looking around.

The early birds were already heralding the dawn. She recognized the dry, rattling chatter of a mistle thrush and the peremptory *tew-tew-tew* of a pair of ouzels. She saw a flash of rusty brown she thought might be a nightingale, but as it was silent, she could not be sure. Smiling, she set about making her breakfast, using some of the grain she had carried with her in a leathern sack, the flask of goat's milk, and the pack of dried berries Donya had gifted each girl. It was a feast and she felt herself making a quiet chuckling sound way in the back of her throat like the ouzel, and the realization caused her to laugh aloud.

Before leaving her campsite, she checked carefully that there was no sign of her stay there.

Except for my smell, she reminded herself, for Catrona had always said a cat might be able to track one of Alta's hunters, but no one else should.

Belting on her sword, she hoisted her pack, patted the knife at her hip, and started off down the trail.

Around a great bend in the track that followed the meandering of the river, she came upon a meadow so broad she could not see the other side. Unexpected and beautiful, the meadow made her lose her breath. The expansive green was sprinkled with tiny white flowers.

Jenna sang out in delight, a high crowing that she turned into a song of triumph. *So, I had been that close all night long and had never known it. But to come upon it in the day, with the flowers open and the sun shining down, was much the best way to do it*, she thought.

Her song masked any other sound she might have heard, and that was why the hand on her shoulder startled her. She put her own hand to her knife, drew it, and turned in the same instant, bringing the knife up in the swift, clean motion she had practiced so often.

Pynt stepped back just as quickly, though Jenna's longer arms meant the knife slashed Pynt's tunic, up and over the heart.

"Some welcome!" Pynt said, putting her hand over the ripped tunic breast and breathing a sigh of relief when she realized the shirt beneath was still whole.

"You—you startled me!" was all Jenna could manage before dropping her knife and enfolding Pynt in a tremendous embrace. "Oh, Pynt, I could have killed you."

"No one can kill her shadow," Pynt said, her voice trembling and a bit muffled against Jenna's hair. She moved out of Jenna's embrace. "My fault, really. I should have known better than to come upon you that way. But I thought you knew I was behind you. Alta knows I made enough noise." She grinned broadly. "When I am in a hurry, I am a regular twig breaker."

"What are you doing here?" Jenna asked, a tinge of anger in her voice. "Is this another of your *secret* ways?"

"You did not expect me?" Pynt looked bewildered. "But I thought you agreed. When I winked, you winked back. You knew there was no way I was going to stay with those two and let you go off alone. Selinda stares off into space and plunges into rabbit holes every third step, and Alna chatters as endlessly as Donya." She paused. "Without you, I could not stand them. And . . . " She sighed. "I could not let you go off alone."

"Oh, Pynt, think. *Think!*" Jenna pleaded. "Use your head. Those two will never find the way on their own." She shook her head. "Selinda still thinks the sun rises in the west."

"Of course they will," Pynt answered. "It is all one trail, no turns, until Calla's Ford. All they have to do is follow the river. They can both use their knives, so there is no danger. And they have each other, you know. Often girls are sent out on their own because there are no others the right age ready to go."

"I could follow the way on my own, Pynt."

Pynt looked stricken. "You do not want me here?"

"Of course I *want* you here, Pynt. You are my dearest companion."

"I am your shadow," Pynt reminded her quickly, a bit of her old spark returned.

"You are a twig breaker," said Jenna. She punched Pynt lightly on the shoulder. "But you did not think this all the way through."

"I have been thinking about this since old Serpent Mouth said you had to go a separate way."

"*Old Serpent Mouth?*" Jenna put her head back and began to laugh.

Pynt joined her and soon the two of them were so helpless in their laughter, they had to unbuckle their swords and throw down their packs. They rolled in the meadow grass, crushing hundreds of white lily bells beneath them. Each time one of them stopped laughing, the other would think up a new name for the priestess, both scurrilous and silly, and the laughter would begin anew. They went on this way until at last Jenna was able to sit up, wipe a hand across her eyes, and breathe in deeply.

"Pynt . . ." she began seriously and, when Pynt still giggled, said more sternly, "Marga!"

Pynt sat up, sober-faced. "You have never called me that."

" 'Pynt' is a child's name. We are on our mission year. Now we must both be adults."

"I am listening, *Jo-an-enna.*"

"Marga, I meant it—about thinking things all the way through. What do you suppose they will do to you—to us —when they find out we disobeyed Mother Alta? Have you thought about that?"

"They will not know until we return in a year, and by then we will have done so many glorious deeds and become so grown up, *Jo-an-enna,* that we will be forgiven." She grinned at Jenna with a crooked smile and head cocked to one side that made her irresistible.

Jenna shook her head again. "You are impossible, Pynt."

They stood up, brushed each other off, and Pynt picked three white flowers out of Jenna's hair. Then, shouldering their packs, they buckled on their swords and started off through the meadow, singing jauntily.

THE SONG:

Come, Ye Women

Oh, come, ye women of the Isles,
And listen to my song,
For if ye be but thirteen years,
Ye've not been women long.

And if ye be threescore and ten,
No longer women be,
Or so say all the merry men
Who count so cruel-ly.

But women we be from our birth,
And will be till we die.
Our counte is made so differently
To give the men that lie.

Oh, come, ye women of the Isles,
And listen to my song,
For we be women all through life,
Where life and love are long.

THE HISTORY:

"Very little music from the early Alta worshippers survives today. Because of the destruction by fire of most of the Hames in the tragic period of the Gender Wars, there are no large manuscript sources before the Covillein Booke of the sixteenth century. Fragmentary sources from earlier periods contain a handful of lullabies, several mangled ballads, and one instrumental dance scored for the 'tembala,' an instrument no longer extant. From the scoring, the tembala appears to be a stringed instrument of the guitar family with five melody strings and two drones."—Arne von Tassle, Dictionary of Early Music, Vol. A.

It is clear from the passage above that Dr. von Tassle, the world's greatest authority on Early Music of the Isles, believes categorically that little music from the Alta Hames has survived till today. In flagrant disagreement, Magon—who readily admits that he is no music expert—cities modern Dales balladry and songs as proof positive that a vital and prolific musical heritage is preserved in the Highlands and Valleys. In yet another reference-poor monograph ("Music of the Spheres," Nature and History, Vol. 47), Magon insists that there were four major categories of Alta music: religious tunes, lullabies and everyday songs, historical balladry, and dialectics.

His thesis concerning the religious tunes is, perhaps, the only tenable one. Certainly songs (which he cites) such as the fragmentary plainsong "Alta," with its plaintive refrain "Great Alta, salve my soule," could possibly be traced to religious ceremonies. But the song itself is such a close relative to the seventeenth-century "Lyke Wake Dirge" of the North Country that it is more than likely a modern reconstruction of that old song.

When Magon tries to link the charming and famous "Catte Lullaby," which had been found scribbled on the battered flyleaf of a sixteenth-century ballad book, to the early Garunian period of the Hames, he is sailing in choppier water. It is almost certainly a composed song, though, like many others of the time, patterned closely on the old oral-tradition tunes. Magon does not, for example, seem to realize that the word "catkin" has no written source prior to the mid-sixteenth century and was certainly not used to mean "kitten" or "little cat" at that time, further invalidating his early dating.

The ballads that Magon cites in the section on historical balladry are of little interest tunewise, as they are derivative of famous standing ballads of later composition. As to their historicity—well, he simply offers the same old shaky thesis about the White Goddess, the albino girl of exceptional height and strength who single-handedly both destroyed and saved the Alta worship system. Magon states this thesis but offers no more historical evidence when talking about the ballads except the internal evidence of the rhymes themselves, which any scholar knows is difficult to count on given the mutability of folk rhyme. We should as soon trust legends.

As to the dialectic songs, such as the infamous "Come, Ye Women," with its preposterous pornographic double entendres on

*the words "counte" and "lie"—it has already been well proved by
von Tassle, Temple, and others that this song is a nineteenth-
century fake, composed at a time when feminist agitators were
once more on the rise throughout the Isles, linking themselves
backward in time with the Alta Luxophists.*

*So once again Magon's reputation as an academic and
scholar has been proved to be a tissue of thinly woven cloth, the
threads tattered and worn.*

THE STORY:

Walking through the meadow proved to be more work than
either Jenna or Pynt had thought. If they went straight across, they
would leave a trail of crushed lily bells that even a child might
follow, and Catrona's first rule in the woods had been: *No tracks,
no trouble.* Besides, the ground was spongy and it made loud
sucking noises as they walked, noises which provoked Pynt to
giggles. So they backtracked and went, instead, along the tree line
that circled the enormous sward.

By the time the sun was directly overhead, they had gotten
only a third of the way, and the flower-covered green still
stretched endlessly before them.

"I have never seen an ocean," Pynt grumbled as they
marched along. "But it cannot be any larger than this."

"Why do you think it is known as the *Sea* of Bells?" Jenna
asked.

"I thought that was just a name, like the 'Old Hanging
Man.' It takes a great deal of imagination to see a man's face in
that rock," Pynt said.

"How would you know? You have not seen any men."

"I have, too."

"When?"

"When we were helping at Selden. At the flood. They are a
hairy lot."

"Lumpy, too," Jenna said, walking with an exaggerated swagger.

Pynt giggled.

By evening they could see a faint smudge on the horizon which Jenna thought might be trees.

"The end of it, I think."

"I hope."

"We can camp here tonight and make it to the end of the Sea of Bells by midday tomorrow."

Pynt sighed. "If I never see a white lily bell again it will be too soon."

Jenna nodded her agreement.

"White is a boring color."

"Thank you," Jenna said, flipping the end of her braid into Pynt's face.

Pynt grabbed the braid and yanked it. "Boring, boring, boring," she taunted.

Jenna pulled back until the braid stretched between them, then suddenly stepped forward and doubled over, butting her head into Pynt's stomach. Pynt sat down on the ground quite hard, but as she had never let go of the braid, she pulled Jenna down with her. They both burst into laughter.

"Now . . . I . . . know . . ." said Jenna, in between deep breaths, "why the first thing warriors do after their final Choosing is to cut their hair."

"You could tuck it into your shirt."

"And then it would stick out of my tunic like a tail!"

They both began to laugh again.

Pynt tried to look serious and failed. "You could be known as the White Beast of Selden Hame."

Jenna shrugged out of her pack and unbuckled her sword. She stood up and crouched over, swinging her arms low enough so that her knuckles grazed the ground. "I am the Beast. Fear me," she said in a low, growling voice.

Pynt gave a high-pitched scream, like the squeak of a wood rat. "Oh, do not hurt me, White Beast," she cried out in mock fear. She dropped her own pack and sword, then began running around in circles. "Oh, help me! Help me! The Beast is here!"

Jenna chased her in ever-decreasing circles until at last they collapsed together in a tangle of arms and legs, with Jenna on top, laughing.

Jenna got up and pulled Pynt to her feet, giving her a fierce hug. "I *am* glad you found me, Pynt. I *am*."

Later in the evening they camped on the ground because there had been no cat sign or bear sign or sign of anything larger than a rabbit. Pynt uncharacteristically talked of her fears as the small fire crackled and the thin line of smoke unwound like a gray thread from a skein.

"I am sometimes afraid that I will not be brave in a real fight, Jenna. Or that I will laugh at the wrong moment. Or . . ."

"I am sometimes afraid that you will never shut up and go to sleep," Jenna mumbled.

"I am sometimes afraid that . . ." Pynt continued, ignoring Jenna's comment. But when she realized that Jenna had fallen asleep, she sighed, turned her back to the fire, and went to sleep herself.

They rose to a morning so fogged over that they could not see the meadow, though they had slept not ten feet from it under the overhang of trees. The fog seemed to get inside of them as well. They found themselves whispering and moving about on tiptoe, as cautious as little animals in the undergrowth.

"No twig snapping today," Jenna said, her voice scarcely audible.

"None," Pynt agreed.

They collected their gear and buried the fire, brushing its remains into the dirt so that there was no sign of their overnight stay. Jenna rebraided her hair and Pynt ran quick fingers through her black curls. Then, squatting on their heels, knees touching, they whispered their plans.

"It will be slow going until the fog clears," said Jenna, her voice hissing on the word *slow*.

"*If* it clears," answered Pynt.

"It will clear," said Jenna. Then, as an afterthought, she added, "It *has* to."

"Do you remember the story Little Domina told us?" Pynt asked. "We must have been eight or nine years old. When we camped out and she scared us so much, you got sick and threw up your dinner."

"And you wet your blanket and cried all night."

"I did not."

"You did. Only I was not sick and I never threw up."

"Yes, you did."

Jenna was quiet for a moment. "The story was about a Fog Demon. With a monstrous snout and wide horns."

"It strangled runners by stuffing streamers of mist down their throats," Pynt added.

"It was just a story," Jenna put in quickly. "We were silly to be so frightened. We were very young."

"Then if it is just a story, why are we still sitting here?" Pynt asked.

"We could walk," Jenna said. "And not run."

"Yessssss," hissed Pynt.

"It is *only* a story," said Jenna.

"And the fog will be lifting soon anyway," said Pynt. "It always does."

There was a sudden crackling sound from the woods, as if a number of twigs were broken at once.

"What was that?" asked Pynt.

"A rabbit?" Jenna's voice was uncertain.

"A Fog Demon?"

There was a scrabbling behind them. Neither of them dared to move. A red squirrel ran up to Jenna's foot, stood up on its hind legs, and chittered at her. Then it ran off, scurrying in a zigzag pattern back toward the woods.

"A squirrel," said Jenna, relief evident in her voice. She stood. "We are only frightening ourselves this way. There is nothing out there but the forest and . . ."

"And that boring meadow," said Pynt, standing and buckling on her sword. "Now, if only we knew which *way* the boring meadow lies . . ."

"That way," said Jenna, pointing.

"No, that way," said Pynt, pointing in the opposite direction.

They were still arguing when a slight breeze lifted the edge of the fog like a hand lifting a comforter and they could see the meadow's edge, with the weak sun, a ghostly white, sitting on the horizon's lip.

"That way," they said together, pointing in a direction that neither of them had guessed before, away from the sun, westward and slightly north.

But the fog did not disappear. In fact, it settled more firmly around them, tucking them in. The result was not comfort but a cold, continuing layer of fear. They stuck to the edge of the forest and whenever they halted, even for a moment, they set their swords down on the ground pointing in the direction they were to continue in, the only steady markers they had.

The birds were still or had long since flown out of the fog. The small animals had all gone to earth. A silent, motionless white world surrounded them and nothing they did seemed to make a difference. The silence was broken only by the shuffling of their feet through the leaves and the sound of their breathing. They walked shoulders touching, afraid to lose contact with each other, even afraid to stop talking, another tenuous link in the fog.

"I do not like it," Pynt said, every few feet.

After the tenth time, Jenna ignored Pynt's complaint, babbling instead about life back in the Hame and about her anger at Mother Alta. Pynt's antiphonal response broke in at regular intervals.

By lunch they still had not reached their goal, or at least they assumed it was lunch, for both their stomachs growled at once. It was a loud, unlikely noise in the fog.

"I have nothing left to eat in my pack," Jenna said. "And there is only a little milk in my flask. It is quite sour."

"I do not even have that," complained Pynt. "I was

counting on ferns today, and mushrooms, and perhaps a squirrel for tonight."

"We will find nothing in this fog," Jenna said. "So we will just have to go hungry."

"In another day we could have cheese. From your sour milk!" Pynt tried to laugh at her own feeble joke, but the fog thinned the sound until it was but a hollow mockery.

They did not stop but walked on, their remarks to each other less and less frequent, as if a Fog Demon had, indeed, stoppered their mouths with streamers of mist.

Once Pynt tripped over an exposed tree root, falling heavily onto her knees. When she rolled up a pant leg, she clicked her tongue at the large bruise already purpling her right knee. Moments later, Jenna walked into a low, overhanging branch and spots, like black blossoms, bloomed before her eyes.

"You are too tall," Pynt whispered. "That branch sailed miles over my head."

"You are too small, so things on the ground rise up to meet you," Jenna answered.

It was their first exchange in almost an hour.

And still they walked.

The fog began to grow darker, as if it were nighttime instead of day. Their shirts were soaked and Pynt's curls had plastered in wet tendrils against her back. Their leather vests and leggings smelled dank and sour.

"Is it night already?" whispered Pynt. "How long have we been walking?"

"I have no idea," Jenna said. "And I do not—wait!" She put her hand on Pynt's arm, drawing her close. "Do you hear that?"

Pynt strained into the mist. "Hear what?"

Jenna was silent for a moment longer, turning her head back and forth as if trying to catch a sound. "*That!*"

There was a low, thrashing noise behind them and then, as if on the thrasher's trail, a high, faint *yip-yip-yipping.*

"A cat?"

"Too noisy."

"A bear?"

"Not noisy enough."

"Is that meant to be comforting?"

"It is meant to be truthful. *Hush.*" The sound had moved away from them and Jenna turned completely around trying to locate it again.

"Gone," she said. "Whatever it was, it is gone now."

"I counted two *whatevers*," said Pynt. "Not one."

"Is *that* meant to be comforting?" Jenna asked.

"It is meant to be truthful," Pynt said.

They walked on.

When the sound came again, it was somehow in front of them. Or else they had gotten turned around. Neither of them was certain.

"There it is," whispered Jenna.

"There they are," Pynt said at the same time.

The thrashing was closer, as if twigs and brush, brambles and briars, were being knocked about with careless disregard for the trail. And along with the thrashing was the sound of heavy, frantic breathing. Farther away, something sounding very much like an enormous animal charging through the woods was accompanied by a thunderous cry. "*Garoooooom! Garooooooooom!*"

Instinctively, Jenna and Pynt shrugged out of their packs and stood back-to-back, their swords in one hand, knives in the other.

"Oh, Jenna, I am terribly afraid," Pynt whispered.

"You would be stupid not to be," Jenna whispered back.

"Are you afraid?"

"I am not stupid," Jenna said.

Something larger than a cat and smaller than a bear scrambled out of the fog, tumbling at their feet, and breathing in high, sobbing gasps.

Jenna bent down, knife in her right hand leading the way. Her heart was *thud-thudding* so loudly in her breast, she was sure Pynt could hear it. She stared into the mud-stained face of a boy who could not have been more than fifteen or sixteen years old.

"Who . . ." she began, her tongue suddenly stuttering over

the familiar syllables. Bright eyes, wide, frightened, and incredibly blue, stared back at her.

"*Merci . . .*" the boy cried. "Sisters of Alta, *ich crie merci. Ich am thi mon.*" His voice was ragged and torn.

"What is it saying?" whispered Pynt from behind Jenna.

For a moment Jenna could not speak; then she looked over her shoulder at Pynt. "*It* is a boy. Slightly older than us. And he is speaking in the old tongue, though I cannot think why."

The boy sat up, his fear tempered by curiosity. "Isn't that how you Altites speak? That's what I was taught. And that if I ever needed aid from you, I was to say *Merci, ich crie merci, ich am thi mon* and you'd be forced by your vows to help me."

"We have not taken our vows yet," said Pynt. "We are only thirteen years old."

"Only thirteen? But she . . ." He gestured toward Jenna. "She looked older." He stared at Jenna, then shrugged. "My mistake. It must have been the white hair."

Pynt spat to one side. "You know nothing, boy."

"I know a lot," he argued. "And I'll know a lot more when . . ." He hesitated and let the sentence trail away.

"No one speaks in the old tongue except the priestess," Jenna said. "And in prayers. Or when we read from the *Book*."

"The *Book of Light?*" He seemed to have forgotten his fear in his excitement. "Have you seen it? Have you touched it? Have you read it? Or . . ." He seemed to search around for the right words, then shrugged and plunged ahead. "Or can you read?"

"Of course we can read," Jenna said with disgust. "Do you take us for savages?"

The boy shrugged again, this time in a kind of apology, and stood. Just as he got to his feet, there was a thunderclap of noise nearby, and an enormous double-headed horned creature burst out of the fog screaming indecipherable curses.

"Oh-oh!" muttered the boy, scrambling away from them and disappearing once more into the fog.

But Pynt and Jenna stood their ground.

"Back to me!" Jenna cried, and Pynt moved immediately to stand with her.

At Jenna's cry, the creature reared up once, towering above them, a black monster in the swirl of white fog. Then it charged toward them, a long, sharp weapon scything down from above.

"Duck!" Pynt screamed, scrabbling under the musky-smelling belly of the beast and coming up the other side. She thrust her sword toward the horned head of the creature. Leaping at the last, she hit something and crashed at the same moment into its huge, sweaty body. For a moment the breath was knocked from her and she fell backward onto her pack, spilling its contents. She pushed herself into a desperate somersault to get out of the way of the beast's flailing legs, and when she stood again, her sword was gone. Whether it was in the creature's neck or lying on the ground somewhere, she could not have said.

The great animal lay on its side, and all Pynt could see in the fog were its struggles to get up again. Then she heard the clang of steel on steel, and she made her way quickly around the beast toward the sound.

Jenna and another horned creature were in full battle. It was the ringing of their swords against each other that Pynt had heard. For a moment she did not understand, and then in sudden illumination realized that the horned creature had been the rider. What had fallen had been its steed, which was even now struggling to its feet.

But Jenna seemed to be losing the fight, for the demon was bigger and stronger than she. Forgetting her own fears, Pynt ran silently behind the hulking horned fighter, bent down, and threw herself against its knees. The backs of its legs were fleshy, but when she grabbed the front, she found they were unbending and hard, as if the creature wore leathern armor. She pushed against its knees again and this time it fell heavily backward on top of her. At the last minute, she reached around and knifed it in the thigh.

Jenna leaped on top of them both and thrust her sword unerringly into the creature's neck.

The demon shuddered once, made a small mewing sound, and was still.

"What . . . what kind of creature is it?" Pynt asked, when

Jenna had rolled the heavy body off her. Her arms ached and both her legs felt as if they had weights attached. There was a sharp pain in her side. "Is it a Fog Demon?"

Jenna was breathing hard. Her sword still thrust awkwardly from the creature's throat. She squatted by the body, put her face in her hands, and wept.

Pynt crawled over to her and put her arms around Jenna's legs. "Why are you crying?" she asked. "Why now, when it is all over?"

"This was not like hunting rabbit or squirrel," Jenna whispered. "I do not think I can bear to look at him."

Pynt nodded, stood up, and went over to the creature's body. She thought to roll it over in order to hide the hideous brown snout and bulging eyes. But as she tugged at Jenna's sword, the edge of the blade slipped up through the brown flesh, severing the chin. Only then did she see that the leathery brown face was no face at all but a mask. Slowly she peeled the mask back, revealing the face beneath. It was an ordinary face, the beard red and gray, the teeth broken and yellow, the right cheek crisscrossed with old scars. Pynt ripped the mask away completely and the horns, part of an elaborate helmet, came off in her hand.

"Jenna, look!"

"I cannot."

"It is not a demon, Jenna. It is a man."

"I *know* that," Jenna whispered. "Why do you think I cannot look? Looking at a dead demon's face would be easy."

"His name," said a voice behind them, "is Barnoo." It was the boy, who had returned silently. "He was known as the Hound. He'll hunt no more." He knelt by the dead man but did not touch him. "Strange . . . even dead he frightens me." Shivering, the boy reached out a tentative finger and poked at Barnoo's hand. "Cold," he said. "So cold, so soon. I thought it would take longer. But then, the Hound was always cold. Cold-blooded, he and his brothers, and the master they serve." He stood up. "I think I'm going to be sick."

Jenna stood up as well and shrugged meaningfully at Pynt.

They listened while the boy was noisily but efficiently sick somewhere in the bushes behind them.

At last the noises from the bushes ceased and the boy found them again, looking somewhat drained but calm.

"I never thought it would be the Hound who would die. I assumed it would be me," he said. "My only hope, in fact, was to lose him in the fog, a small hope at best. He was known throughout the land as a great tracker."

"*The Hound*," said Pynt, nodding.

"How did you know about the fog?" asked Jenna.

"Everyone knows fogs are frequent around the Sea of Bells. So when I found out he was on my trail, I headed straight here."

"*We* knew nothing about the fogs."

"And we know nothing about the Hound. Or about you," said Jenna pointedly. "Why was he hunting you? Are you a thief? You do not look like one. Or a cutthroat?"

"He looks even less like that," said Pynt.

"I'm . . ." He hesitated. "I'm Carum. I am—or was, at least, before I had to run for my life—a scholar. Alive I'm a threat to Lord Kalas of the Northern Holdings. Lord Kalas . . . who wants to be king!" There was unhappiness in the boy's voice, and bitterness he tried to disguise. "I have been running all spring."

Pynt reached out to touch his arm. At the last moment, they both drew back.

"We'd best bury him," the boy said. "Else his brothers will find him when the fog lifts and they'll make further black marks on my long tally sheet."

"Are his brothers as big?" Pynt asked.

The boy nodded. "And as ugly."

"And—they are very much alive," Jenna muttered to herself.

They began to dig a grave using their knives carefully, a long, time-consuming task. Carum stripped the dead man of a dirk at the belt and another in his boot. He also found a small spadelike ax in a throwing sheaf under the Hound's arm and they used it as well. When the digging was done, they rolled the Hound's body into the hole. The hole would have been too small for the carcass had not Barnoo curled up in his death throes and stiffened that way. He landed facedown in the hole.

Jenna breathed a sigh of relief at that, and tossed the mask after him. Then they threw in handfuls of dirt, aware of the heavy breathing and frequent huffing and stamping of the steed somewhere out of sight in the fog.

As the last clod of dirt was tamped down, Jenna whispered, "Is there something we should say to speed him on his way?"

"On his way where?" asked Carum.

"To wherever you believe he goes after death," said Jenna.

"I believe there's only Here," said Carum. "Nothing after."

"Is that what all men believe?" asked Pynt, astonished.

"That's what *I* believe," said Carum. "And all my reading has not changed my mind. But I can say a few words about what the Hound and his brothers believe, if you'd like."

"Do," Jenna said, "for I cannot wish him a place in Alta's cave or at her breast, which is where I expect to go when I die."

Carum's mouth twisted a bit, almost as if he were trying not to smile. Then he took a deep breath and looked down at the gravemound. "May the God of Fine Battles, Lord Cres, welcome you to his side in the great halls of ValHale. May you drink his strong wines and eat his meat forever, and throw the bones over your shoulder for the Dogs of War."

"What an awful prayer," said Pynt. "Who would want to go to such an unpeaceful place after death?"

"Who indeed," said Carum, shrugging. "Is it any wonder I don't believe it?"

Just then the steed gave a strange, low sound and marched over to them.

"What is that?" whispered Pynt.

"Never seen a horse before?" Carum asked.

"Of course." Pynt's answer came so quickly, Carum smiled. "*Of course,*" he said, his voice full of mockery.

"Well, once anyway," said Pynt. "And they were much shorter. What would we do with such a large beast on our small mountain trails?"

Jenna turned away from their argument and stared out into

the impenetrable fog, remembering the two little foals they had helped rescue from the flooded Selden barn while the body of the mare had floated by, knocking against the pilings. She turned back suddenly. "Is it all right? The horse. Is it hurt? Can it be ridden?"

Carum's voice came to her from the fog. "If it's on its feet, it can be ridden. Kalas' horses are always strong and solid. He knows flesh, my uncle does." This time the bitterness in his voice could not be disguised.

"Can you catch it?" Jenna asked.

"Just grab its halter and it'll come. It's well trained, you know. All of Kalas' battle horses are."

"Well, *you* grab the halter, whatever that is, and then we can start off again," Jenna said, picking up her sword and pack.

"Which way?"

Jenna turned around several times, trying to pierce the fog.

Pynt, on her hands and knees, was too busy looking for the contents of her pack to offer a suggestion. When she found everything she could, she jammed it in and looked around again for her sword. Then she joined the other two, who were still trying to figure out the direction.

They huddled together, a small island in the midst of a sea of fog, arguing over the way. At last Carum sat down in disgust. Only the horse, its gray nose moist and its dark eyes unfathomable, seemed unworried.

"Shall we camp here until morning?" asked Jenna.

"Without food?" Carum's voice threaded up to them.

"And do you want to go off on your own in that fog in the hopes of a handful of mushrooms?" asked Pynt.

"What about a fire, then?"

"We'll go hand in hand to look for wood," Jenna said.

They found only a few dry bushes and made a small brushy fire, as far from Barnoo's grave as possible. The horse stood, silently, all night over the fresh gravemound, its only marker.

The three were asleep long before the fire went out. The horse, in its silent vigil, stayed awake much of the night.

THE BALLAD:

Lord Gorum

Oh, where have ye been all day, Gorum, my son?
  The bull, the bear, the cat, and the hound,
Where have ye been all day, my pretty one?
  And the brothers have pulléd me down.

I've been far afoot, with my staff in my hand,
  The bull, the bear, the cat, and the hound,
I have been out walking my dead father's land,
  And the brothers have pulléd me down.

I looked in the mountains, I looked in the sea,
  The bull, the bear, the cat, and the hound,
A-looking for someone a-looking for me,
  And the brothers have pulléd me down.

What have ye for supper, Lord Gorum, my son?
  The bull, the bear, the cat, and the hound,
What have ye for supper, my pretty young one?
  And the brothers have pulléd me down.

I've nothing for supper, and nothing to rise,
  The bull, the bear, the cat, and the hound,
But fed on the look in my own true love's eyes,
  And the brothers have pulléd me down.

What will ye leave to that true love, my son?
  The bull, the bear, the cat, and the hound,
What will she leave you, my handsome young one?
  And the brothers have pulléd me down.

My kingdom, my crown, my name, and my grave,
  The bull, the bear, the cat, and the hound,
Her hair, her heart, her place in the cave,
  And the brothers have pulléd me down.

THE STORY:

They awoke to birdsong and a sky the color of old pearl. Pynt laughed aloud on rising but Jenna cast a suddenly shy glance at Carum, who had rolled into a ball at her feet and looked at once young and grownup in the lambent morning. He had long dark lashes that seemed to fan and shadow his cheeks, and his right hand lay across his nose, the long, shapely fingers hanging limp. Jenna was careful not to disturb him by stretching.

Pynt came over and stared down at him. "I thought . . ." she began, but Jenna shushed her with a finger to her lips. Then Pynt whispered, "I thought that men were all hairy and lumpy."

Jenna turned away, whispering over her shoulder, "That is because *he* is still a boy." But her heart sent a different message as she walked into the woods, casting about until she came upon some of the wild mushrooms that Pynt loved best. She was especially glad she found Pynt's favorites, the fleshy ones that were as good raw as cooked.

A twig snapped behind her, and Jenna turned. "See," she said to Pynt, "here are the ones you like."

"I found some ferns," Pynt said. "If we only had water, we could cook them up."

Jenna shook her head. "No fires and no time," she said. "Without the fog to mask it, we cannot chance a fire and if the Hound's brothers are, indeed, on his trail, we need to leave this place and its ghosts, quickly."

Pynt nodded her agreement, and they bent to the gathering

of mushrooms. When their hands and their leather pockets were full, they stood and headed back to the camp.

Carum was gone.

The ground was scuffed, but just a little. It *could* have meant a fight.

"What is it?" Pynt whispered. "The other brothers? Or Lord Kalas? Not many, I would say."

"We should never have left him alone," Jenna said fiercely. She clenched her hands, crushing the mushrooms. They dropped the food on the grass by the fire. "He cannot have gotten far. Surely we have enough woodsense to trail a scholar. And look, they have not taken the horse." She bent over, casting about for his track, and discovered a place where he seemed to have staggered off into the undergrowth, for the branches were broken and the trillium trampled underfoot.

They had not gone far when they heard a noise; both dropped to the ground as one. Inching forward, they saw the back of Carum's head, his light brown hair tangled. With one hand he was scratching his head and with the other . . .

"Alta's Hairs!" said Jenna disgustedly.

Pynt sat up and laughed.

Carum's head snapped around and he spotted them, his cheeks a bright flush. "Haven't you ever seen a man relieving himself?" Then he laughed, too. "No, I suppose not." He turned his head away again.

"We thought . . ." Pynt began.

"Explain nothing," said Jenna in a tight voice. She stood, stared at Carum's back with hooded eyes, then turned and stalked back to camp. "Come, Marga," she called.

Pynt scrambled to her feet and followed.

After their meager breakfast, they headed along the wood's edge toward the end of the lily meadows, taking turns on the horse. Its broad back stretched their muscles painfully and the heavy leather saddle rubbed sores on their thighs. After a try or two, both Jenna and Pynt decided to walk. But Carum chose to ride as if he were born to horseback, or as if the added height lent him courage in the girls' company.

"Tell me about the Brothers," said Jenna, one time that Pynt was astride the horse and she and Carum walked along together companionably. Carum was leading the horse by its halter. "So that I do not come upon them unaware." She had forgiven him the morning's scare and embarrassment—as long as he did not mention it.

"They really *are* brothers, of a single mother, though it's said they each had a different sire. One can readily believe that, seeing them together, for in all things but one they're as unalike as strangers. But in their devotion to Lord Kalas, they're as one. The Bull, the Bear, the Cat, and the Hound."

"The Hound I have met," said Jenna, keeping her voice calm and the memory of the dead man's back hunched over in his grave out of her mind. "What of the others?"

"The Bull is ox-strong and as stupid. He tries to do with his arms what his head cannot. He can work all day and not tire. I've seen him turn a mill wheel when the ox falters."

"And the Bear?"

"A hairy man, as large as the Bull, but smarter. A *little* smarter. His hair falls down to his shoulders, and his chest and back are likewise covered as if with a hair shirt."

"Attractive," said Jenna, half smiling.

"But the Cat, he's the one to be wary of. He's small and light on his feet. Once he leaped across a chasm, from rock to rock, with a pack of the king's hounds after him. The pack fell to its death. They cried all the way down. I heard them in my sleep for weeks." Carum's eyes squinted in the sun and Jenna could not read them.

"But though he's half the size of the others, he's the one I fear the most."

"More than Lord Kalas?" asked Jenna.

Carum shrugged as if to say they were to be equally feared.

"Then tell me about him, this dread Lord Kalas, so that I will know him if I meet him."

"You wouldn't want to meet him," Carum said. "He's tall and so thin they say he must stand twice to cast a shadow. His breath smells the sweet rot of piji."

"Piji?" Jenna asked.

"It is an addiction the poor know nothing of," said Carum.

"We are not poor," said Jenna.

"You don't know piji," Carum replied. "Therefore you are poor!"

"If that is a scholar's argument, then I am glad I know only the one book!" She laughed lightly and punched Carum on the arm. "What more of Kalas?"

"*Lord* Kalas," reminded Carum, ignoring the touch, though his cheeks seemed to grow pinker. "If you leave off his title, he'd as soon have you leave off your head."

"A pleasant man," said Jenna. "What more?"

"He has red hair and a red beard."

"The Hound had a red beard," mused Jenna. "Does red run in your family of villains?"

"No more than white runs free through the Alta Hames, I imagine," replied Carum.

Jenna nodded. "You are right. I alone have white hair. And I have always hated being so different. I longed to be just like the others and instead I have been called a tree overshading the little plants below."

"You *are* tall," said Carum. "But I like that. And your hair is . . . is marvelous. Promise me you'll never cut it."

"I will cut it when I take my vows," said Jenna. "A warrior cannot chance long hair in battle."

It was Carum's turn to muse and he was silent for a long while. Then he spoke in a strange, faraway voice. "There was a tribe of warriors—men, not women—in the East across the sea about . . ." He seemed to be calculating, bit his lip, then smiled. "About seven centuries ago. They wore their hair in long, single braids. They tied the scalp locks of their defeated enemies into the braids. Sometimes they used their hair to throttle their foes, when silence was the key. That's what the historian Locutus wrote. He added, *And in that way they were never weaponless*. They were called . . ." He hesitated again. "No, I've lost their names. But it'll come to me."

"You carry a great deal in your head, packed tight for travel," said Jenna, smiling.

"That, my lady," Carum answered, sweeping his arm in front of his body in an elaborate bow, "is a fine definition of a scholar: a bag of information packed tight for the road."

They laughed loudly and Pynt, from her high seat on the horse's back, called down, "What is so funny?"

"It is nothing, Pynt," said Jenna. When she turned back to Carum to smile again at him, she missed the look that passed over Pynt's face.

Pynt dismounted. "I do not want to ride anymore."

"Then I shall," said Carum, putting his hands on the horn of the saddle and swinging himself easily into the seat.

"How does he do that?" asked Jenna, her voice filled with admiration.

"*Why* does he do that?" muttered Pynt.

They reached the meadow's end by the time the sun stood straight overhead. Casting a glance backward at the great sweep of the Sea of Bells, Jenna sighed.

"Before we go farther, we need to take stock," she said.

"*And* find something to eat," reminded Pynt.

"And explain to my stomach that my throat hasn't been slit," said Carum. He slid off the horse's back and led it to the meadow's edge to graze. When he wandered back, Pynt and Jenna were in the middle of an argument, and Pynt was saying, "And *I* say we should leave him."

Carum pulled a smile across his face and said cheerily, "You don't want to leave me, because I know a shortcut to Nill's Hame."

"How did you know we were going there?" asked Pynt.

"Do not be stupid, Pynt. What other Hames are along this route?" said Jenna. She turned to Carum, all the while pulling on her braid. "Thank you, Carum, but we know the way. The map is up here." She pointed to her head. "And besides, you cannot come into the Hame. No men are allowed."

"I know that," Carum said, "but I'm going farther along the same road, to a place where *only* men are allowed. It's a place of sanctuary where even the Brothers and Kalas—"

"*Lord* Kalas," interrupted Jenna, stroking her finger across her throat. "Remember your head!"

He grinned. "Lord Kalas wouldn't dare violate those walls. I'll be safe there. So I can guide you and . . ."

"And we can keep you out of trouble!" said Pynt.

"*Three are better than one where trouble is concerned,*" Carum said gently. "At least that's what we say."

"We say the same," said Jenna. "Is that not strange?"

"Then I can go along?" His face betrayed his eagerness.

"After we eat," Jenna said. "But do not leave the horse out in plain sight. Just because we have not seen any trace of the Brothers does not mean they have missed us."

Carum nodded.

"We shall each take a different path, going only within ear of this place, to find something for our meal."

Carum collected the horse and by the time he got it tied to a limb of a middle-size oak, the other two had disappeared into the forest. He looked around, found a wide deer run, and followed along it as quietly as he could.

Not an hour later they met again near the horse and poured their woods' bounty onto a kerchief that Jenna spread. Pynt had collected several dozen mushrooms, not the great white puffs of which she was so fond, but a darker variety that had a nutty flavor. Jenna had discovered a squirrel's cache of nuts and a little dell of ferns, but she left the ferns since smoke from a fire for the boiling of them would have stained the bright, clear sky and given them away at once. Carum had filled his pocket with berries.

"Berries!" Pynt laughed.

Jenna explained. "*Spring berries are for dye and dying.* That is what we say in the Hame. The eating berries are not yet ripe and these others"—she counted through his meager store

—"these are all poisonous. Though some—like this Bird Berry" —she touched a small hard black pebbly fruit—"can be steeped in hot water over several days for a strong purgative. And this"—She touched a larger, bright red berry —"which we call *Step-o'er-me-lady*, can be mashed into a greasy salve for burns."

"Berries!" Pynt laughed again.

Carum looked down at the ground.

"Oh, hush, Pynt," said Jenna. "Carum knows much more than either of us, just not what is here in the woods."

"And *what* does he know?" asked Pynt.

"He knows about warriors who use their braids to strangle their foes, which is what I shall do to you if you do not shut up." Jenna held her white plait between her hands like a noose and gave Pynt a wicked look.

"The Alaisters!" Carum said triumphantly, looking up with a grin.

"What?" Pynt and Jenna turned to him at the same time.

"That's the name of the tribe. The Alaisters. I knew I'd come up with it after a time."

Jenna squatted on her heels and picked up two mushrooms. Stuffing them into her mouth, she muttered, "Just don't eat the berries, scholar."

They ate quickly and quietly and when they were done, swept away any sign of their makeshift lunch. Carum went over to the horse and untied it.

"Bring the horse here," Jenna called.

Smiling, Carum led the cross-grained gray to her. "Do you want to ride now?"

"None of us will ride anymore," Jenna said. "We are going to send the horse across the meadow. That way." She pointed south. "He will make a wide trail and lead any followers away from us."

Carum looked over his shoulder nervously. "Have we been followed?"

Pynt laughed. "If we had, we would not now be standing here out in the open. Trust us."

"But there *will* be followers. Following you or following the

Hound. And well you know it. I have worried all this morning about taking the horse with us, and you both should have been worrying, too. But I think, with Alta's help, we will use the horse to confuse the trail." Jenna threw her right braid over her shoulder for emphasis.

"*You* did not look worried," scolded Pynt.

"Why didn't you say something?" Carum's face clouded over. "It never even occurred to me . . ."

"That is because scholars worry about the past, Carum, while warriors must worry about the future. It is possible we will have no future if we keep the horse," Jenna said, her tone low and sensible. "So tell me, horseman, how do we best encourage the beast to ride off that way?"

Carum laughed. "Trust *me*," he said. Dropping the horse's reins, he went over to a flowering bush, cut and stripped a switch. Then he came back to the horse, patted it once on its nose, and whispered into its ear. Turning it around so that its head was facing south, he brought the switch down hard twice on its flank, shouting, "Get on home!"

The horse shied, kicked out its rear feet, and missing Carum's thighs by a scant inch, galloped off across the meadow, leaving a swath wide enough to be read by even the most reluctant trailers. It did not stop until it was hundreds of yards away, where it put its big nose down and began to crop the grass.

"What did you whisper into its ear?" asked Jenna.

"To forgive me for the switching," Carum answered.

"I do not think it forgave," Pynt pointed out, "if its aim was any indication of its intent. Had it connected, I doubt there would be many new scholars of your line."

Jenna smothered a laugh and Carum scowled.

"I thought you Altites knew nothing of men," he said.

"We know we do not spring from flowers or cabbages or from the beaks of birds," said Jenna. "Our women give birth so we know where babies come from. *And* how they are made. We choose . . ." She stopped, for Carum's ears were beginning to turn red from embarrassment, but Pynt had no thought to spare his feelings.

"We choose to use men but not to live with them. To serve them for wages as guards if need be, but not to stay otherwise in their service." Although she said it with conviction, it sounded more like a litany, and Carum began to protest.

"Your mouth says that, but . . ." he began. Jenna put her hand on his arm to stop their argument.

"The horse has not moved on," she said.

Carum walked a few feet into the meadow and shouted, "Gee-up home, you misbegotten son of a she-ass!"

The horse lifted its head and, with a mouthful of grass and lilies still hanging from its jaws, took off south. Soon it was just a moving dot on the horizon.

"*Wonderful!*" said Pynt sarcastically. "Your shout should have alerted every follower within miles."

Carum ignored her pointedly and turned to Jenna. "There was no other way."

Jenna nodded and turned to Pynt. "What is wrong with the two of you? First you shout, then he shouts. You speak with fire and he answers with ice. We cannot go on this way."

"Then send him off," muttered Pynt, not entirely under her breath. She walked a few steps away.

Carum drew in a deep breath, then spoke softly so that only Jenna could hear. "Never mind, Jenna, we'll be at the Hame soon, and I'll be gone. And don't worry about the horse." He raised his voice at the end so that Pynt, hearing him, looked back. "Kalas' horses are well trained and he'll find his way home eventually."

"And home is . . ." Pynt's curiosity overcame her anger and resentment.

"North," Jenna said. "The Northern Holdings, you said. Alta's Hairs! That horse will be going the same way we are."

"No, Jenna," Carum interrupted, putting his hand on Jenna's shoulder. "That *was* home for Lord Kalas once. But now he's taken over the High King's palace in the South Downs and calls it after himself. The wine cellar my . . . king so loved has been made into a dungeon. And Kalas squats on the throne for the past year like a toad in a hole, waiting for a coronation that will not—if the gods forbid it—ever come."

"I thought you believed in no gods," said Pynt.

"I'll believe if there is no coronation sanctioned by the priests. But in the end, even that won't matter. A man who sits on a throne long enough even though he wears but a helm is still called *Your Majesty*. The people's memory is short when mercy and justice are short. I fear Kalas *will* be king ere long."

The girls stared at him as he spoke, for the words seemed to lay a mantle of majesty on him, though it was sorrowing majesty at best. When the wind ruffled his hair, he seemed, somehow, taller and yet—at the same time—stooped.

"Oh, Carum," Jenna said, and there was a real sadness in her voice, loss echoing loss.

Carum seemed to shake himself suddenly free of the oratory and shrugged. "Never mind me. We scholars sometimes invent an appropriate metaphor and, other times, we simply talk because we love to hear the sound of ringing words."

Pynt said nothing for the longest time, but at last she cast a glance at the lowering sky. "Where is that shortcut you promised?"

Where the meadow ended, the ground was boggy, sucking eagerly at footfalls. Jenna led them back into the woods so as not to leave a pattern of prints, and they came around the northern edge where the great oak and beech forest gave way to newer growth. There was a real track now on the meadow's far side, not just deer paths. The track was wide and well worn, with roadside bushes and flowers that bespoke a nearby civilization: the prickly raspberry patches, the yellow spikes of toadflax, and the tiny, pensive blue and purple heads of heartsease nodding in the rising breeze.

They found a clear spring, and bent over to drink one at a time, long eager draughts. Then the girls rinsed out their skin bottles carefully before filling them again with the water.

"We must stay off the road but close enough to it that we do not lose the way," said Jenna.

"Why not let Carum walk in the woods, keeping us in sight? No one is searching for us," Pynt argued.

"Because we undertook his guardianship," said Jenna. "He cried us *merci*. And though that is not something we have yet pledged, you and I, I guess it will be one of the seven vows we will take in less than a short year's time."

Pynt nodded, but muttered, "Could we not guard him as well from the road?"

Jenna shook her head.

"All right," Pynt said at last. "Into the woods, then." She turned abruptly and entered the woods first without snapping a single twig.

Carum followed after and Jenna, after checking the road both ways, came last.

They walked along as quietly as possible, all comments contained in the kind of hand signals the guards at the Hame used, which left Carum out of the conversation entirely. It was the road, not fifty yards to their right, that silenced them, but Carum did not seem to mind. He walked along almost oblivious of his surroundings, caught up in his own thoughts.

Single file, with Pynt in front and Jenna in the rear, they moved in a rhythm dictated by the density of the undergrowth. Twice Carum let a branch snap back into Jenna's face and, turning to apologize, received only a scowl and a dismissing wave of her hand. Once Pynt stepped in a small depression, twisting her ankle, though not severely. But the accidents, small as they were, served as warnings. Silently, they watched the ground as well as the branches, glancing only occasionally off to the right to check the road.

Brambles caught at their clothes and hair, slipping without incident off the rough skins that Jenna and Pynt wore. Carum, in loose weave, had the most trouble and often they had to stop and help him untangle himself from the thorns. But silently, always silently, the road so close by a stopper in their mouths.

The silence in the end was what saved them, and the fact that, for once, they were not moving ahead but standing in a knot trying once again to unhook Carum's shirt from a high raspberry bush. The sound of hooves galloping nearby was a thunder underfoot. They crouched down instinctively, huddled together, while a dust of riders raced by, going north.

As soon as the riders had passed, Pynt whispered, "Could you see?"

Jenna nodded. "At least a dozen," she said under her breath, "maybe two."

"There were twenty-one," said Carum.

Pynt and Jenna looked at him. "How can you be so sure?"

"I counted. Besides, a company of horse is always twenty-one, with a captain at its head."

"And," Pynt said, the sarcasm a hard edge in her voice, "I suppose you also happened to notice who was in charge!"

Carum nodded. "The Bull."

"I do not believe it," said Pynt, her voice growing louder until Jenna had to silence her with a hand on her arm. Then Pynt whispered, "They went by too quickly and we were kneeling here on the floor of the forest."

"*You* were kneeling," Carum pointed out. "I was caught upright by the thorns."

"He is right," admitted Jenna.

"Besides," continued Carum, "only the Brothers ride those big cross-grained grays. And the Bull is so large, he towers over his men. *And* his helmet gave him away."

"His helmet," Jenna whispered, her face marking the memory of the other helmet and the sound it had made *thunking* down on the dead man's back. She was silent for a moment longer than necessary, then whispered fiercely, "We must move even deeper into the woods. If *we* can see *them*, then . . ."

She did not have to finish the thought. Both Carum and Pynt nodded, united at least on the danger. Pynt ripped Carum's shirt from the thorns without regard for the cloth, and led them further into the forest where some of the old, great oaks still stood sentinel.

Carum had promised them the trip to the Hame would take only a day, and they had hoped to get there by evening. But the woods, even the edge of it, slowed them down considerably. Twice more that afternoon a company of riders raced by, once from the north and once up from the south. The first had been a silent ride, all dark purpose. The next time the riders were shouting, though their words were lost in the dust and clamor of hooves. Each time the three in the woods moved deeper into the shadows of the trees.

"We will try and rest now," Jenna said. "And we will move only at night. Even if it takes an extra day or two. Carum must be kept safe."

Pynt nodded and, under her breath, muttered, "And we will be safer, too."

They found a hollow tree with a large enough hole that all three of them—with a bit of sorting out of arms and legs—could sleep as comfortably as kits in a den. Pynt reminded Jenna of a story they had heard in Selden Hame about a sister who had lived for a year in a hollow tree, and Jenna smiled at the tale. Carum fell asleep in the middle, snoring lightly.

THE HISTORY:

We are more certain of the makeup of the armies of the G'runians than of anything else of that period, since the Book of Battles *is quite clear on the subject. The* Book of Battles *(hereinafter referred to as the BB) is the only extant volume discovered in the old script. It was translated by Doyle even before her monumental work on Alta-linguistics. It is best to remember, however, as Doyle herself reminds us in her Introductory Notes, that work on the BB is far from over. Many words are, as yet, untranslated and the idiomatic phrases are often puzzling. But the BB brings us closer to that dark period in the history of the Isles than any other single rediscovered object.*

The BB is dedicated to two gods: Lord Cres of the dark and

Lady Alta of the light. This is the earliest literary reference to Alta, firmly placing her within the Garunian pantheon of gods where, as Professor Temple advises us in his book, "she reigned as a minor goddess of childbirth and song." Even more puzzling, then, her position as dedicatee of the BB, though it would be wrong, as Magon would have it, to conclude that it is "further indication of Alta's warrior status."

The BB begins its descriptions of the armies with the following invocation. (The translation is, of course, Doyle's.)

> *Come, lover of the light,*
> *Come, my strong right arm,*
> *Follow me down into the dark walkways.*
> *Be my sword, my shield, my shadow.*
> *Be my Blanket Companion.*

A curious prayer, and the most curious part of all is the phrase "Blanket Companion," which Doyle translates baldly, having—as she says—no notion of the idiomatic usage. She suggests, however, that the phrase has more to do with the homoerotic impulses of long-term soldiery than with actual battles, war, or the makeup of the armies.

The BB delineates three types of forces. Paramount was a warrior caste, a hereditary guard known as Kingsmen who "ate before the king." (Doyle states that it is unclear whether this means the Kingsmen ate in front *of the king—i.e., where they were placed at the table—or that part of their job was to serve as food tasters, so that they ate their food earlier than the king.) According to the BB, the sons of a Kingsman could choose to be in the guard, but the eldest had to become a member or forfeit his life. (The phrase "offer his naked neck to the king's sword" is used.) There has been much debate about the origins and the state of antiquity of this curious caste. Baum argues for the simple equation: nobles=Kingsmen in his treatise "Might Makes Right: Noble Ranking and Noble Favors in the Early Dales" (Nature and History, Vol. 58), while Cowan, always searching for a more intricate answer, holds forth the provocative idea that the Kingsmen represented the retention of arms in the hands of a conquering people who have, by their conquest, reduced an entire population to serfdom. (See her footnote #17 in the article "Orbis Pictus," Art 99.) The Kingsmen were a mounted guard, the only soldiers allowed horses, and they rode in groups or troops of twenty that were paired (perhaps Blanket Companions?) under a single leader. These leaders were known by animal names, such as the Hound, the Bull, the Fox, the Bear. (In fact the BB cites twenty-seven such names.) The leaders of this select horseguard were known, collectively, as the Brothers, and the men of the guard colloquially—and only amongst themselves—as the Sisters. (Which nomenclature, Dr. Temple points out convincingly, most likely gave rise to the mistaken belief that there were women in the armies.)*

The second type of armed force was the provincial troops that served under a governor appointed by the king. These troops were called Queensmen, a sop perhaps to the matriarchal system so recently overthrown, though they owed their allegiance not to the queen but to the provincial governor(s). Arguably, this was a dangerous system, laying as it did the groundwork for insurrection. Several times in the early history of the Garunian rule of the Isles, according to the BB and corroborated by folk tradition, governors (or Lords) revolted against the king, and the basis of their power was the loyalty of the Queensmen. (See Cowan's "The Kallas Controversy," Journal of the Isles, History IV, 17.)

The third type of armed force was the Mercs, or mercenaries, a small but significant soldiery. Fearing to arm the conquered peoples of the Isles, the Garunians banned mass conscription, turning instead to hirelings from the Continent. These soldiers of fortune often made vast amounts of money fighting for the king, settling afterward on the land and raising families who were identifiable by their patronymics as sons and daughters of mercenaries. The BB cites several names as typical of such soldiery: D'Uan, H'Ulan, M'Urow, the initial letter identifying the company in which the mercenary had served.

THE STORY:

Jenna awoke first out of a shallow sleep and realized it was the moon that had awakened her. In only a day or two the moon would be full, and in the clear night sky it was a beacon. The hollow tree was on the edge of a clearing, so the clearing itself was well lit. Something dark and small moved past the tree cautiously, turned once, then seeing Jenna's movement, raced away.

Her first thought was to her stomach. They had eaten only handfuls of mushrooms and nuts for days. But a fire and hot food would be impossible, and she did not dare light a torch. It would be another long period of hunger before they came to the Hame.

She touched Pynt lightly on the shoulder, and the touch was enough to wake her.

"Hush, come with me," whispered Jenna.

Pynt was careful not to wake Carum, slipping her legs out from under his. She followed Jenna to the clearing.

"Are we leaving him now?" Pynt asked.

"What do you think?" said Jenna.

"Just checking." Pynt laughed quietly.

"While he sleeps a bit longer, we should see if we can find something to eat."

"Would you believe I have a pocket full of nuts?" Pynt asked.

"No," said Jenna.

"Just checking again." This time Pynt laughed out loud.

"Hunger makes you giddy," Jenna remarked.

"And it makes *you* sour," said Pynt. "For that alone we had better find some food."

They separated quietly, Pynt moving northward into the forest and Jenna searching the clearing's edge.

Pynt found five potherb plants and pulled them up. The root bulbs were small and round and sharp-tasting, but delicious. She nibbled one as she continued searching. She came upon thistle in the usual way—by backing into it. But she remembered Catrona's verse about it:

> *Downy head and thorny spine,*
> *On the roots you safely dine,*

which meant the young, tender roots would be good to eat. Avoiding the prickers, she cut away the roots and chewed thoughtfully on a piece. It tasted a great deal like celery.

Meanwhile, Jenna had found some birds' nests, all but one empty. There were three eggs in that nest and, hoping the young birds had not yet begun to develop, she stole the eggs. A handful of walnuts, still in their coverts, completed her share of the feast.

They met back at the tree and woke the sleeping Carum, who grumbled until they mentioned food. Luckily the eggs were liquid. After showing Carum how to bore a hole in the shell with a knife point, Jenna and Pynt each took an egg themselves and eagerly sucked out the contents. After only a moment's hesitation, Carum did the same.

"I never thought such a meal would taste good," said Carum. "But it's greater than any feast I've eaten."

Jenna smiled, and Pynt said, "At the Hame it is said that *Hunger is the best seasoning.* I do not think I ever understood that before."

Carum laughed. "I understand it, too." He chewed on the thistle root a while, then said, almost to himself, "In the moonlight you two look like shadow sisters, black and white."

Jenna clapped her hands. "We are," she said. "Did you know that Pynt is called 'shadow' in the Hame because . . ."

Pynt stood up abruptly, tumbling her share of the walnuts onto the grass. "It is time to go. Before—Jo-an-enna—you give away all our secret, private things." She threw a shell angrily and went back to the tree to pick up her pack and sword.

"She is tired and hungry and . . ." Jenna began.

"She is jealous," Carum said.

"Jealous of what?"

"Of you. Of me. Of us."

"Us?" Jenna looked puzzled for a moment, then said very slowly, "There is no *us*." She stood up.

Carum reached up for her hand and she ignored it, so he stood on his own. "Jenna, I thought . . . I felt . . ."

"There is only a woman of Alta and a man who cried her *merci*. That is all." She turned her head away quickly, seeking out Pynt, who stood silently waiting by the tree.

The silence stretched out endlessly as they walked through the midnight forest, Pynt in the lead. They cast long shadows whenever they crossed open ground, the shadow limbs touching in intimate ways none of them dared consider. As if to underscore their silences, the forest seemed alive with small noises. Leaves dropped mysteriously to the ground, crackling. Little animals scurried unseen through the undergrowth, rustling the grass. A night bird called over and over from a low, overhanging branch, in ever-descending loops of sound. And their feet kept up a steady susurration.

They walked hours in the same speechless way, their mouths stoppered by their feelings. Jenna turned time after time to say something to either Pynt or Carum, and found she could not begin, sure that whatever she said would be wrong. So she continued to say nothing, her head down. Trudging through the woods, she scarcely noticed her surroundings until a single, high, fluting birdcall stopped her.

Carum, unalerted, continued walking and crashed into her back. They both leaped away, and Jenna fell against Pynt, who had already turned.

Pynt caught her and whispered, "It is too early for thrush. The sun is not yet warming the woods and there is no light save the moon."

Jenna nodded, signaling to Carum to be still.

The birdcall came again, tremulous, insistent.

"Ours or theirs?" Pynt's question threaded directly into Jenna's ear.

Jenna's response was to put her hand to her mouth and whistle back a darting, twittering reply.

"Good call!" whispered Pynt.

A shadow unwound behind them and hissed. "Sssslowly. Turn slowly so that I might identify you."

Jenna and Pynt obeyed, raising their hands and making the goddess sign quickly with their fingers, but Carum did not move.

The shadow laughed and when it came full into the moonlight, resolved itself into a tall, youngish woman with a vivid brown scar running down her right cheek. Her hair was cut in a high crest and she was wearing the skins of a warrior. Unnocking the arrow, she put it carefully into the quiver on her back in a single fluid motion. Then she struck her breast with her fist. "I am Armina, daughter of Callilla."

"And I am her dark sister, Darmina."

Carum turned to look behind them and there was a second woman, almost a twin of the first, with her hair in a high black crest and a dark scar on her left cheek.

Armina spoke again. "You two are, I think, missioning. But who is this scarecrow you have with you? A boy but not a boy. A man almost. Quite pretty."

Darmina laughed. "For a scarecrow."

"He might be fun in the dark," Armina said.

"Or with a candle by the bed," her dark sister added.

"If he is a bother to you, we could—" Armina stopped speaking suddenly but her grin continued.

"He *is* a bother," said Pynt.

"But a bother we take on willingly," Jenna added quickly.

Armina and Darmina nodded.

Pynt struck her own chest in imitation of Armina's greeting. "I am Marga, called Pynt, daughter of Amalda."

Jenna followed suit. "Jo-an-enna, called Jenna. Daughter of . . ." She hesitated, swallowed, then began again. "Daughter of a cat-killed woman, daughter of Selna."

Pynt added, "*And* daughter of Amalda, too."

"He is Carum," Jenna said, gesturing with her head.

Armina and Darmina walked around Carum several times, clicking their tongues against the roofs of their mouths as they did.

"Close enough to make him interesting, sister," said Darmina.

"There are several in the Hame who like bull calves," Armina replied. "But—alas—he cannot come in. Too close to a Choosing."

"What a pity," Darmina said.

"Pity, my pretty," Armina added.

Jenna pushed between them. "Leave him alone. He cried us *merci*."

Carum laughed. "They're only teasing, Jenna. I like it. No one has ever admired me for my body before, just my mind!"

"*Merci?*" Darmina shook her head.

"You have not taken vows yet," said Armina. "Am I right?"

Pynt nodded.

"So—it means nothing. Just a boy and a couple of girls at play. But if you two have spoken for him already . . ."

Pynt looked over at Jenna, and Jenna's face was stone. "We may not be fully vowed yet, but we of *Selden* Hame take such pleas to Alta's altar seriously. We have killed a man for him already."

"A Kingsman," Carum added suddenly.

"Are you sure?" Armina asked, rubbing her hand up through the crest of her hair.

Darmina echoed her. "A Kingsman?"

"If Carum says it is so," Jenna told them, "it is so. He is a scholar and he does not lie."

"Think you scholars do not lie, little sister?" asked Darmina.

Armina chuckled. "One may lie by saying or by *not* saying." She glared at Carum. "Tell us of this Kingsman, boy."

Carum squared his shoulders and stared back at her. "He wore a helm and rode a cross-grained gray. He carried a sword and a dirk at saddle and at knee. Does *that* identify him for you?"

Armina looked over at Pynt. "True?"

Pynt nodded.

"And what did the helm look like?" Armina asked.

"It had antlers," Pynt said.

"Antlers?" Armina shook her head. "I know of no Kingsman who wears an antlered helm."

Jenna interrupted. "From afar they looked like antlers. But I held the helm in my hand and can say different. Not antlers but the great chewed ears, lifted, of a giant hound. With a snout and snarling fangs."

"The Hound!" The sisters spoke together.

"So *he* said." Pynt's head jerked at Carum for emphasis.

"You killed The Hound!" Darmina's voice was low.

Jenna nodded. "We did, Pynt and I. It was not . . . pleasant."

"I can believe that," Armina said. Her mouth worked without sound for a moment, the scar stretching and bunching in an ugly fashion. "So you killed The Hound. Well, well, young missioners. Such news you bring. We must go to the Hame, and at once."

Darmina put her hand on her sister's. "What of the Choosing? And bringing *him* in?"

"We will take him directly up to Mother Alta's chamber by the back stairs. She will know what to do." Still clutching her sister's hand, Armina turned to Jenna. "I wonder, young missioner, what terrible thing you may have brought to our doorstep. And I wonder, too, whether we but compound it by bringing you in. Come."

She threaded her way through the forest, with Darmina, visible only when the moonlight pierced the canopy of trees, right behind. Pynt followed after. Jenna, leading Carum by the hand, made up the rear.

It was fully light by the time they reached the Hame, and only Armina was there to guide them. Where the forest ended, there was a wide clearing rimmed around with berry bushes and several plantings of herbs in straight, marked rows. A wide road ran by the wood-and-stone gates, but it was empty of travelers and the dirt, hard-packed, not recently disturbed.

They walked quickly to the gate and Armina called up a password in the old tongue. Slowly the gates were pulled inward, but not before Jenna had gotten a good, long look at the ornate carvings on the front.

"Jenna," whispered Pynt, "it is the same scene as the tapestry in Mother Alta's room. Look—there is the game of wands, and there Alta collects the children, and there . . ."

They were ushered inside and the great gates slammed shut behind them. Now they stood in a vast, almost deserted courtyard. Only one sister hurried across it, her back to them, holding a full basket of breads heaped high. From the corner of her eye Jenna could see another yard, somewhat smaller, off to the right where three girls her age were lined up with their bows. The steady *thunk-thunk-thunk* of arrows hitting an unseen target squarely came to her, but Armina had already disappeared through an archway on the left. Pynt pulled Jenna to the door and pushed her through.

"Come on," Pynt urged.

Carum followed without a word.

They trotted after Armina through a maze of halls and rooms, more than four times the number at Selden Hame, and climbed two flights of stairs as well. For Jenna and Pynt this was a new experience, for Selden Hame was all on the flat, and they exchanged delighted glances. But Carum mounted the twisting stairs with an air of knowing.

"Castle-born," Pynt muttered at his back, as if that were a curse.

Jenna was still marveling at the complexity of the Hame when Armina stopped suddenly before a door and signaled them with a raised hand. They moved cautiously up to the door, which was even more ornately carved than the outside gate. Only instead of figures, the door was inscribed with symbols: apple, spoon, knife, needle, thread . . .

"Eye-Mind!" Jenna said. "Look, Pynt, the signs are all from the Game."

Pynt traced around the knife sign with her finger.

"Now we go in," Armina said, nodding at them, and her great crest of hair swayed slightly. "In to speak with the Mother."

Jenna drew in several long breaths, ending the Spider breath with which she had climbed the stairs and beginning the deeper *latani* breathing. It soothed her. She could hear Pynt matching her breath for breath.

Armina smiled. "Frightened? Of the Mother?" She pushed through the door into a darkened chamber and dropped to one knee so quickly Carum stumbled into her. The girls, still breathing deeply, walked in more slowly and knelt by Armina's side.

Jenna peered into the dimly lit room, trying to follow Armina's gaze. Between two covered window slits was a large chair. Something—someone—stirred in the chair.

"Mother, forgive me this intrusion, but I come with three whose presence may be a danger. It is for you to say."

There was a long hush. Jenna could hear Carum swallowing. Pynt swayed a bit by her side. Then the figure in the chair gave a sigh.

"Light the lamps, child. I was just napping. Your sisters damp them when I sleep—as if day or night has meaning for me. But I can smell that the lamps are out. And I like the small, hissing sounds they make."

Armina stood and lit the lamps with a torch she fetched from the hall, then drew aside the cloth from each of the windows as well. The light revealed a small, dark figure in the chair, as small as a child, but old. Older, Jenna thought, than anyone she had ever seen, for the woman's face was as brown and wrinkled as a walnut, and crowned with thin, white hair. Her blind eyes were the color of wet marble, gray and opaque.

"Forgive, Mother?" Armina said, but her question carried no deference.

"You scamp, Armina, I always forgive you. You and your dark sister. Come here. Let me feel that foolish head." The old woman smiled.

Armina moved over to the priestess and knelt before her, lifting her face to the old woman's touch. "I am here, Mother."

Mother Alta's fingers, like little breezes, brushed across Armina's face, ran down the scar, and then floated up to the brush of hair. "Who have you brought me? And what the danger?"

"Two girls on a mission, Mother, and a boy they say cried them *merci*," Armina replied.

"The girls, from what Hame?" the old woman asked.

Armina turned and looked at Jenna.

"Selden Hame, Mother," Pynt said before Jenna could answer.

"Ah, the small Hame in the Borderland Hills. How many there now?" She stared at them as if she could see them.

"Forty light sisters, Mother," said Jenna.

"And forty dark," Armina said, chuckling.

"Thirty-nine," Pynt said quickly, delighted to have caught Armina out. "One, our infirmarer, is a Solitary."

"And four missioners and five girls," Jenna finished.

"We have four hundred, light and dark," Armina said. "And many, many children. Many missioners, too, though I doubt they go to so small a Hame as Selden."

"We have only once or twice seen a missioner," admitted Jenna. "But we know about missioning. We know about . . ."

"*Girls!*" Mother Alta said sharply, and raised her hands, which had been hidden in the voluminous sleeves of her robe. Jenna saw with a kind of fascinated horror that each hand had a sixth finger stretching straight out from the side. She could not keep her eyes off the hands. They seemed to be weaving dark fantasies in the air.

"Now, Armina, you are the older by several years, for your mission is five years gone. Act as a guide and a guard; be my eyes. If there is danger, we must be ware afore time." Her hands disappeared again into the cave of sleeves.

Armina's face darkened for a moment from the scolding; then the mischievous grin reasserted itself. "Mother, the taller one is the one with the lower voice. She stands nearly as tall as I do."

"Taller, since you have that crest," said Pynt.

"That, then, is the smaller one?" asked the priestess.

"Yes, Mother, she is smaller in all but mouth. Slight and

dark. Like a woman of the Lower Dales. The boy is reasonably good-looking, fine-featured, none of your barbarian stock. They say he is a scholar and in danger, though what danger a scholar could possibly get into, only Alta knows. Reading the wrong volumes, I suppose. But he is *himself* the danger to our Hame. The girls have killed the Hound in his cause."

The old woman's head came up and her hands flew out of the sleeves again. "The Hound? Are you sure?"

"We . . ." Jenna began, but Carum's hand reached out and touched her on the arm, silencing her.

"Mother Alta," Carum began, his voice strong, "I am sure because I knew the Hound well."

"Did you?" murmured Armina.

"*How* did you?" asked Mother Alta.

"I . . ." He hesitated and darted a quick glance at Jenna. "He was seeking me because I am . . ." He stopped again, drew in a deep breath, and finished, "I am Carum Longbow, a scholar and the king's youngest son."

Jenna's eyes opened wide and Pynt elbowed her in the side. Jenna moved away from her, staring at Carum.

"*So!*" said Armina.

"The Hound hunted for a vicious master," said Carum.

"He hunted for Kalas," Mother Alta said, head nodding.

"You know!" His head began to nod in rhythm with hers. Putting his hands in front of his chest, he said, "Mother, *ich crie thee merci!*"

"It seems, young Longbow, that scholars do not know everything." Her smile added wrinkles. "You have already cried to one Altite, and one is surely enough. If they have killed the Hound who hunted you, indeed what more could they do?"

"These girls have not yet taken their sacred vows, Mother," reminded Armina. "And a vow to a king's son must be . . ."

"We did not know he was a king's son," Jenna said, sharply.

"If we had . . ." Pynt added, but let the rest of her sentence trail off, for she did not know what they would have done.

Neither one mentioned that the Hound had been killed because *he* had attacked *them*.

"What is a vow, Armina, my child," asked Mother Alta, "but the mouth repeating what the heart has already promised? These two young hearts will be no stouter next year, nor their mouths any more truthful after their vows than before. Carum Longbow cried them *merci* as a man, not as a son of this person or that. And they have killed in his cause, because they took on his protection. What can be more binding than blood? What can be more sacred than that? The Goddess smiles."

Armina looked down at the floor and was silent.

"Now, imp, do not sulk. I can hear your angry short breaths. Bring us food that we may sit and gossip of the Hames." Mother Alta chuckled. "And you will share with us, Armina, child of my child."

Armina looked up. "But, Mother, what of the danger?"

"Think you that Kalas' men will look for the boy here? We will dress this young cock in hen's feathers and if he is as fine-featured as you say, if he is young enough to be beardless yet . . ."

"I am, Mother," said Carum. Then he flushed, realizing that it sounded as if he were praising himself.

They all laughed then, Carum a beat behind.

"Now, Armina, get us that food. And some sweet wine. And do not forget a savory for after. But ware—not a word about our guests save that they be missioning. I do not want this young bull calf amongst the heifers undisguised. I wish to discover what I can without the added danger of tongues wagging. If we have one fault here in this Hame, it is that we can keep nothing secret."

"I will say nothing, Mother," Armina promised, "and I will get the food at once." She rose directly and went to the door, where she turned. "There is rhulbarbe pie, your favorite." Then she left, whistling.

Mother Alta sighed. "If she keeps her promise, it will be the first time." Then, bringing her hands once more out of her sleeves and gesturing to them, she said, "But come, my children, closer to these old ears. And tell me how you met and what has transpired since."

* * *

A succession of kitcheners left food outside the door on platters decked out with red and gold flowers. Pynt and Jenna helped Armina bring in the plates but ate so eagerly, they scarcely noticed the decorations. And so intent were they on the tales they were spinning for the priestess that the profusion of sweet breads, tangy rabbit stew, and salads of spring lettuce and small onion bulbs went down without comment. The priestess ate with quiet precision, scarcely moving.

They found themselves admitting everything to her, even Pynt's disobedience, even Jenna's disgust at the killing, even their worry at Carum's disappearance into the forest to relieve himself.

After the third time Pynt made excuses for deserting Selinda and Alna, Mother Alta sighed with annoyance.

"Enough of your excuses, child. You have told me not once but over and over that you are Jo-an-enna's shadow and that dark must follow light."

"Yes, yes," Pynt answered.

"Dear child," Mother Alta said, leaning forward in her chair, "though loyalty is prized, Great Alta reminds us that *A foolish loyalty can be the greater danger.* You will find understanding from me but not expiation. We do not yet know what your loyalty will cost."

"Did she actually say that?" Carum asked, breaking into the conversation. It was his first entrance in many minutes. "Great Alta, I mean. Did she actually say that? Or is it written?"

"If she herself did not utter those words, still they are well said," the priestess answered, her mouth twisting with private mischief. "But the words are written down in the *Book of Light,* chapter thirty-seven, verse seventeen, in a quite ordinary hand." She raised her left hand and wriggled all but the sixth finger.

"There is nothing ordinary about that hand," Carum said.

"Ordinary—extraordinary," mused Mother Alta, her head nodding down. Then she looked up, her marble eyes shining. "We are—do you not all feel it—at a moment in history, a nexus, a turning where the ordinary *is* extraordinary. I *know* these things. There is a light in the room, a great light."

"But, Mother," protested Pynt. "You are blind. How can you see a light?"

"I do not *see* it, I feel it," Mother Alta said.

"Like the feeling in the forest right before a storm?" asked Jenna.

"Yes, yes, child. You understand. And do you feel it, too?"

Jenna shook her head. "Yes. No, I am not sure."

"Well, never mind. It is gone now, that feeling," Mother Alta said, her voice whispering off. "Fading . . . fade . . ." Her head nodded once and she was asleep.

"Come," Armina said, standing, "we must leave her to her rest."

"Is she all right?" Carum asked.

"She is old, old past counting, Longbow," Armina said. "And sometimes she is not quite lucid. But today she was —somehow—transformed. Visitors are always good for her, but you three seem special somehow. I have not seen her so—so *animated* in a long time." She bent and quietly began replacing the dishes onto the trays. "She will want to talk to you later, I know."

They helped carry out the trays with as little noise as possible, but nothing seemed to disturb the old woman, who sat upright, eyes closed and mouth slightly open, fast asleep in the chair.

As the door closed behind them and they placed the trays against the wall, Jenna asked, "But should we not move her to her bed? Will she not fall out of the chair?"

Armina shook her head and the great crest of hair waved. "She is tied into the chair. She will not fall."

"Tied! But that . . . that is . . ." Pynt fumbled for the right word.

"*That* is her own request," Armina said, her voice gentle in the extreme. "For if she fell, she could not help herself. She cannot walk, you see."

They went to Armina's room by a dark back stairs, passing no one on the way. It was a pleasant, open room, with a narrow window through which afternoon sunlight streamed. A large bed, its head under the window, the covers rumpled, filled much of the space. On one side of the bed stood an oaken wardrobe, on the other a table with a lamp. Half a dozen piles of clothes were on the floor.

Armina went over to one pile and pulled out a pair of baggy brown britches. From another she chose a red shirt; after holding it to her nose for a moment, she discarded it on a third pile and picked instead a loose blue shirt and a blue scarf.

"There," she said. "These should do. Put them on."

Carum looked around. "Here? With you watching?"

"*Over* your other clothes," Armina said. "I shall want them back when you are gone, and we cannot leave you running naked down the halls of refuge—" She stopped and laughed. "Though it *is* a thought."

He slipped into the trousers and shirt and looked helplessly at the scarf. Armina tied it expertly around his head. The blue brought out the color of his eyes.

"There," she said as she stood back to admire him. "No one would ever guess you are a prince." She looked over at Jenna and Pynt, who had watched the whole thing from the bed. "And no one will guess he is a man, either, not with those long lashes and those eyes."

"Enough!" Carum said, snatching the cloth from his head. "It's bad enough that I have to wear these things. I won't be laughed at."

"Laughter, dear boy," Armina said, turning to him, "is called the goddess gift in this Hame. And it is well known that women can laugh at themselves, whereas men . . ."

"The first thing a scholar learns," Carum said, "is to beware of any sentence that begins *It is well known!*"

"And the last thing a scholar learns is humor," said Pynt.

"Enough," Jenna said. "All of you. Enough. *Wicked tongues make wicked wives*. And that bit of wisdom comes from the Lower Dales."

"Upper, actually," Carum said.

"If you think my tongue is wicked, wait until dark.

Darmina's tongue is twice as fast as mine." Armina stopped, tried to catch control of her thought, then exploded into laughter. When she caught her breath again, she shrugged and winked at Jenna and Pynt. "Private joke. *Her tongue is twice as fast!*" She began to laugh again, and the girls looked wide-eyed at her and completely mystified.

Carum's eyes narrowed. His shoulders went down and his head up. "I don't mind women making randy jokes," he said, "but . . ."

"Alta's Hairs!" Armina ran her hand up through her hair. "He is a prude as well. What fun we shall all have."

Carum finished thoughtfully, ". . . their jokes *and* their curses should at least have the grace of originality. Come on, Jenna, Pynt. We're going."

"But where?" asked Pynt.

Jenna stood and pulled Pynt up beside her. "Carum is right. We must go and find Mother Alta and tell her it is time to get Carum to his refuge. Hospitality is one thing, safety another."

"He is safe here," said Armina.

"But is the Hame safe with him here?" asked Jenna.

Pynt thrust her chin forward. "He is *our* pledge, after all. He cried *us merci*. We must go on." She grinned. "But we could pack some food. That rhulbarbe pie was wonderful."

Armina shrugged. "I did not think you even noticed. Very well, I will take you back to Mother Alta. You will never find the way on your own."

"You are talking to three who got through the Sea of Bells in a fog," said Pynt.

"That is child's play compared with the maze of this Hame. Why"—and Armina smiled—"they say there is one young missioner from Calla's Ford who was lost twenty years ago in our halls." Her voice got very low. "*And she has never been found.*"

"Can you never be serious?" asked Carum.

"What for?" Armina asked, shrugging again. "*Laugh longer, live longer*, the hill people around here say. But, Longbow, before we go out into the halls, put the scarf back on. It is what makes you look the part. Besides"—and she laughed again—"it goes so well with your eyes." Her laughter was so completely without malice that they were forced to laugh with her, first Pynt, then Jenna, and at last, though reluctantly, Carum.

They followed her out of the room and swiftly traversed the mazing hallways, nodding pleasantly at the women they passed. Armina led them up a broad flight of stairs and past many rooms, until they stood at last before the priestess' carved door once again. The trays of food they had left in the hall were gone.

"There, would you have found it?" Armina asked.

"You took us a different way," said Jenna. "We might have found the old route."

"We *would* have found the old route," said Pynt.

"Or we could have gotten lost *and never found*," Carum put in, in the same sepuchral tones Armina had used before.

"You see," Armina said with a broad grin, "now Longbow will live longer!" Her face turned suddenly serious. "But mind, you must sit there quietly until she wakes on her own. She is not so sweet-tempered if you wake her beforetime. *I* know!"

But the old priestess was already awake when they went in, being fussed over by two older women who were arranging her robes and combing her hair, not without some resistance from Mother Alta.

"Leave me," she said to them, dismissing them imperiously with a wave of her hand. The blue priestess sign in her palm showed plainly. "I would talk with these three missioners alone. Armina, guard the door. I do not wish us to be disturbed." Her voice now held an edge of authority. All three women jumped to do her bidding.

When the carved door snicked shut behind them, Mother Alta's hands once more disappeared into the sleeves of her dark robe. She nodded her head and her voice was the same soft burr as before. "Come, children, and sit. We must talk. I have been giving your problems much thought."

"But you were asleep, Mother," Pynt said.

"Is it not written that *Sleep is the great unraveler of knots?* And do not ask in what volume, young Carum. I forget. But this I know, I do my best thinking there, where color and line explode behind my sightless eyes. All becomes clearer to me, as a traveler sees his own home more clearly in a foreign land."

They sat by her feet and awaited instruction.

"Let us first breathe the hundred-chant," Mother Alta said. "And you, Longbow, follow as best you can. It is an old Alta exercise that calms the mind and frees the senses, making one fresh for the new work ahead. With it, the Goddess smiles."

As the deep breathing began, Jenna felt strangely lightened, as if her real self had been pulled free of the body to float above it. The chanting moved into the twenties and thirties, and she seemed to range around the priestess' room without moving, her mind remarking upon the furniture she had not noticed before: the slat bed with its two pillows; a large wooden wardrobe incised with goddess signs; a copy of the *Book of Light* on a stand, its raised letters casting strange shadows in the fading light of day; and a mirror covered by a red-brown cloth the color of dried blood. The chanting bodies below her moved toward the seventies and eighties, and Jenna found herself ranging over them, her translucent fingers reaching down to touch each upon the very center of the skull, where a pulse beat beneath the shield of skin and bone. At the touch—which only she seemed to notice —Jenna found herself drawn down inside each of her companions in turn. Mother Alta was as cool as a well, and as dark. Armina was all sparkling points, like the bright flames and embers of a wood fire. Pynt, on the other hand, was a windstorm, blowing hot, then cold, then hot again in quick and dizzying succession. Carum was . . . She was drawn down and down and down to his center, passing pockets in him, some restful, some fretful, some filled with a wild, engulfing alien heat that threatened to entrap her. She pulled herself away and fled up into the air again, turned, and faced her own chanting self. That was, somehow, the strangest of all, to watch herself, unaware, a secret mirror of . . .

The hundred-chant ended and Jenna opened her eyes, almost surprised to find herself anchored once again in her own flesh.

"Mother," she began huskily, her voice scarcely above a

whisper, "a strange thing has just happened. For the time of our hundred-chant, I was—somehow—free of my flesh. I floated above the room, searching for something or for someone."

Mother Alta spoke slowly. "Ah, Jo-an-enna, what you feel is the beginning of womanhood, the beginning of true twinning, though you are much too young if you are only now missioning. Such *enlightness* happens on the Night of Sisterhood, when the soul ranges for a moment, finds the mirror, and plunges into the waiting image. Light calls dark, the two parts of the self are made whole. Did you find the mirror, child?"

"It . . ." Jenna looked around the room and saw that the mirror was, indeed, covered. "There is a cloth over it."

"Then how . . . strange, my child. Strange that you are so young for this. That it is daylight. That the mirror is masked." Her chin touched down on her chest and, for a moment, she seemed to sleep.

Armina stood and quietly went out the door.

"What did it feel like, Jenna?" whispered Pynt. "Were you frightened? Was it wonderful?"

Jenna turned her head to answer, but Carum's hand was on her arm.

"The Mother wakens," he said.

The priestess' opaque eyes were open. "I do not sleep," she said, "but I *do* dream."

Pynt whispered into Jenna's ear, "Armina said she is sometimes not lucid. Is this one of those times?"

"Hush!" Jenna commanded.

"More lucid than ever I was, dear Pynt," the old woman said. "Remember, child, that one who has no sight is gifted extra hearing. It is nature's way."

"Forgive me, Mother," Pynt said, her head lowered. "I meant no . . ."

Mother Alta's hand crept from her sleeve and swept away Pynt's embarrassment with a quick gesture. "We must all think, now. What brings us together?"

"We came back, Mother, to tell you that we must get Carum away from here," said Pynt.

"I fear I am a danger to your Hame. We saw riders . . ." Carum began.

"Oh, there is more to the puzzle than these few pieces," Mother Alta said. "Something is missing. The Game is incomplete. I cannot recall all the parts." She began to mumble to herself. "Light sister, dark sister, needle, spoon, knife, thread . . ."

Pynt elbowed Jenna.

The old woman's head snapped up. "Come to me, Pynt, and tell me of yourself. Not *what* you have done, for that I know. But *who* you are." The old woman gestured to her.

Reluctantly, with Jenna pushing her, Pynt inched closer to the priestess and knelt so that her head was within reach of the six-fingered hands.

"I am Marga, called Pynt," she began, "daughter of the warrior Amalda, whose dark sister is Sammor. I have chosen the way of warrior and hunter. I . . ." She giggled as the priestess' hand ran down her face.

"Good, good, child. My eyes are in my fingers. They tell me you, Marga called Pynt, have dark, curly hair and a quick smile."

"How do you know I have dark hair? The eyes in your fingers cannot tell you that."

"By the coarseness of the strands. Dark hair is always coarser than light. Light hair has a fineness to it, and red hair often confuses."

"Oh."

The old woman smiled. "Besides, Armina told me you were dark like a woman of the Lower Dales. I may be old, but my memory is still sharp. *When* I am lucid."

Pynt's cheeks flushed and the old woman laughed.

"Are you embarrassed, child, or are you disappointed that my magic has such a mundane explanation?"

Pynt did not answer.

"Never mind. Go on, child."

"I have a scar on my right knee from wrestling with Jenna when we were seven, right before the Choosing. And my eyes are dark."

"Almost violet," put in Jenna.

"And . . ."

"And you have a fine scar under your chin. More wrestling, Pynt?"

"I fell in the kitchen in a game of Seek and Find. It bled forever. At least it seemed so at the time."

"Good. That is all I need to know of you now. Jenna?"

Jenna slid over to Pynt's place. In passing, Pynt winked and whispered, "It tickles."

"I am not ticklish."

Carum cleared his throat but said nothing.

The priestess' fingers started over Jenna's face. "Speak, child."

"I am Jo-an-enna, called Jenna, daughter of a cat-killed woman and fostered to Selna, the great warrior of Selden Hame, and her dark sister Marjo. I am named for her, I think."

"You think—you do not know?"

"They died when I was but an infant."

"And then who fostered you at the Hame, thrice-mothered child?"

Her voice faltered. "No one."

"*Our* Mother Alta would let no one else foster her. It was the shame of Selden Hame," Pynt put in. "My mother, Amalda, would have had her gladly. But there was something awful that happened when her foster mother died. Something so awful, they were not allowed to talk of it. And . . ."

"Enough, Pynt," Jenna said.

"Let her tell," said Mother Alta.

But Pynt bit her lip and was still.

The priestess' hands returned to Jenna's head. The right hand made the goddess sign over her; then the sixth finger of the hand caught in Jenna's hair.

"Are you dark, too, Jo-an-enna? Your hair is not fine enough for light, yet Pynt calls you her light sister."

"And I call her White Jenna," Carum put in. "At least I call her that to myself."

"*White* Jenna?" The priestess was suddenly still, as if

listening to a song no one else could hear. At last she asked quietly, pausing between each word, "And . . . is . . . your . . . hair . . . pure . . . white?"

"Yes, Mother," Jenna replied.

Mother Alta smiled triumphantly. "The final piece of the Game!" she said. "And if I were not blind, I would have known it at once." She sang out a low plainsong of five lines in a voice that rang clearly through the room.

THE SONG:

Prophecy

The babe as white as snow,
A maiden tall shall grow,
And ox and hound bow low,
And bear and cat also.
Holy, holy, holy.

THE STORY:

When the song ended and the echo of it was gone as well, Jenna started up. "I am *not* the White Babe. Our Mother Alta said I was, but I reject that utterly. Look at me. Look!" She turned to her friends, her voice pleading. "Do I look like something from a prophecy?"

Carum reached up and pulled her down beside him. "Hush, Jenna," he said, stroking her hand. "Hush. This is just an old woman's whim. Let *me* deal with this. It is scholar's work." He spoke to the priestess. "That is a Garunian prophecy, Mother.

The white babe and the bowing of hound and ox and the rest. But no one takes it seriously, no real scholar." He smiled.

"Ah, young Longbow, and did you think you were the only scholar, the only *real* scholar, on the Isles?"

Carum's cheeks flushed. "Of course not. But I surely didn't expect to find one here."

"Here, in this backwater, you mean? Amongst the warrior maidens? But we are not all warriors here, much as I must look the part to you." She chuckled pleasantly. "Some of us must cook and some of us must clean and some of us must keep the rota of events, just as it is amongst you of the outer world. And *some* of us"—she leaned forward—"*are* real scholars."

Settling back in her chair, she continued. "Who knows what I might have been in your world, Carum, for I am a daughter of a Garun lord. Yes, even I. But look at my hands, look deep into my eyes, and you will see the signs of my abandonment." She held her six-fingered hands before her face. "I was a babe wrapped in cloth of gold and left on a heath long years after white-haired Alta had reaped the hillsides. Still the women of the Hames, to honor her, culled that forbidden crop. I was brought to this Hame and raised up to lead. Years later, when my father's line had come to its barren end, a messenger sought out all the Hames to ask whether a blind child with twelve fingers had miraculously weathered the years. But my foster mother and sisters would not give me up, nor would I have gone if asked. I had pledged myself to Alta, and Alta's I remain." She stopped and tapped a finger to her mouth.

"It was clear to all that I was a strange child bound for a stranger destiny than death on a hillside. Yet no one knew what role I would play. I chose to study, and was curious about my father's world, learning of it as I had learned all else, with my ears, the good, strong daughters of the mind. I have learned—through these ears, Carum—more than you shall ever through your eyes."

"I apologize for my thoughtlessness, Mother," said Carum, striking a fist against his chest.

"It is youth's privilege to be thoughtless," Mother Alta

replied. "But also youth's privilege to learn. Think, Carum Longbow. You and I *may be* kin in blood, but we are kindred souls. We seek connections, we look for links. You see, I know the Garunian prophecy."

"Only the plainsong, Mother. And it is much discredited."

She laughed. "You think I know only the plainsong, child? No, indeed. I know the entire prophecy: about the virgin in the winter, though we say here at the Hame that *virgin* is just another word for a girl. So it could be that the babe's mother was more or less a child herself. And I know about the mothering three times. And all the rest. Know you Alta's prophecy so well?"

He shook his head. "I don't know it at all," he said. "Much of Alta is closed to outsiders."

"And so we desire to keep it," she answered. "But I can tell you this much: what our prophets wrote is the light sister to your dark. We hold—and we believe it utterly—that there will be a child as white as snow, as black as night, as . . . what color are your eyes, Jenna?"

"Black, Mother," Jenna replied. "But . . ."

"As white as snow, as black as night, as red as blood."

"What is red about her?" asked Carum.

"Do I know all? The language of prophecy is the language of puzzles, is the language of riddles, is the language of dreams. What is said is not always what is meant. Often we come to understanding long after the events have occurred. Perhaps the red was the Hound's blood. Perhaps it will be Jenna's first flow. But like the Garunians, we say clearly that this one shall be queen above all and she shall begin the world anew. The one great task laid upon Mothers of every Hame is this: to wait for her, to look for her, the white child, the Anna."

"The *Anna*," mused Carum. "The white babe, the great white goddess."

Nodding, Mother Alta continued. "Many thought I was marked for the Anna myself, for my hair turned white overnight when I was eighteen. And to look upon me was to be sure I had been touched by Alta's heavy hand. Long we waited and nothing more occurred, till at last my sisters pitied me for being naught but an unnature, a freak. Yet I, alone, never lost hope that I might be part of the workings-out of the prophecy. If not the Anna herself, at least her forerunner, her guide, the one who sings her praises. *Holy, holy, holy.* And now the Anna is here."

"No, Mother. Not here. Not me," Jenna cried. "I am not that white babe. I am only Jenna of Selden Hame. When I have a cold, my nose runs. When I am hungry, my stomach growls. When there are beans in the stewpot, I make a stink. I am no Anna. I am just a girl."

"The signs cannot be ignored, my child," Mother Alta said. "Much as you would like to. Though it is true there have been thrice-mothered girls before. And there have been white babes with hair the color of snow and eyes like watered wine. But the Hound bowed down. That cannot be forgot—the Hound bowed down."

"He did not bow, Mother. He died," Jenna said. "With my sword in his throat and Pynt's knife in his thigh."

"And what greater obeisance?" Mother Alta asked.

"Might as well say the white-haired babe will have red hair," Jenna said unhappily. "Might as well say a goat and a horse will bow to her."

"Might as well," murmured Pynt.

Mother Alta chuckled, a low, cooing sound. "Prophecies speak to us on the slant, child. We must read them through slotted eyes."

"*You* read them," Jenna said. "I will not."

Carum, who had been listening to the exchange with a faraway look in his eyes, suddenly turned to the priestess. "Mother Alta," he said slowly, "the prophecy also says that the white babe will begin the world anew. That's the point of the whole thing, isn't it? But to do that, one must first . . . must first . . ." He hesitated.

"Spit it out, boy!"

"First one must destroy the old, and that I can't see Jenna doing."

"Ah, Longbow, on the slant. See the world on a slant . . ."

she murmured and fell asleep with a strange smile on her face, as quickly and as quietly as an infant taking a nap.

They looked at one another and, as if on a signal, all stood, opened the door carefully, and slipped out into the darkening hall.

Armina was outside the door. "Well, what did she say? Is she still asleep?"

"She . . . she asked us about our lives. Who we were. And—yes—she is asleep. But she said we must . . . must find refuge for me," Carum said.

Jenna and Pynt said nothing, their silence conspiring to agree with him.

Armina looked puzzled for a moment. She blew air into her cheeks and the dark scar puffed out. Then she smiled. "Refuge. Of course. But first we must all eat. It will be a long trip otherwise. I will take you back to my room and bring the food there. No one else must know our plans. When it is dark, we will start out and that way I shall have Darmina for company. It is the last night before the full moon."

They followed her down the stairs. The wall sconce sent shadows bouncing along behind them, and they were silent for the entire time. Feeling like conspirators, they entered Armina's room and sat uncomfortably on her bed, and stared up guiltily. She smiled at them from the door.

"I will be back soon. With the food." Then she closed the door behind her. Instead of the comfortable snick, the door let out a strange, ratcheting sound.

Jenna leaped up and ran to it, trying to push it open. She turned back to her companions with a stricken look. "She has barred it. She has barred the door. It will not open." Then she turned again to the door and hammered on it, shouting, "Armina, what are you doing? Let us out."

Armina's voice strained through the thick oaken barrier. "You did not tell me the truth, sisters. Mother would never send you elsewhere for refuge. Not without telling me. I will speak with her when she wakes. Until then, stay quiet. *This* is a place of refuge. No harm will come to you here."

Jenna put her back to the door and looked at her friends. "And what do we do now?"

In the end they did nothing. The door was impassable and the single window, while wide enough for Pynt, was too narrow a slit for either Jenna or Carum. Besides, it was too high for escape, even with all the bedclothes and Armina's few leggings knotted together. What appeared to be the second floor was really the fourth, for the back end of the Hame was built on a cliff which fell off abruptly into a swift-flowing river. Neither of the girls could swim.

It was well after dark, with the moon grinning through the window slits, when Armina returned. She and her dark sister opened the door and barred it with their swords, sliding the tray of food into the room with their feet before speaking.

"Mother still sleeps," Armina said. "You will see her first thing in the morning. Your visit tired her. So eat well, and rest."

Darmina smiled at them. "The bed is wide enough for two—or three, if you are so minded."

Armina looked at the window, where the bedclothes were still knotted and the end wound several times around the sconce. She laughed. "I see you have used your time well. When I was younger, I used to slip out of the window and dangle over the river. It was what we all did, before we were allowed to play at the Wands. But in those days we were on a lower floor and the drop was not so deadly. Except . . ."

Darmina took up the narrative. "Except there was one girl, a silly twist named Mara, who had wet hands and a weak heart."

"It matched her chin. She let go. She screamed all the way down until the water covered her mouth." Armina's free hand ran up through her crest of hair.

"She could not swim," Darmina added.

They ended together, "And her body was never found."

"Another one of your ghost stories?" asked Carum.

"Call it a warning tale," Armina answered. "Besides, there are guards."

"Why, Armina?" asked Pynt. "Why not just let us be on our way?"

"Twice this evening Kingsmen have been to our gates asking about Longbow, calling him by name and describing him by a few choice birthmarks."

Carum blushed.

"Twice we have sent them away knowing nothing," Armina continued. "They are not singling *us* out. They are asking the same questions in all of the villages as well. But Longbow cried us *merci*, and so we must shield him."

"He cried *us!*" Jenna pointed out.

"And in so doing, cried us all," Darmina said. "Did not Mother Alta tell us that?"

"But you . . . you were not there this afternoon when she spoke with us," Carum began, looking first at Darmina, then at Armina. "Or at least I think it was you." He pointed to Armina, who smiled.

Darmina took up that smile and answered him. "Do you not understand yet, *scholar*, that what my light sister knows, I know?"

Armina lowered her sword a fraction of an inch. "We wait for Mother to awaken. She will tell us what we must do. My mother, Callilla, says there is a secret passageway out of here, through the priestess' room and down along the river. But only Mother Alta knows the way."

"Then for our sake, or Alta's sake, or the sake of the Hame," cried Carum, "wake her."

Both sisters shook their heads.

"We cannot," said Darmina. "The Mother is exhausted. If we wake her before time, she will be muddled and it will avail us not. And soon enough it will be morning." She gestured with the sword toward the window, where the moon had already traveled beyond the window slit. "So sleep. And sleep well. We will have much to do tomorrow."

So saying, the sisters backed out of the door, slammed it, and slid the heavy bolt across it once more.

"What do we do now?" asked Pynt.

"What *can* we do?" said Carum.

"We can eat!" Jenna said. "And worry after."

They broke for the tray and sat around it, and, after the first few bites, relaxed enough to eat the meal slowly, savoring the steaming pigeon pie, the pickled eggs, and the rose-colored wine. When there was nothing left but a few slivered bones and the gillyflower that had decorated the platter, they stopped.

Pynt belched daintily and lay down on the bed. Jenna crawled up next to her. Carum looked longingly at the empty side of the bed, then lay down on the floor, under the window, and covered himself with a piece of the knotted blanket. He was conscious of the sound of the girls' breathing, steady and sighing, from the bed. The floor was hard under him. He thought he could feel a nail unevenly hammered into the boards. Just when he had resigned himself to a sleepless night, he slipped reluctantly into a dream. It concerned Jenna, who was tied to a chair, her long, white hair blowing across her face as if stirred by a sea wind. She was crying out to him, but the voice was an infant's, high, frantic, wordless, and thin.

They were awakened not by the sliver of morning sun through the window slit but by Armina's voice.

"Mother Alta is awake and asking for you. It is a good sign. She remembers all. Come."

They roused quickly, and Pynt and Jenna took turns with Armina's combs. She had brought them water in a pitcher and a bowl. The scented water felt cool on their faces. With his back to them, Carum waited until they were done, then ordered them outside.

"Men seem to take forever cleaning themselves," remarked Pynt as they waited.

"Perhaps they have more to clean?" mused Jenna.

Armina laughed. "I take it, then, you spent a *quiet* night."

"We slept," Jenna said.

His face clean and his hair combed, Carum stepped out into the hall. "What I'd give for a real bath," he said.

"That can be arranged," said Armina. "In daylight or at night?"

"As long as there's plenty of hot water, I don't care about the time."

"*Not care?*" Armina laughed out loud. "Oh, you *are* innocent of Alta's ways, boy."

Pynt and Jenna giggled and Carum blushed furiously.

"But we have no time for baths or . . . other things. Mother wants us now." Armina led them quickly up the back stairs.

Mother Alta's door was open and the old woman was waiting for them.

"Come in, come in quickly. We must talk of Jenna's future."

"But what of my future, Mother?" asked Pynt, settling herself down at the priestess' feet. "And Carum's?"

Mother Alta reached out toward her and Pynt shrank back from the touch. "Child, if Jenna is who I say she is, then her future is all of ours. She is the rushing river and we are carried along. But you, dear child, must learn to think before you speak, not to push ahead. Use your head in front of your heart, else you will have no future at all."

Pynt's lips pursed, and she shrugged away from Mother Alta's words.

"Pynt," Jenna began, "do not be hurt. That is no more than what A-ma has always said to you."

"And you, Anna," Mother Alta said, shifting slightly in her chair. "You must learn to listen more to the musings of your heart, to lengthen yourself by your own shadow. Heart and head working together is always the best way."

"Mother, for the last time, I am not the Anna. I puzzled it over all this past night, praying to Alta for guidance. And . . ."

"And?" The old woman leaned forward in her chair.

"And I found no greatness in me. Only the memories of an ordinary childhood."

"What do you think the Anna should have?" asked Mother Alta. "Thunder and lightning at her birth? An animal in the woods to nurse her?"

"*Something*," Jenna begged. "Something out of the ordinary."

"And would you recognize it, Jo-an-enna, if this something extraordinary happened to you? Or would you excuse it, lopping off the unwieldy parts to fit it into your ordinary life? Do not worry. When you and I are long in the Cave, there will be poets and storytellers who will gift you such a birth."

Jenna looked down, unable to meet those marble eyes. She tried to concentrate on the priestess' words, but there was an awful pain in her stomach, almost as if she were hungry. And an angry buzz in her ears. Then she realized the buzz came from the window. She glanced over at it.

Mother Alta, too, had stopped to listen.

Noting their attention, Pynt stood up and went over to the window, standing on tiptoe to see out.

"What is it, child?"

"A knot of men and horses, Mother, in front of the gate. They are shouting, though I cannot make out their words. The guards atop the gate are shouting back. One man is on a gray horse and . . ."

Carum leaped up and ran to the window. "Oh, the gods! Kingsmen! And that is the Bull himself. Now we're for it."

"The Bull," said Pynt, "has a spear and is shaking it at the guards."

"There's something on the spear tip," said Carum.

"I see it! I see it!" Pynt said excitedly. "Oh, Alta's eyes!" She dropped down from the window and turned slowly, a strange look on her face. Then she found their packs where they had left them the night before, upended her own, dropping the contents on the floor. Pawing through her meager possessions, she gave a horrified cry.

"What is it, Marga?" asked Mother Alta.

Jenna ran over to the window slit herself. Tall enough to see out without straining, she stared at the scene below. "I see him. I see the Bull. What is it? Oh, Pynt, no!" She turned. "It is my light doll, Pynt. The one I gave you."

Pynt's voice was an agony. "I cannot find it, Jenna. It must have dropped from my pack."

"When, Pynt, when?"

"I cannot remember. I had it . . . I had it when I was first trailing you. I slept with it in my arms."

Jenna said nothing, remembering vividly how she had spent the night in the crotch of the tree with Pynt's doll wrapped in her embrace.

"And I never took it out again, just jammed it on top of the pack. And then we met Carum and . . ." Pynt stopped, horror written all over her face. Putting her head in her hands, she shuddered.

Though Mother Alta's eyes could not read Pynt's face, she understood the sudden silence. "You remember, child."

Pynt looked up. "In the fight with the Hound, I tripped over my pack and it spilled. I gathered everything up after we buried him. At least I thought I gathered everything up. I must have missed the doll in the fog."

"Oh, you *twist!*" said Carum in disgust.

"Quiet, Longbow," Darmina said. "She was fighting in your cause."

Jenna took up the tale in a quiet voice. "We could not stand to sleep close to the grave and so we moved on a bit and did not look back in the morning." She hesitated.

"Yes, that is what must have happened," said Mother Alta, nodding. "Those men, Kingsmen, came upon Carum's old trail and followed it to the site of the fight and the grave with its dreadful contents. And there was the doll nearby. Who but a young Altite would have a doll so deep in the woods? Surely not the boy they were seeking! We at Nill are the closest Hame, so of course they came here."

"Mother, I am sorry . . ." Pynt began.

"There is no blame, daughter," Mother Alta said. "No blame at all. You are simply playing out your part in the prophecy. What will be was written long before you were born."

Pynt began to weep openly.

"Now listen to me, my children, it is clear there will be a battle. These men are in no mood to be cozened. And they are no fools. We must try to buy some time. In the daylight our forces are halved. And—"

Carum interrupted. "You don't *really* mean the dark sisters aren't here until night?"

Armina laughed. "Why do you men have such trouble believing that?"

"It is mere superstition. There are other tribes, down in the Dales, who believe that their mothers are filled by the god of the river and they give birth at the flood. And the Besarmians say that the son of their god comes down once a month in the shape of a bee to . . ."

"Darmina is no superstition. She is real. You saw her. You talked to her, you . . ."

"Children, we have no time for this. Carum will believe what he will. So it has been through the years. Men see and do not understand. Their minds belie their ears and eyes. Come, now, Armina, I need you to go down and tell Zeena to keep the gate closed no matter what. And bring the little ones here to me." Mother Alta stopped and ran her curious hands across her eyes. As the door closed behind Armina, Mother Alta suddenly cried out, "Oh, that my blindness brought us to this place. If I had guessed earlier, I might have . . . I might have . . . I am old, my children. And blind. And helpless." Two large tears ran down her cheeks. Then she looked up at them with her sightless eyes. "No—not *so* helpless. For the *Anna* is here. So the ending begins. But so, too, the beginning."

Jenna and Pynt looked at each other, shaking their heads. Carum put his finger to his temple and touched it, nodding.

"Come here, Jo-an-enna," commanded Mother Alta.

Jenna glanced at her companions once more, then moved closer to the priestess, who reached out to touch her hands.

"Listen carefully, for if this is indeed the end, you must understand what lies ahead. The prophecy says that you shall be queen and not queen, and that you shall carry three babies."

"Mother, I am but thirteen years old," Jenna said.

"And not yet to your woman time, I suspect," Mother Alta said, cocking her head to one side as if listening for the sound of Jenna's nod.

"Not yet," Jenna whispered, blushing furiously.

"But if you are to be a queen, then you must know a king. I suspect your meeting with this young Garun princeling Longbow is no coincidence but further proof."

"Mother," Jenna whispered urgently, "he is but fifteen or so." She took her hands away from the old woman's and held them swiftly at her side.

Carum cleared his throat. "I am seventeen, Jenna."

"Does he look at you?"

Jenna was silent, embarrassed.

"You tell me so with your silence."

"I am Alta's own."

The old woman chuckled. "So am I. So are we all here. Yet still there are babes in our cradles, and not all are fostered. The girls go down into the towns for long nights. The world turns ever and the sun goes east to west. *Queen and not queen.* What can that mean but that you will bear a king sons but not sit on the throne. Sometimes prophecies are easy to unriddle. Sometimes."

"But the fight, Mother. What shall we do?"

"You shall get the boy from here. The Kingsmen must not find him at Alta's door. Better that they not suspect you are the white one spoken of in their own prophecy, the one before whom Hound and Ox and Bear and Cat bow down. Take him from here, you and your dark sister."

"Pynt? You mean Pynt is in the prophecy, too?" Jenna grabbed onto the old woman's hands thankfully, almost tugging her from her seat.

But Mother Alta looked away, as if listening, and Jenna listened, too. The sounds outside were louder, angrier.

"Quick, my child, take this ring." She slipped the great agate ring from her tiny bird-talon finger. It barely fitted on Jenna's pinkie. "You must go from Hame to Hame to warn them. Say this: *The time of endings is at hand.* Say it to the Mothers. They will know what to do. Repeat it."

In a little voice Jenna said, *"The time of endings . . .* oh, Mother Alta, I am not who you think I am."

"Say it!"

She whispered, *"The time of endings is at hand."*

"Good. There is a map of all the Hames. Can you read maps?"

"We both can," said Pynt.

Mother Alta ignored her and spoke to Jenna alone. "Go to the mirror." She gestured with her head to the great covered mirror. "Touch the goddess sign, turning it to the left. A small drawer will open and in it will be the map. Every Hame is outlined in red."

It was Pynt who leaped up first, crossing to the mirror. A sliver of morning light touched the cover. She took off the cloth and stepped back, shocked at her own blanched reflection. Then she found the carved goddess sign and moved it to the left. There was a loud click and the sign leaped open, disclosing a little dark cubbyhole. Reaching in, she found a piece of parchment and removed it.

"I have it, Mother," she said.

"Give it to the Anna."

Pynt handed it to Jenna, who opened it. It was a map outlined in spidery black writing. The names of the seventeen Hames were in red. Jenna folded it back along the deep creases and slipped it into her tunic.

"Let no one else take it," Mother Alta said. *"No one."*

"Not even Pynt? You said she was my dark sister."

"Only if you are dying. Only then."

"Only then," Jenna whispered, though she could not quite take it in. Dying? How could she think of it? Even when she had been fighting the Hound, she had not thought about the possibility of death, only what it might feel like to be wounded. "Only then," she whispered.

"Now go."

"What of you, Mother?"

"My children will care for me. And I care for them. So go now. The time grows short."

Jenna nodded and started toward the door. "Alta's blessings, Mother," she said, looking over her shoulder. She signaled the others to her.

"Wait," Carum said. "Armina said there was a secret passage. We could go out that way."

"There is no such thing," said Mother Alta. "Armina has these . . . little tales she likes to tell. Her own fancies."

"So we have learned," said Carum.

"Will we meet again, Mother?" asked Jenna.

"We will surely meet again in the Cave," the old woman said. It was her only benediction.

Jenna turned and went out the door, the others following her. As they went down the stairs, the thread of Mother Alta's reedy voice followed them to the first landing, singing the song of burial.

> In the name of Alta's cave,
> The dark and lonely grave . . .

They met Armina on the landing. She was carrying an infant in each crooked arm and there were two little ones clinging to her jacket. Behind her trailed a dozen or so girls past the age of First Choosing, each holding a sleeping babe. Beyond them were five older girls and they, too, carried babes not quite at the toddling stage.

Jenna, Pynt, and Carum put their backs to the wall to let the processional pass.

Armina smiled. "The Mother wishes to bless them," she said as she went by. "And to keep them from any fighting."

The children were silent as they filed past the landing; one golden-haired little one in the arms of the next-to-last girl waved to them. Jenna waved back.

"I've never seen such quiet children," remarked Carum.

"Alta's babes are ever so," said Pynt.

* * *

At the final turning, they came into the Great Hall, a high-ceilinged, light-filled room with great vaulted wooden ribs that held up the roof. Candelabra hung on long chains from the roof beams, swaying slightly.

The room was abuzz with women at work on weapons. A group of them squatted in a semicircle, honing knives rhythmically and chanting. Over to the side, in a small alcove hung with bows, a group of ten women was testing bowstrings and nocking arrows. They were speaking softly to one another, and one had thrown her head back and was laughing. By the great hearth, small knots of three and four women huddled together, talking intensely as they plaited ropes.

"We will be in a *real* battle this time," Pynt remarked.

"Was the slaying of the Hound not real enough for you?" Jenna asked.

"You know what I mean, Jenna."

"Well, I don't," Carum said. "Blood is blood."

Pynt turned on him. "You do not know? I thought scholars knew everything. I mean sisters side by side, the way the ballads tell of it." She began to recite the first lines of *Krack's Ride:*

> I sing the arrow's song,
> The eager, whistling flight,
> I sing the sword's sharp tune,
> And sisters side by side . . .

"You are like that arrow," said Carum. "Too eager."

"What do you know of it, who loses his meager dinner over a killing?"

Jenna put her hand on Pynt's shoulder. "He is right, Pynt. We should not be so eager for killing. Who knows—we may be the ones killed."

"And what if we are?" asked Pynt. "Then we will go directly to Alta's cave." She glared at Carum.

"Where you will throw the bones over your shoulder for the Dogs of War, I suppose," he countered.

"Shut up, *scholar*," said Pynt. "I say only what we all say before a battle."

"Then you say it because you are afraid. Not because you believe in the beauty of battles."

"Of course we are all afraid," Jenna said. "We would be stupid to be otherwise. And *that* is what all this bickering is about. But the battle is not ours. You both heard the Mother. We must get you away from here, Carum, and when you are safe, our task is to take a long route around to warn all the Hames."

Pynt turned her head away and stared at the floor. "If it were our own Mother Alta, I would disobey her again. But this one is no Serpent Mouth, is she?"

"No, Pynt, she is not. And Carum cried us . . ."

". . . *merci*, I know. But could we not get him to his refuge and hurry back here for the fight?"

Jenna shook her head.

"Then we will do what Mother Alta says. But still, I feel we will be in the thick of things and they will sing of us long after we are gone," Pynt said.

Carum snorted. "You'd like that! *The Battle of Pynt and White Jenna*, accompanied by nose flute and tembala."

"No, scholar, I think it will be called *How the Dark Warrior Marga Saved a Princeling's Insignificant Skin*."

"I will write one myself," said Jenna, "though I have no gift for balladry, and I shall call it *The Day Jenna Knocked Heads*."

Carum laughed and, to her surprise, Pynt laughed, too, and when Carum held out his hand, Pynt took it.

"But which way will we go?" Pynt asked.

As they were puzzling that over, a tall, long-nosed woman came over to them.

"I am Callilla," she said, "the mother of Armina. There is a back door Mother Alta wishes you to know."

* * *

On the landing, Armina turned to the little ones. She pursed her lips and whistled once, stopping them all.

"Soon Mother Alta will speak to you and you must listen without comment. What she says, you must do—as always. Big ones, help the little ones. There may be dark times ahead, and fearsome. But we are Alta's own. We will not be afraid." She nodded at them.

The girls nodded back, solemnly.

Armina led them to the carved door and pushed it open with her foot. The children filed into the room in front of her. Then Armina entered and kicked the door shut behind.

"We are ready, Mother," she said.

Mother Alta smiled at the children, who stood waiting for her command. She lifted her arms. "Sit, my babes, and I will tell you a story."

They sat at her feet.

"Once, long ago, before you were born, the first Mother Alta of Nill's Hame was told in a dream of a great battle to come. She dreamed that all the children were saved because they lived like little creatures in a warren. And so she had a secret tunnel built against that time." She smiled again and put her finger against her lip.

Some of the littlest children imitated her gesture.

"Today is a special day," said Mother Alta, "for we are going to find that secret tunnel. It will be your safe passage. Armina shall lead you there and there you shall wait. Food has been placed on shelves and you shall stay in your warren, eating when you are hungry, sleeping when you are not. Some of you shall be little rabbits, who shall it be?"

Only seven of the girls raised their hands.

"Good," said Mother Alta, as if she had counted them with her sightless eyes. "And we need some little moles, too."

Two girls raised cautious hands.

"And some little jumping mice?"

A host of other hands went up.

"And you older girls will be foxes and hedgehogs to keep the little ones in line. Do you understand?"

They nodded and she heard the movement of the air where they had agreed.

"When the food is gone, one by one the foxes shall emerge and check to see if all is safe. If it is not, return to the warren until you are called. One shall save you. You will know her by her white hair. She is the Anna, sent by Great Alta."

"But, Mother," piped one of the four-year-olds, the golden-haired child with the sunny face. "We have seen the Anna already. She was on the stairs."

"You will see her again," promised Mother Alta. "She will come for you with a sword of fire and a heart of flame."

"Will you come, too?" persisted the child.

"The warren is only for little creatures."

"But you *are* little," the child said.

Armina hissed through her teeth to shut her up.

Mother Alta smiled again. "I will not enter your warren, but I will guard the way."

The children nodded.

Mother Alta leaned forward in her chair. "Armina, line the children up before my mirror."

It took no more than a minute for all the children to be so aligned.

"Now touch the goddess sign and turn it to the right."

At Armina's touch, there was a loud, groaning sound and the floor beneath the mirror's carved legs slid open, disclosing a dark stair.

"Look into Mother Alta's glass once, where someday you shall find your dark sisters, then go down the stairs. Armina shall lead you and light the way."

Armina took the lamp from the wall, lit it, and—first looking into the glass—led the children down the stairs. As the last of them disappeared, Mother Alta sighed and brushed away the tears that had pooled in the corners of her marble-colored eyes.

THE LEGEND:

There was once a noddy old woman of Nilhalla's Crossing who had so many children, she kept them in an underground warren as if they were rabbits or mice. No one knew the children were there, indeed no one even suspected it, for the woman was as ugly as early spring and twice as windy.

One day the old woman died. Of distemper, some said; of pure meanness, said others. When the guardsmen went to bring out her body for burial, they found the warren entrance and lifted up the great wooden door barricading it.

Thirty-seven half-starved children of all ages scattered out, but they had lived so long under the ground in the dark like animals, they were blind, every one. And their long, unkempt hair had turned white. Ever since, Nilhalla's Crossing has been known as the Home of the White Babes.

This is a true story. It was told by Salla Wilmasdarter, whose great-grandfather had been a guard at the Crossing around the time the old woman's warren was uncovered.

THE STORY:

Callilla led them across the Great Hall, threading a line between the busy women and into the kitchen, which was three times the size of the kitchen at Selden Hame.

Pynt gasped at it, but Jenna kept her eyes on Callilla's back. Carum trailed behind.

"Jenna," Pynt whispered, "they are heating great vats of oil."

"And water," said Jenna.

"You did not look."

"On the slant, Pynt. You have to use your woods' eyes everywhere."

"Do not lecture me, Jo-an-enna."

"Then do not be stupid, Marga."

"And do not call me stupid."

Suddenly Callilla turned right and stopped before a plain door. "Here," she said.

They clustered around her.

"This door opens onto a narrow, steep path that goes down to the Halla."

"That's the river," Carum said.

Callilla nodded. "The Halla is swift and unforgiving, so you must take care."

"I cannot swim," said Pynt.

"Nor I," admitted Jenna.

"Well, I can," Carum said.

"No one needs swim the Halla," Callilla said, "though all our girls are taught early to traverse it at its calmest points. The path may be steep, but it is well trod. Our guards patrol it daily. No one else knows of it. Once you get down to the river, you must simply follow its line until you come to a stand of birch. Turn east, and you will come, in the space of a full day's journey, to Bertram's Rest."

"My refuge," Carum added.

"And will it really be safe for him there?" asked Jenna.

"Bertram was a great saint of their religion, a fighter who gave up fighting. His sanctuaries are never violated by the Garunians, whatever the provocation. They are a strange people, and their gods are bloody, but they are honest for all that. However, women are not allowed in their sanctuary halls, so you will have to leave him there and go on about your missioning. It will be a hard year for you if this is but the first of it."

"We have a greater mission now," Pynt said.

Jenna touched her tunic over the breast and could feel the map crackling beneath, but said nothing.

"What about food?" asked Carum.

"You will find what you need in the woods," Callilla said. "We have no time for provisioning beyond these." She bent down and picked up three full wineskins from the floor. "And I found some goat cheese for you. Bread also." Reaching into a deep tunic pocket, she brought out a leather-wrapped packet and gave it to Carum. "It is but a day's journey. How hungry can you get? For the rest . . ."

"We know," Carum said. "Nuts, mushrooms, and roots. No berries."

Callilla smiled reluctantly. "Good. Then you shall need for nothing." She pulled open the door. "Alta's blessings on you, hand and foot."

The girls nodded and slipped through the door, but Carum turned and whispered loudly. "And may the eyes of Dark Morga see you long after and may his fins stoke the water over your back."

Callilla looked blank.

Carum grinned. "A safewell blessing from the Morganians. They live on the southern coast of the Continent and eat only what comes from the sea at low tide. Strange people. Nasty diet. But honest!" He turned and disappeared after the girls. Callilla's short, barking laugh followed him.

The path began at the door, for, farther up, the sheer wall of the Hame and the cliff met in a single steep drop. Even on the path there was little room between the wall on their right and the drop-off to the Halla on their left. They walked carefully, listening to the low growling of the river far below them, surging angrily between its banks.

Pynt slipped suddenly on some loose pebbles and fell backward, catching herself at the last moment and hurting her wrist. She got up and angrily brushed off the back of her clothes despite the pain.

They could hear the tumbling shower of dirt and rock for only a moment before the noise of the river overwhelmed it.

Once they were past the Hame's steep wall, the path widened a bit, though there was still a small cliff, half again as tall as a man, on the right. Then the path took an abrupt right-hand turn and before them was a twisted fir tree jutting out across the path. Its roots held deep into the cliffside like the fingers of a clutching hand, and the fanning branches obscured the way ahead.

"Under or over?" asked Jenna.

Pynt peered under the tree. "Under. There is enough room."

Unbuckling her sword, Pynt pushed it under the tree, then followed it, crawling along on her belly. Jenna was next, and Carum last, the food packet in his hand. As he started to stand up, Pynt put her hand out.

"Hush. Wait. I hear something."

"That's just the river," Carum said.

"I hear it, too," Jenna whispered. "Hush!" She drew her sword from its scabbard. In the sunlight it seemed to catch fire.

"Probably the Hame guards," Carum whispered back. "Callilla said no one else knows the path." He stood and began to brush off his clothes.

"Get behind me," Pynt said softly.

"I'm already behind you," Carum said. "I've been behind you all the—" But he did not get to finish his sentence, for there was a high whistling and an arrow whizzed by his shoulder to embed itself in the tree.

"There they are!" came a shout. "Three more of Alta's bitches."

"Those aren't guards," Carum said. "They're . . ."

Another arrow flew by, this time passing through his shirt and pinning him to the tree.

"Damn!" Carum shouted, pulling himself loose by ripping the shirt.

"Duck!" screamed Pynt. She pushed Carum toward the tree, nearly sending him over the cliffside instead. He scrambled under the gnarled trunk, then turned. Pynt's sword hand and arm were partway under, but she had stopped. He grabbed her hand, careful of the sword, and pulled her through, surprised at her dead weight. When she was on the other side, he saw the arrow sticking out of her back, broken off halfway.

"Pynt!" he cried, drawing her to him.

She did not answer.

He picked up her sword and straddled her, waiting.

A sword and then a hand emerged from under the tree. Carum raised his sword to strike, then saw it was Jenna's arm and stopped. She scrambled the rest of the way under the tree.

"It's Pynt," Carum cried. "She's been hit. An arrow under the left shoulder."

"Alta's Hairs," Jenna cursed quietly. She bent over Pynt's body. "How bad is it?"

"I don't know. But she doesn't move."

"Oh, Pynt, say something," Jenna begged.

Pynt groaned.

"She needs water," said Carum. "And that arrowhead has to come out. And . . ."

"She needs to be back at the Hame."

"She's not heavy. I could carry her."

"You get her back there," Jenna said, "and I'll cover your retreat."

"No—you get her back there. I'll cover *your* retreat."

"I am better with a sword," Jenna said.

"And you think I'm better at retreating?"

"Why are we arguing?" Jenna cried.

"I don't want anything to happen to you."

"It is a narrow cliff and I have the advantage of that tree," said Jenna. "Just take Pynt. Now. If she dies, I will never forgive you."

Carum hefted Pynt's body onto his back. She cried out once and then was still. He heard the shout of the men on the other side of the tree and started back up the path as quickly as he could. Pynt seemed heavier at every step, but still he ran. Pebbles shot out from under his feet, skittering over the cliff. He ran until he came to the Hame door and, balancing Pynt on his back, pounded on the door with both fists. A peephole slid open, then shut, and then the door began to move. Carum and his burden fell inside.

Someone took Pynt from him and when he stood again, he saw that the door was shut.

"But Jenna is out there," he cried. "Open the door."

No one moved and so Carum ran over to the door and tried to open it. Locked, it did not move.

"Move this god-rotted door!" he shouted.

Callilla played with a lock and the door opened. Jenna fell toward Carum, her sword dragging, something bloody and horrible clutched in her left hand.

"I do not know . . ." she began, trying to catch her breath. "I do not know if this was the hand that sent the arrow into Pynt's back, but it is a hand that will surely do no more damage to Alta's own." She flung it down, her eyes wild. "He foolishly put it under the tree first as he tried to crawl through."

Callilla pushed the hand with her boot. "Not so foolish, perhaps. It might have been his head!"

Carum stared at the hand. With the dark hairs on its back and the crabbed fingers, it looked like some strange, bloody creature. On the middle finger was a great ring with a K engraved in the middle. Looking up, Carum stared at Jenna wildly. "It's the Bull's ring, Jenna, with Kalas' crest. Many a time I had a buffet from it. The Bull was my swordmaster before he joined his brothers in Kalas' service. Jenna, don't you know what this means? Now Ox and Hound have both bowed down. Ox and Hound. Mother Alta is right. The prophecy *must* be true. You *are* the White Babe, the Anna."

The women began to murmur, but Jenna ignored them and knelt by Pynt's side. The infirmarer, short and stocky, with gray flecks in her hair and worry lines etched across her brow, was already looking at the wound.

"It is deep," she said to no one in particular. "And badly placed. Near the heart."

"Will she die?" asked Jenna, her voice breaking.

The infirmarer looked over at her, as if surprised to find she had been talking to someone. "I cannot say with any certainty. But for now I must get her up the stairs to my hospice and clean the wound. The arrowhead must be removed. After that I might be able to say with more accuracy."

Pynt coughed and groaned almost at the same time. She tried to sit up but the infirmarer pushed her down with a gentle but firm touch.

"It is you who are being stupid now, Jenna," Pynt whispered hoarsely. "I will not die. How can I? You would be lost without your shadow." Then her eyes rolled back and she was still.

"Is she dead?" Jenna cried.

"She has only fainted," said the infirmarer, "for the pain is great and that is nature's way of easing it. Now she must go upstairs and"—she looked at Jenna—"she is to have no visitors. Trust me, child, you cannot do her any good right now."

At the infirmarer's signal, three of the younger women gathered Pynt up and carried her away. Then the infirmarer turned and pointed at the hand which still lay on the floor. "Get that thing away. It will soon gather disease to it and it might frighten the children. We who are Alta's heirs do not revel in such bloody keepsakes."

Carum bent down and tugged the ring off the stiffened hand. "I will keep this until I can fling it at Kalas' feet. We Garunians, unlike you Altites, revel in such reminders." He put the ring into his pocket and turned away quickly, hoping he had been fast enough so that no one could see the color of his face, which he knew had whitened at the feel of the dead hand.

But Jenna had seen. She touched him on the back, whispering, "Carum, do not be ashamed at your disgust. If I had not been blood-crazed, I would never have brought that hand into this hall. But battle fever had hold. I did what I did without thinking. You, though—you think too much."

He turned around, his face composed at last, but before he had time to answer he caught sight of Callilla behind her, anger and fear fighting in her face.

"We must talk. And quickly. Before those men gather their courage and try this door."

"The door is well defended," said Carum.

"It can be," admitted Callilla. "But do we keep it ready to be opened for our guards, or do we barricade it?"

"We saw no guards," Jenna answered.

"No bodies either," added Carum.

Callilla nodded grimly. "The Halla has cradled Alta's own before."

"The men who chased us cried out, *Three more of . . .*" Carum stopped.

". . . *of Alta's bitches*," finished Jenna.

Callilla turned to two women standing nearby. "Who stood guard today?"

"Mona," said one.

"And Verna with her."

"Oh, sweet Alta, salve them," murmured Callilla. "And Verna just past her seventeenth spring. Their mothers must be told. I fear the worst."

The two women nodded solemnly and left.

"How many men?"

Carum shrugged. "We didn't wait to count them."

"At least three," said Jenna. "And one of those now sorely wounded."

"He was the leader," Carum added. "Which might slow them down."

"Or might provoke them further. There is never any way of knowing which, so we must prepare for a swift attack." Callilla looked beyond them and shouted, "Clea, Sari, Brenna—to me."

Three young women came running.

"Is it true, Callilla? About Verna?" asked one.

She nodded.

"Hush, Clea. Do not ask more," the larger of the three girls said.

Callilla said quietly, "Remember what Alta, in her great wisdom, reminds us. *Not to know is bad, but not to wish to know is worse.*"

The girls all looked at the floor, waiting.

"Now you must do this. Sari and Brenna, you barricade the

door and stand watch here until you are relieved. Clea, you must alert all the door wardens that the time of a great fight is at hand. We all know what to do." Callilla dismissed them with a wave of her hand, then turned to Jenna. "It is written in the *Book* that *The day on which one starts out is surely not the time to begin one's preparations.* You will find this Hame well prepared."

"I can see that," Jenna said.

"Then we must prepare also for another escape route for the two of you. I will send Armina to you when she returns from Mother Alta. Tonight you will go by a road even the watchers outside our gates will not guess at or follow. Darkness will be our helpmeet."

"The moon is all but full, Callilla," Sari said over her shoulder as she struggled with Brenna to move a large chest in front of the door.

"Then they shall have both dark and light to aid them." She signaled to Jenna. "Meanwhile, you two can help us with our fortifications."

They worked all afternoon ceaselessly, helping the Hameswomen set strong barriers against the other doors and nail shut the narrow first-floor windows. Carum took a long turn at fletching new arrows, while Jenna helped haul up water from the courtyard well.

"If there are fires," she explained to Carum, "the Hame will be well prepared."

Only once did they try to visit Pynt in the upstairs hospice, but were turned away by the infirmarer at the door.

"She sleeps," they were told. "But I have gotten out the arrowhead, which, by luck, was not poisoned. She has taken a tisane I brewed which will help her sweat out any fever the wound produces. The wound itself I have treated with a poultice of figwort, which we call HealAll. You may believe I have done everything in my power to make her comfortable."

"*Comfortable!*" Carum said. "That's what the physician said of my mother for the month it took her to die."

"Will Pynt die?" asked Jenna.

"We all die at the last," said the infirmarer. "But do not measure the shroud before there is a corpse. Your friend is in Alta's good and gentle hands, those same hands that hold a nestling and take the fawn from the doe." The lines in her forehead deepened as she spoke.

"I hope," Carum whispered to Jenna as they left, "that she is more original with her medicines than she is with her words." He held tightly to Jenna's hand, which lent comfort to them both.

There was an early dinner in shifts in the kitchen. Jenna and Carum ate during the second round, sitting with Armina and two of her friends. Armina finished picking at the drumstick on her plate and pushed away the bones. Turning her back on her friends, she spoke urgently to Jenna.

"When the attack comes or night falls, whichever is first, I will take you upstairs. There is another way, more difficult of course than the back path, but surely no man will find you there."

Carum interrupted. "Why didn't we go there first?"

"You will see."

Jenna pushed the uneaten fowl around on her plate.

"Battle does not make you hungry," Armina commented. "It makes me starved."

"My stomach argues both ways," said Carum. He was reaching for another wing piece when there was a flurry of shouts from the Great Hall and the muffled *thud-thumps* of someone hammering on the gates.

"This is it, then," Armina said, rising. "They will be busy at the front for a long while. Those doors are a foot thick at the least and there are wicked spikes on the tops of the walls."

"Armina, are you coming?" asked one of her friends.

"I have charge of these two," Armina said, nodding at them.

"Alta's luck, then."

"You, too."

"You know," Carum murmured, "they'll have rams, the Kingsmen. And a great sling for boulders. The gates won't outlast such implements of war."

"We know," said Armina. "A number of our women have

served in the king's armies. Your way of fighting is not unknown to us."

"Blanket Companions!" said Carum.

"My mother, Callilla, was one. I am the result." Armina smiled faintly. "But the walls will buy us time. And if they are breached, still the men will find us no easy prey." She stood.

"But the children . . ." Carum said. "And the wounded."

"We have a place for them. Never fear. Come."

They followed her out of the kitchen, through the Great Hall, and up the wide front stairs to the second floor. She turned right, then left, then right.

"I'm lost again," Carum whispered to Jenna, who did not answer.

Armina stopped, flung open a door, and went in. They followed at her heels and were surprised to find themselves in a kind of playroom, with toys for young children scattered across the floor.

"We have nothing like this at Selden Hame," murmured Jenna, looking at the half-dozen small wands and jumping ropes, hoops, and balls.

"The windows aren't boarded up," Carum said. "Isn't that dangerous? Kalas' men could come in that way."

"Think you so? Then look!" commanded Armina.

They peered out. It was a sheer drop down to the Halla, tumbling nearly a hundred feet below.

"Oh, no," said Jenna immediately. "I cannot swim."

"I can," said Carum.

"I shall rope you together," Armina said as she knotted together four of the jump ropes, testing each knot by pulling against it. "These are very strong. And you shall each carry a kicker."

"Kicker?"

Armina went over to a standing wardrobe, pulled the doors open, and searched through the contents of an upper shelf. She turned back with two large pieces of wood the shape of shovel heads, though twice as big. "We use these to teach our little ones how to swim. They are held so." Gripping the flat edge, she raised the kicker overhead. "And then you kick with all your might. The wood floats, you see. As long as you hold on to it, you will not go under."

"*I* will go under," said Jenna.

"Even should you do so, remember, you will still be roped to Longbow, and he can swim."

"A little," admitted Carum. "In quiet pools and in the palace baths. I have never tried a swift river. An *unforgiving* river."

"You must *jump* in," Armina said. "There is no other way."

Carum turned to Jenna. "It has to be all right, Jenna. The prophecy doesn't talk about the Anna dying. She's to become queen and . . ."

"For the goddess' sake, I am no Anna," Jenna said angrily. "But I *am* a warrior of Great Alta's. And as I have pledged myself to your safety . . ." She drew in a deep breath and looked steadily at Armina. "We will jump."

"First we must get the ropes ready to tie around your waists. Carum, you mount that window and I the other," said Armina. "Then I shall fling you an end outside."

Carum climbed onto the windowsill and, straddling the spanning bar, leaned out. Meanwhile, Armina had climbed up onto the other and flung the rope toward him. It took three tries before he could catch it, but at last he drew the rope in and secured it loosely to the bar. Armina did the same with her end, then jumped back down.

"Now, we must fasten your sword to your side, Jenna. The river is a grasping sort. It will take it from you if it can."

"I can do that," Jenna said. She found another jump rope and began to twine it around herself and the sword, knotting it securely.

Armina picked up the kicker boards and set one by each window. "There is not much danger in this, really. It is more frightening than anything else. We older girls—as a test of courage—often come up and leap into the Halla. *Without* the kickers."

"So you told us. And of the girl who was never found," said Carum.

"That was just a tale. To frighten you."

"You've succeeded," said Carum.

"The only real danger," Armina said, "is that you might not get out of the river in time. There are some rapids after a bit."

"Rapids?" asked Jenna.

"Rough water, great whirlpools and eddies. And then there is a waterfall. You must be sure to get out early enough *and* on the right side."

"And how will we know when these rapids are approaching?" asked Jenna.

"You will know."

"Then we'd better go," said Carum. He looked at Jenna, who nodded.

"I am ready," she said, then added, "I think."

"Carum is right. You must go quickly. Carum, you get up first and tie the rope to your waist. Then, Jenna, you do the same. Less time to worry that way. I shall hand you up the boards and then count to three. On three, leap together. Oh, and you must leap at the same time, or one will drag the other." Armina thought a minute. "There is one other thing."

"Now she tells us," said Carum.

"Do not leap straight down or you shall hit the rocks. Leap out."

"Anything more?" asked Carum as he climbed up and stepped over the spanning bar.

"Do not scream. It might alert any Kingsmen about. It is getting dark and they will not be close enough to see you leap, but why take chances? And may Alta hold you both securely in her hair."

Jenna nodded, climbing onto the windowsill. "And to you, too, Armina. And all in this Hame. May you fight bravely and may I see you again." She turned, stepped over the bar, untied the rope, and secured it around her waist with a double knot.

Armina handed them each a board and began the count. "One . . . two . . ."

Jenna felt something hot and hard in her stomach, and her

mouth tasted salty. She knew that a woman of a prophecy would
never feel such fear.

". . . three!"

Jenna leaped slightly ahead of Carum but not so much that
the rope pulled taut between them. She felt the rush of wind by
her ears and a strange scream flew all unbidden from her mouth.
There was a thin echo of that scream and Jenna realized, only as
she plunged into the icy water, that Carum had been yelling as
well. She hoped they had not been heard.

Water rushed suddenly into her open mouth and the board
leaped like a wild thing from her hands. Flailing about, she tried
to find the surface of the river, but with her eyes closed it was all
guesswork. Then, thinking she was out, she breathed in and
swallowed a mouthful of water, and then everything was black and
full of cold bubbles. Just as suddenly her head was in the air, and
Carum was pushing a board into her hands. She heard, as if from
far away, his shout, "Breathe, Jenna, please breathe." She gulped
in air and coughed out water almost at the same time. Then she
pulled herself partway onto the board, conscious of its solidity
under her, but she was too weak and confused to kick. Carum put
his arm around her, lifting his body partly onto hers, and kicked
for them both.

After a while, Jenna's eyes cleared of the film of water and
she could see again. Her heart, while still pounding, was no longer
racing quite so madly, and the fear that had inhabited her throat
and bowels no longer threatened to spew forth. Breathing deeply,
she called to Carum over the noise of the river in a raspy voice,
"We . . . we are alive!"

"Of course we're alive," he shouted back. "I told you I could
swim. Now kick, Jenna." He slipped away and she was suddenly
conscious of the loss of his body on hers. "Kick, I say!"

Jenna began to kick and the board moved noiselessly through
the water ahead of her. "It works!" she cried, turning her head
toward him.

Carum swam by her side, as graceless as a waddling pig, but
still managing to keep pace with her and her board. They were

both helped along by the force of the river, and the banks on either side hurtled by with frightening speed. Scarcely had they sighted one possible landmark when they were beyond it.

"How will we know when we are nearing the rapids?" Jenna shouted.

"Armina said we'd know," he called back.

The noise of the river was such, they barely made out one word in three, but after several more tries they understood each other. Then they rounded a turn, and suddenly the noise of the river seemed to double while the water boiled about them with white pockets of foam.

"I think we've found it," Carum shouted.

"What?"

"I think we've found it."

"What?"

With an effort, he kicked closer to her, grabbed her shoulder, and headed her toward the right side.

"Just go over there."

They were nearer the left bank than the right, the east bank, but they fought toward the right with the last of their strength. The river drew them steadily forward. Suddenly Carum was spun away from Jenna and the rope went taut between them. He was turned around several times into a deep eddy that drew him down and then popped him up again like a cork till the rope snapped him back to Jenna's side.

Just as he found a footing on the rocks, Jenna was spun about in the same swirling water and the board was torn from her grasp. It shot straight up in the air and splashed down inches from Carum's head. He ducked, nearly fell back into the channel, then steadied himself and hauled on the rope between them, dragging Jenna toward him. She was so exhausted he had to half lift, half drag her to the shore.

They flopped down on the slippery grassy slope, breathing heavily. Jenna coughed up water twice without lifting her head from the bank. Then she sat up suddenly, turned a greenish face toward Carum, and was sick in the grass. She lay down again, unable to move away.

"There . . ." Carum said, breathing deeply between words, "now . . . we . . . are . . . even . . . for . . . my . . . getting . . . sick . . . in . . . the . . . woods."

It took Jenna a full minute to answer. "Not . . . amusing," she muttered.

"I'm only trying to laugh and live longer," he replied.

This time she did not bother to respond.

Carum sat up slowly and looked around. Then he crawled on his hands and knees up and over the embankment. Ahead of him was a long meadow pied with the pensive blue, purple, and yellow faces of heartsease. Off to the right was a copse of graceful, white-barked trees, almost ghostly in the fading light.

"The stand of birch!" Carum called down to Jenna. "The birch that Callilla said to watch out for."

Jenna sat up at last and tried to wring the water from her braid, but her hands had no strength yet. "We could have passed hundreds of such stands while we were drowning," she said.

"Do you have a better idea of where we are?"

"None at all."

"Then let's assume we are only a day's journey to Bertram's Rest, Jenna, because that way we'll both sleep easier."

Jenna shook her head. "How can either of us sleep easily, knowing that Pynt may die, knowing that the Hame is in danger, and knowing that we have no idea where we are or that we may be found by the Kingsmen at any minute?"

"I don't know, Jenna," Carum said, "but I'm going to try."

She nodded, too tired to argue, and in fact they both fell asleep within minutes on the riverbank, in plain view of any passersby.

THE HISTORY:

The Garunian religious practices are much more thoroughly documented than any other group of the Dales from that period.

There are two reasons for this. First, the Continental ancestry of the Garunians provides us with a broad base from which religious history explorers may make their speculative forays. After all, though only two authenticated Garunian documents have been found in the diggings in the Dales, there are at least twenty such (including a book of gnomic sayings) discovered by Dr. Allysen J. Carver during her twenty years of barrow work in the Continental border towns. Second, of the two Dalite documents, one is the famous essay "Oblique Prophecies" (or, as Magon persists in calling it rather too colloquially, "Prophecies on the Slant," thus diminishing its considerable power) by the scholar-king Langbrow II, in which the system of refuges, or Rests, is mentioned.

These walled monasteries, which were part religious retreats, part sanctuaries, part prisons, were considered sacrosanct by the Garunians, and many a wanted man apparently holed up in them, possibly (though not probably) for years. Langbrow cites a number of proverbs, some too obscure for parsing, but two seem clear enough: In the wrong, in the Rest *and* Better in the Rest than in the Battle. *Both Magon and Temple, for once, agree on the meaning, that felons and army deserters alike took advantage of the immunity such Rests offered. Magon further hypothesizes —a bit freely considering that the length of the document is but three pages—that once a man was hounded into a Rest, he was often there for life.*

THE STORY:

They were, in fact, less than a day's journey away, for they began, after seven hours of sleep, with the moon still overhead. Following close by the path, they did not stay directly on it; caution, an old habit, claimed them.

So it was a bit past noon, the sun ripe above them, when they crested a small rise and saw Bertram's Rest in the valley below.

The Rest was a series of low stone buildings in the shape of a broken cross with neat gardens and fruit trees nestled in each crook, the whole surrounded by a set of double walls. While smaller by far than Nill's Hame, the Rest was still larger than Selden.

"That's it!" said Carum. "All Rests are built that way, in the bent crux sign." He started to stand and Jenna pulled him down by the shirttails.

"Wait!" she said. "We always say *They stumble who run ahead of their wits*. Let us watch a moment or two."

He knelt down again and as they watched, a troop of horsemen raced out of the western woods and gathered restlessly before the gates. Long minutes later the horsemen, on some signal, spun around and sped away toward the rise where they were huddled.

Jenna grabbed Carum by the arm and pulled him into the densest part of the underbrush, careful not to leave a trail that the seasoned traveler might read.

Farther on they came upon a small cliff with a tiny dark cave pocking the face. They pressed in, though it was barely big enough for the two of them. It was full of animal droppings and sour-smelling, but they stayed in it until darkness had wrapped around the woods, and the riders, whoever they were, were long gone.

A full moon rode high in the sky and the valley was starkly illuminated.

"We might as well have crossed by day," Carum said, "for that moon is as strong as the sun."

But without a hope for clouds, and under a sky bright with a powerful moon and the scattering of stars, they raced across the grassy meadow. Luck was with them; if there were watchers, they slept at their posts.

The walls of the Rest were higher than they had seemed from the hill, so high it would take a scaling ladder to mount them. They were topped by cruel-looking spikes.

"A welcoming sort of place," Jenna commented.

"Remember, it's got to keep people out as well as in," Carum said.

"I thought your people respected the sanctuary."

"My people are not *all* people," Carum said.

The gates were wood set into the stone walls with iron brackets. They were good, solid, unadorned gates, the only decoration a peephole about halfway up.

Carum hammered on the door with both hands while Jenna, sword unsheathed, stood guard. For a long time nothing happened.

"They cannot want to help those in need very much if they do not open their doors," Jenna said.

"Jenna, it's the middle of the night. They'll all be asleep."

"All? Are there no guards?"

"Why should there be guards? No one in the Dales would dare violate a Rest."

"I would have thought no one would violate a Hame filled with women and children. But Pynt has an arrow in her back, and Verna and the other sister are missing, and we have had to swim an unforgiving river."

"*That* was a Hame and *this* is a Rest," Carum said.

"And you are a king's son who had to cry me *merci* from his own kind."

Carum looked down. "I'm sorry, Jenna. You're right. That was a stupid thing to say. A wicked, un—"

"Unthinking?"

"Unthinkable thing to say. And there should be someone up. Or we can get someone up." He turned and hammered on the gates again.

At last there was a grinding noise and the peephole cover slid aside. They could see a single eye staring through. Carum moved in front of Jenna and shouted up at the eye.

"We seek sanctuary: I for what time I need, and my companion for the rest of the night."

The door opened slowly, drawn inward just a crack, and an

old man, with deep creases around his mouth like parentheses, stood in their way.

"Who asks?"

"I am Carum Longbow, the king's . . ."

"Ah, Longbow. We have been wondering if you might make your way here."

Carum stared. "How did you know?"

The old man's head moved back and forth like a clockwork doll. "Your brother Pike, who lies within, had hopes. And there were Kingsmen here just hours ago asking of you. Of course we sent them on their way."

"Pike here? And you say *lies*. Does he sleep—or is he wounded?"

"Wounded, but nowhere near dying."

Jenna stepped forward. "Please let him in. You can talk once the gates are closed behind."

The old man peered closer at Jenna. "This is the companion you spoke of?"

"Yes."

"But she is a woman."

"She is an Altite warrior who pledged herself to save me."

The old man made a *tsking* noise with his tongue. "Highness, you know we have no women here."

Carum drew himself up. "She stays. I am the king's son."

"But not yet the king, nor likely to be unless your brother dies. And only the king can make that request. She cannot tarry here. It is the law." His head went back and forth again, more like palsy than an answer.

Jenna put her hand on Carum's arm. "Go inside, and quickly. My charge is done, Carum Longbow. You are safe now, and I am free of my vow to you."

"Free of the vow but not free of me, Jenna."

"Hush, Carum," she said. "We both have other missions now, I to my sisters and you to your brother. And to your life. We were companions because danger tied us one to the other with bonds as strong as the ropes that held us in the Halla."

"I won't let you leave so quickly. Not like this."

"Carum . . ."

"At least kiss me good-bye."

"Why?"

"Why not?"

"Because . . . because I have never kissed a man before."

"You said I was a boy."

"I have never kissed a boy before."

"That's not a good enough reason. I never ate bitter roots before I met you. You never swam a river before you met me." He smiled, and held out his hands.

She nodded imperceptibly and moved into the compass of his arms. His lips touched hers softly and when she thought to move away, his hands were on her arms, steadying her, so she moved, without quite meaning to, even closer to him until their bodies were pressed together and she began to tremble. She pulled back a little and took her mouth from his.

"What is this?" she whispered.

Carum smiled ruefully. "I'd call it love."

"Is that . . . is that a scholarly definition, Carum?"

"It's a guess," he said. "I've never kissed a girl before. But from what I've read . . ."

"What have you read?" Her voice was still a whisper.

"That the Carolians, who worship only under an open sky, say that *love* was the first word God memorized."

"What a strange god."

"No stranger than this," Carum said, kissing her once again without touching her anywhere but on the lips. Then he stepped back. "We *will* see each other again, my White Jenna."

"Oh," Jenna said, unable to say more until the door had closed between them, and then all she could manage was to whisper his name.

It was only when she got back to the forest's edge and drew out the map that she found it had been ruined by the water. Knowing no other route to a Hame but the ones she had already traveled, she knew she had to turn back toward the river and retrace her steps. At Nill's Hame they would give her another map or at least set her on the track to the next mission Hame.

Without Carum, she did not feel the need to leave the path. One person alone, she reasoned, could disappear quickly into the woods. One person alert, she convinced herself, would hear an army on the road.

She moved swiftly, stopping infrequently, gathering what edibles grew along the path. She slept only a few hours, a sleep that gave her little rest, for she dreamed of Carum, who fell to his knees and cried out, "Holy, holy, holy," refusing her embrace.

By midmorning she found herself back by the fir tree that groped across the path like a disfigured hand. A dark stain, half under the tree, the size and shape of a serving plate, was the only reminder of the violence that had occurred there. Crawling under, she held her breath, for she feared what might wait for her on the other side. But when she came through, she was alone.

There was a strange silence, broken only by the river's surging, though in her mind she heard again the screams and cries that had last accompanied her at this place. Those voices haunted her, and she ran quickly to the Hame's back door. She pushed against it and it was solid and unmoving and, though she breathed thankfully for that—it meant no Kingsmen had gotten through this way—she did not hammer on it in case the enemy were inside.

Instead, she went back down the path, scrambled once more under the tree, and ran along the path until she came to the place where the cliff was lowest. Hand over hand she climbed up the face, her sword banging against her legs and threatening, at every move, to entangle them. It took her a long time to achieve the top, where she lay panting and grateful on the grass, waiting to catch her breath. Then, slowly, she began to crawl through the high grass toward the front of the Hame, conscious all the while that she could be seen from the tops of the walls.

As she crawled, she realized that everything except the grass right around her was still. Too still. Surely there would be the sounds of voices or the cries of cocks or the bleating of goats floating on such still air. Fear trembled through her and for a moment she did not dare move again.

To calm herself, she took three deep *latani* breaths, no easy task lying on her stomach, then pushed herself to her knees. In a crouched-over position, she ran to the wall and put her hand on the stone. Its very solidity lent her courage.

Turning the corner carefully, she gasped, her stomach knotting, a strange metallic taste flooding into her mouth. The carved gates were in splinters, the walls breached. Tumbled about like fruit from a bowl, the heavy stones had their dark, hidden faces up to the sun.

Jenna waited, hardly daring to breathe at all, for minute after minute, straining for some sound. But that deathly pall lay over all. Three more deep *latani* breaths, and she moved forward at last, stepping carefully between the fallen stones.

There were bodies scattered everywhere throughout the courtyard: men in full battle armor, women in their warrior skins. She stopped at one body after another, brushing impatiently at the flies, hoping to find someone, some*thing*, alive.

Everywhere, she thought distractedly. *They are everywhere.*

The women who died facedown she turned over, looking for someone familiar—Armina, Callilla, or the priestess herself.

Near the well, her hand over her face as if shutting out the sun, lay a young woman in trews. There was a small hole in her throat. Jenna stared down at her.

Such a small entrance to let in death, to let out life, Jenna thought.

She knelt and pushed the hand away and recognized Brenna, though she had seen her only the once.

"Alta's mercy," she whispered, wondering where that mercy had been scant hours before. She felt more for that one corpse suddenly than for all the others. "I swear, Brenna, I shall give you a burial if I can find someone to show me your Hame's Cave."

She stood and continued to search through the courtyard, her shadow dancing oddly by her side, until she realized she was moving in peculiar starts and stops. That was when she first knew she was incapable of taking it all in, the heartbreaking horror of it. There was simply too much of it, too much death. And she realized, too, that she was terrified to go inside the Hame.

She forced herself to squat down and breathe deeply, though the air was filled with a sweet-sharp smell. The sun beat down on her and she began the hundred-chant, trying to steady herself for what further horrors lay ahead. As she counted, she felt again the strange lightening, and she was pulled slowly from her body to float above the courtyard. She looked down as if from a great height at the chanting figure swaying slightly in the midst of the scattered corpses. But when she sailed down to touch one body after another, she found no entrance, no living self to be drawn into. At last she spiraled down, down, down toward her chanting self just as the final number was reached.

Standing again, she walked purposefully toward the broken door into the Hame.

She found Callilla in the kitchen, her throat slashed, and five dead men around her. Armina was on the main stairs, an arrow in her back and a broken sword at her feet. Behind her were three men whose faces had been scored by her nails and whose throats had been pierced with a knife.

Jenna sat on the step by Armina's head and stroked the crest of hair. "Laugh longer, live longer," she whispered hoarsely. And only then the tears came, gushing out of her eyes, along with great gulping sobs. She wept uncontrollably, not only for Armina, but for all of them, her unknown sisters who had died defending themselves against the Kingsmen. The Kingsmen, who wanted Jenna for the killing of the Hound, and Carum for . . . she realized for the first time that she did not even know why they wanted Carum. Only that they did. They wanted him so badly they had slaughtered an entire Hame of women to find him. And to find her. This horror, then, was their fault, Carum's and hers. Just as Mother Alta had said: she *was* an ending. An entire Hame gone.

An entire Hame! And Pynt, too! Jenna leaped up and, turning, took the stairs two at a time, trying desperately to remember where the hospice room was. Somewhere on the second floor, that much she knew. She could not make herself believe the men would kill a wounded girl lying in a hospice bed.

She opened door after door, stepping over corpses of women and their pursuers, for the women of Nill's Hame had taken more than their own number into the dark Cave.

A tall, bearded man with a face as seamed as wood and a bloody throat lay against a closed door, blocking it. Jenna kicked him aside.

"And are you throwing bones over your shoulders for those bitter dogs now?" she shouted. "May they rip your throat out again." She opened the door and saw it was the hospice. Three dead women lay on the cots and one, her eyes bandaged, was under a table. None of them was Pynt.

"Pynt!" Jenna screamed. The room echoed with the name but there was no answer.

She raced out the door, leaped over the dead man, and ran down the hall, flinging doors open and shouting wildly into each room. One door was already ajar. When she looked in, she saw it was the playroom from where, two days before, she and Carum had leaped into the icy flood. She went over to the windows and stared down at the Halla below, coursing mindlessly between its banks. When she turned back, the scattered toys looked like the corpses of playthings.

Slowly something else teased into her mind, something beyond the horror and the blood.

"The children!" she whispered. "I have seen no dead children!"

Leaning against the window frame, she tried to remember what it was Armina had said to them about the children, but when she tried to picture Armina speaking, she could only see her body stretched out along the stairs.

"I must think," she said aloud. "I *must* remember." She forced herself to recall the dinner and the fatal hammering at the doors. That was when Armina had told them something about the children. But what was it she had said?

And then she remembered. ". . . a place for them. Never

fear." The children, she had said, and the wounded. Jenna bit her lip. She had seen the wounded murdered on their cots. No safety there. Then she said, speaking her thoughts aloud, "But surely not *all* the wounded. In a battle of this size, things would have gone on for hours. So there *must* have been others, moved earlier. To the place Armina mentioned. If only she had named it!" She thought, suddenly, *Perhaps Pynt is there as well.*

Afraid to hope too much, she nevertheless allowed herself a faint glimmering. Leaving the playroom, she finished her search of the second floor and then, finding the back stairs, mounted to the third.

There were fewer bodies here, as if the fighting had not reached so far or, she thought grimly, as if there had been fewer fighters left. And then she came to Mother Alta's carved doors. They were shattered, split down the middle. Cautiously she stepped inside.

It was here some sort of stand had been made. The last of the wounded were clustered at Mother Alta's feet, almost stacked up, their bandages soaked in newer blood. The infirmarer, her own head encased in a linen binding, had fallen across the priestess' lap. Mother Alta's fingers were entwined in hers, the sixth finger alone outstretched. The priestess' marble eyes were wide open and staring.

But Pynt and the children were gone. The realization came to Jenna suddenly. The men must have taken them, taken the screaming, hysterical children and . . . Here her imagination failed her utterly. She simply could not guess what grown men would do with several dozen children, some still babes in arms.

For the rest of the day Jenna carried the corpses of the women down to the kitchen and the Great Hall. She carried them reverently, as if by doing so, somehow, she could excuse her guilt. She laid them side by side, leaving room between for their dark sisters. The last one she brought down was Mother Alta, the small, twisted body weighing less than a child.

She knew that she could not bring them all to the Cave, had she even an idea of where the Cave lay. Instead, she planned to set the Hame afire. It would serve as a fitting memorial for the battle brave.

It was deep into the night by the time she brought Mother Alta down, setting her gently atop the kitchen table and arranging her shrunken legs. She kissed each finger on the six-fingered hands before crossing them over the old woman's breast. Jenna's eyes had grown used to the almost-dark. She lit lamps only at the far turnings of the stairs, for otherwise she would have been burdened with the dark sisters as well as the light. But once she had Mother Alta's body arranged, she lit a candle and placed it at the priestess' head, watching with quiet satisfaction as the corpse of Mother Alta's dark sister appeared, her flickering sixth finger resolving in the full light.

"Sisters side by side," Jenna whispered. Then she lit all the kitchen lamps before proceeding into the Great Hall. Making sure all the corners of the room were well lit, she nodded as corpse after corpse appeared next to their light sisters. Unbidden, the words of the grave prayer came to her lips.

> In the name of Alta's cave,
> The dark and lonely grave . . .

And she thought that those dead sisters would *not* be lonely this night. The memory of the last time she had heard those words came to her: Mother Alta's reedy voice following them down the stairs.

Mounting those stairs one last time, Jenna was suddenly aware just how exhausted she was. She headed directly for the priestess' room, for she had already decided to bring down two final tributes to the courage of the Nill's Hame sisters—the *Book of Light* and the mirror. Standing before the broken door, she took a single deep breath, then went in.

She snatched the cloth from the glass, momentarily startled at her reflection. There were blades of grass in her hair and her braid needed replaiting. Black smudges seemed to be growing under her eyes. She had either lost weight or grown unaccountably taller. Blood spotted her clothing and there was a smear of it across her right cheek. It was a wonder Carum had ever wanted to kiss her.

At the thought of him, she put her fingers to her lips, as if some trace of the kiss still lingered there. *And he is gone, too*, she thought. *Gone to a place where I cannot go.*

She raised her hands toward her mirror self as if pleading, and whispered hoarsely, "Thee to me. Thee to me," the only part of Night of Sisterhood she could remember. "Thee to me."

She meant Carum and Pynt and the children and all the dead women of the Hame. She meant her stepmother A-ma and her foster mother Selna and her real mother who had been cat-killed. And even Selden's Mother Alta. Even her. All the ones who had been part of her life and were gone from her now. "Thee to me." Knowing they were dead or too far for her recalling, still she called. "Thee to me." Tears ran hot down her cheeks, washing away the bloodstains. "Thee to me. Thee to me."

The moon silvered through the window and a small breeze stirred the tendrils of hair at her forehead and neck. In the mirror a mist seemed to form, as if there were moisture in the air, clouding the glass. But Jenna's eyes were so teary, she did not really see it.

"Thee to me," she whispered urgently.

The mist shrouded her reflection slowly, from the edges in, and all the while her hand moved in its beckoning motion and the chant, taking on a life of its own, ran its course.

"Thee to me."

The image, mimicking her motions, whispered back, "Thee to me."

As if in a trance, Jenna stepped forward until she was almost on top of the mirror. Palms out, she placed her hands upon the glass. Instead of the hard surface, her hands touched warm skin, palm to palm. She closed her fingers about the image's fingers and drew the other from the glass.

"It took you long enough," said the image. "I could have been here days ago."

"Who *are* you?" Jenna asked.

"Your dark sister, of course. Skada."

"Skada?"

"It means shadow in the old tongue."

"Pynt is my shadow." Mentioning Pynt's name out loud made Jenna's throat hurt.

"Pynt *was* your shadow. Now I am. And I will be closer to you than Pynt could ever be."

"You cannot be my dark sister. You look very little like me. I am not that thin and my cheekbones are not that prominent. And . . ." She ran her hand nervously down her braid.

Skada smiled, touching her own black plait. "We none of us know how others see us. It is one of the first warnings taught in my world: *Sisters can be blind.* I am dark where you are light. And perhaps I am a bit thinner. But that will change."

"Why?"

"You eat better in this world, of course."

"Your world is different from ours?" Jenna was confused.

"It is the mirror image. But image is not the same as substance. We must wait your call for that."

Jenna shook her head. "This is very different than I expected. *You* are very different than I expected."

Skada shook her head as if mocking Jenna. "What did you expect?"

"I do not know. Someone . . . softer, maybe. Quieter. More pliant."

"But, Jenna, *you* are not soft, quiet, pliant. And though I am many things, I am not what you are not. *I am you.* And what you keep yourself from being." She smiled and Jenna smiled back at her. "I would not have waited so long to let Carum kiss me."

"You saw that?" Jenna felt her cheeks flush.

"Not exactly *saw.* But it happened at night under the moon. So your memories of that are mine."

Jenna touched her fingers to her lips, remembering, and Skada did the same.

"And there are other things I would do differently," said Skada.

"Such as . . ."

"*I* would not have hesitated to claim being the Anna. So that means some part of you desires it, too."

"No!" Jenna said.

"Yes!" Skada answered.

"How can I believe you?" Jenna asked. "How do I know you are not simply a woman of the Hame?"

"Shall I tell you what Carum said? How he carried you out of the Halla? That was at night, too. Moon nights I share with you, Jenna. Forever."

"Forever?" Jenna's voice was scarcely a whisper. "You will not leave?"

"I *cannot* leave," Skada whispered back. "You called and I came and it is done. Sister called to sister, need to need."

Jenna sank down on her haunches and stared at the ground. Skada did the same. "My need . . ." Jenna muttered. Then she looked up to find Skada staring back at her. "My need is to find where the children have been taken. And Pynt."

"I will help you every moonlit step of the way."

"Then first help me take the mirror down. And the *Book*. I want to put the *Book* by Mother Alta's head and the mirror at her feet. But I will break the glass first just in case. No man shall ever find the secret to our sisterhood." She nodded her head at Skada.

Skada nodded back. "You begin the task, sister, and I will have little say in the matter."

Jenna smiled ruefully. "I forgot."

"It will take some getting used to," Skada said. "For me as well. In my own world, except at a mirror or pond, my movements were my own."

Jenna stared at her. "Do you resent me for that?"

Skada returned that stare. "Resent you? You make me—how shall I put it—whole. Without you I am indeed a shadow."

Jenna stood and touched the left side of the mirror. Skada touched the right.

"When I give the signal, lift with me," said Jenna.

Skada almost smiled. "When you lift, that will be signal enough," she said.

"Oh, I understand. Strange—I have been around dark sisters all my life, but gave them little thought."

"Soon you will give me as little. I shall just *be*," Skada answered. "Lift the mirror, Jenna. You talk too much."

Jenna spread her legs apart and bent her back to the task, and Skada heaved with her, but the mirror would not move, as if it were attached, somehow, to the floor.

"That is strange," said Skada.

"Very strange," Jenna agreed. She straightened up for a moment, then bent back to the task, Skada following her every movement. "Let us try again." As she tried to heft the mirror, Jenna's hand was on the goddess sign and her hand moved it slightly to the right. There was a loud, groaning sound and the floor under Jenna's foot began to move. Jenna leaped away from the mirror in alarm and Skada did the same. Jenna pulled her sword from its sheath with a single swift motion and was momentarily startled when Skada's sword flashed back. The moonlight touched the steel and, for a moment, both seemed bathed in a cold fire.

The floor continued its groaning motion, and slid open until it disclosed a stair going down. There was a strange, high cry from below and a child climbed out, blinking in the moonlight. She looked around, first at Skada, then at Jenna.

"The Anna," she cried. "Mother Alta said you would come."

She turned, gave a loud, piercing whistle down the stairs, then turned back and flung herself into Jenna's arms.

The children boiled out of the tunnel like rats from a hole, all trying to talk at once. Even the babies gabbled for attention. Jenna and Skada hugged and petted them each in turn, then gathered them in a large semicircle.

"Is that all of you, then?" Jenna asked. "No more hidden down those dark stairs?"

"Just one, Anna," said one of the older girls. "But she is too sick to come up herself."

Jenna gasped. "How sick?"

"Very sick," said a smudge-faced girl with tangled brown hair.

"Why did none of you bring her up?" asked Skada.

"She is too big for us to move," the brown-haired child replied.

"*Too* big!" Jenna whispered. Pushing hope down, she stood. "Skada, help me."

"Then someone must bring a lamp," Skada said.

The oldest child there, a twelve-year-old with dark braids and a deep dimple in her cheek, lit a lamp. "I will."

They went down the stairs and through a series of dark, dry rooms with cots lined up along the walls. The remnants of food tins were scattered about. The rooms were close and smelled dreadfully.

"Too many babies and too few baths," whispered Skada.

Jenna wrinkled her nose but did not reply.

In the last room, the child cried out, "There she is."

There was a cot against the wall and the figure in it had dark hair, but her back was to them.

"Pynt," Jenna whispered. "Pynt, is it you?"

The girl on the cot stirred, but she was obviously in too much pain to turn over. Jenna ran to the bed and, with Skada's help, turned the bed around.

"Hello, Jenna," Pynt said. Her eyes were dark hollows.

Jenna could not contain her tears. "I said I would be back," she whispered. "In my heart, I said it."

"I knew you would," Pynt said. She smiled up at Jenna, then looked at Skada.

Jenna noticed the look. "Pynt, this is . . ."

"Your dark sister, of course," Pynt said hoarsely. "I am so glad for you, Jenna. It would not do for you to be alone, and I will not be shadowing you for a while. Not for a long while." She closed her eyes and was still.

"Not . . . not dead," Jenna whispered to Skada.

Skada smiled. "Well, they say *Sleep is death's younger sister.* No wonder you are confused."

"Oh—sleep!" Jenna said, and grinned.

They hefted the bed between them and carried it carefully through the dark rooms and up the stairs, setting it in front of the half circle of children.

"But where is Mother Alta?" asked the girl with dark braids.

Jenna squatted down so as not to tower over the children, and Skada squatted right by her side. "Now listen, little ones, what you will find below will break your hearts if you let it. But remember that your mothers are all with Great Alta now, where they wait for the day we can all be together again."

A four-year-old began to snuffle. One or two of the others started to cry. The girl with the dark braids made a strange moaning sound.

"All?" she asked. "Not all."

"All," Jenna said as gently as she could and wishing there were some comfort in it.

A baby, unused to the light and the sound of all the crying, took it up in a thin, high wailing.

Pynt opened her eyes. Without moving more than her mouth, she began to speak, her voice surprisingly strong. "Hush! Hush! You are young warriors of Alta. You are the Mother's own. Would we trouble the mothers' rest in Alta's cave? They are happy there, playing at wands with the goddess herself and taking their nourishment from her breast. Would we make them miss a cast with our cries? Would we disturb their suck? No, no, my babies. We must be strong. We must remember who we are, always."

The snuffling cries stopped at her voice; even the baby was still, soothed by her tone.

When it was quiet, Pynt whispered to Jenna, "They will cry no more. Not a one of them cried in the warren, even when the candles gave out. And I know none of them will cry outside. Lead on, White Jenna. Lead on, Anna. Lead on and we will all be your shadows."

* * *

They broke the mirror with the butt end of Jenna's sword and set fire to the kitchen and the Great Hall. Jenna let only the older girls help. She could not bear for the babies to see the bodies and all the blood. So the children waited by the back door.

Then, with the smoke spiraling behind them, Jenna and Skada carried Pynt's cot, followed by the single line of children.

They chopped through the twisted fir tree that lay across the path, clearing the walk for everyone. And when they came to a low embankment, the children scrambled over easily. With ropes they hauled Pynt's cot up and then, at Jenna's signal, turned toward the Sea of Bells where, beyond, Selden Hame waited. It was the only place Jenna knew of that would take so many children in. Once she got them safely there, she swore she would find another map and warn the Hames.

THE MYTH:

And so Great Alta made the Anna, the White One, the Holy One, out of fire and water, out of earth and air.

"This One that I have made," quoth Great Alta, "shall be sundered and yet shall be whole. She shall be drowned and yet she shall live. She shall burn and yet not be ashes. She shall go down into the earth and up into the air and yet shall not die. She shall be the end of all things and the beginning."

FOUR

THE ANNA

THE MYTH:

Then Great Alta took up the hair that bound the dark and light sisters to her and with a great shears severed the braid. It fell between them into the sinkhole of night.

"Even as I have done, so you must do," quoth Great Alta. "For a child who is wrapped in her mother's hair, a child who wears her mother's clothing, a child who lives in her mother's house, that one remains a child forever."

So the queen of shadows and the queen of light departed, but not before they each took a single hair from the braid, twining it about their wrists, as a token of their love.

THE LEGEND:

The day that Mairi Magoren was playing at Counters, she looked up and saw an old woman trotting down the road with her head going back and forth like this, tok-tok, tok-tok. *Behind her was a long line of dirty, nasty children calling after her.*

"Old woman, old woman," said Mairi, "and where are you going so fast?" For she was thinking that she might give her a drink or a chair to rock in or a kind word, and let the gang of children go by.

But the old woman trotted along without a sound, her white-haired head moving back and forth, tok-tok, tok-tok. *And her shadow on the ground made the same motion,* tok-tok, tok-tok. *And those ragged children kept pace behind.*

And then Mairi saw that the children were bound together with ropes of hair and that she could see right through them to the trees beyond.

That was when Mairi knew she had seen the Hanna Bucca, the Hanna Ghost or Devil, who stole naughty children from their cradles and lured them from their beds and forced them to dance behind her till their clothes were in rags and their shoes in patches and their mothers long dead in their graves.

THE STORY:

They traveled by night, but not because it was safer. How a troop of thirty-three children, ranging in age from infancy to twelve years, hoped to obscure their tracks was beyond even Jenna's fine woodcraft. But they traveled in the moonlight because Skada could be there to help haul Pynt's cot. Once into the deep woods, though, Skada's movements were not to be counted on, and Jenna relied more and more upon dark-braided Petra.

Petra seemed extraordinarily composed for a girl on the edge of missioning, and Jenna was not surprised to discover she had chosen to follow the priestess' way. Jenna tried to remember herself just a year past, but what she recalled mostly was the sound of doors slamming, the angry scraping of chairs being pushed from tables, and endless moody self-examinations. Petra seemed troubled by none of these, being equally at home with the babies as with the still-feverish Pynt. She also had an endless store of tales and songs which she recited in a voice that reminded Jenna more and more of the six-fingered Mother Alta.

They had taken as much food from the Hame as they could pack. Each of the older girls carried sacks or baskets crammed with breads, cheeses, and dried fruits. The younger ones had leather pockets full of *brod*, the hard-baked crackers Nill's Hame was famous for. Jenna had slung a half-dozen wineskins over her back which she planned to refill with water whenever they were near a stream.

"Even if we never make it to Selden Hame," Skada had remarked, "we will never go hungry."

The children had cheered then, the first sound they had made since leaving the Hame, though Jenna had shushed them quickly.

Outlined by the moon, the Sea of Bells seemed an endless realm of closed white flowers and dark, shadowy grass. Jenna was thankful there was no fog.

She and Skada led the children straight across the great meadow, heedless of the matted track they left behind. More important than any trail was speed. The children needed mothering, Pynt needed nursing, and regardless of Skada's joke, there was hardly enough food for more than a few days. Besides, Jenna's head was never long without Mother Alta's voice saying to her, *"You must go from Hame to Hame to warn them. Say this: The time of endings is at hand."* Every repetition brought with it a memory of the horror that had been Nill's Hame, with body after body in the courtyard and on the stairs, and after the thin smoke trailing up from the funeral fires like an unwinding skein of souls.

The first morning they picnicked by the eastern edge of the lily bell meadow. The infants, who had slept all night in the arms of their carriers, were wide awake. But the others were exhausted from their night of walking and fell asleep in the grass, heedless of the babies' happy babblings.

Jenna and Petra took turns standing guard during the day, though there was, thankfully, little to see except a family of red foxes playing some hundred feet away from the sleeping children and a V of wild geese honking northward overhead.

In the evening they all shared a meal of cheese and bread, water and a cache of nuts Jenna had found during one of Petra's turns at the watch. The fruit was saved for treats along the way.

After the meal, Jenna got them all to their feet, saying, "Come, my warriors. Come, my fine woodswomen. Petra will tell us a story and then we will be on our way."

Petra told them the ever-stirring ballad of *Krack's Ride*, singing the chorus:

> *Hallo, hallay, King Krack does ride,*
> *And with him, sisters side by side*

and all the children joined in. Even the infants seemed to take part, waving their arms at the last three words just as the older girls did.

Remembering Pynt's recitation of the opening lines of the poem, Jenna knelt by her cot.

"And how are you doing, my shadow?" she asked.

Pynt managed to raise her head. "I believe I am healing, Jenna. Who would have credited it? Bouncing along between you and Skada, packed in like a pound of *brod* and cheese. But my fever broke in the night and the wound aches only a little, like a tooth gone rotten."

Jenna put her hand on Pynt's head and found it cool, though a bit damp. She tucked the covers gently around Pynt's shoulders as Petra finished the last lines of the poem.

Pynt whispered the chorus along with the children. "*And with him, sisters side by side*. That is a good one, Jenna. It will get them moving quickly, and without fear."

"So she hoped," Skada said, materializing by Jenna's side.

Glancing quickly to the horizon, Jenna saw the moon

making its slow way. She nodded, as if to herself, and said in a low voice, "You are here. Now we can really go."

The moon was no longer full, its edges sloped and faded, but Skada seemed as crisp as ever, her laughter piercing Jenna's moodiest moments. So the first time Jenna tried to hush her along the long march, she would not be still.

"If I quieted, Jenna, you would say the very same things inside your mind, but they would not be half as amusing. Admit it."

"Hush, Skada, I hear something," Jenna said, stopping, her head cocked to one side. Skada stood in the same attitude.

"How you can expect to hear anything beyond the tramping of sixty-six little feet, Great Alta alone knows," Skada said, though she listened as well.

"Will you hush?"

"I am still. You are the one who is flapping."

As soon as they stopped, the line of children stretched out behind them came to a halt. After the last child had quieted, there was still a shallow echo of sound, a crackling of twigs from the line of trees.

Pynt whispered from her cot, "A cat?"

"Too noisy."

"A bear?"

"Not noisy enough."

"Is that meant to be comforting?"

"That is meant to be—oh, Pynt, we have had this conversation before."

Pynt grinned despite the fear.

"How can you joke at a time like this?" Jenna asked.

Pynt pushed herself up onto her elbow. "Jenna, you are always asking *me* to think. You think this time. Think about the last time we heard such a noise, and in the fog."

"It was Carum." Jenna's voice was suddenly soft.

"But it is not Carum now. Still, that is a noise made by someone equally human. *One* someone. Surely we outnumber whoever is there."

Jenna nodded and drew her sword. Skada followed suit.

A voice called out from the bush, "Put up your sword Jo-an-enna. If I had wanted to surprise you, you would never have heard me."

Pynt sat all the way up on the cot, her smile disguising the cost of such effort. "A-ma!" she cried.

Amalda stepped out of the shadows and, as she did, her dark sister Sammor materialized by her side.

Jenna slipped her sword silently back into its sheath, nodding as Skada did the same. They stepped aside so that Amalda and Sammor might get to the cot.

"What has happened to you, child?" asked Amalda.

"I spoke too soon and went first," Pynt said wryly. "Just what you warned me about. I think that *this* time I may have learned my lesson. But, A-ma, why are *you* here?"

Sammor held Pynt's right hand, Amalda her left. "You brought us here, imp," they said together.

"When a runner came from Calla's Ford to say that you had not gotten to the Hame with the other two—," Amalda began.

"See, Jenna," Pynt interrupted, "I told you they would make it on their own."

Unruffled, Amalda continued. "We could not stay at home knowing you had acted so foolishly, knowing that you might have put your life—and others'—in danger. Marga, you went *directly* against the Mother's orders."

"They were bad orders, made to hurt, not to heal," Pynt said.

"They were the Mother's orders," said Amalda, "no matter what your heart told you. In the Dales they say: *The heart can be a cruel master.* And look how cruelly it has served you." She and Sammor fussed at the bandage around Pynt's shoulder and back.

"Even more cruelly served were the women of Nill's Hame," Jenna whispered. She gestured at the exodus fanned out around them, the children waiting quietly for their next instructions.

Pynt bit her lip and looked down.

"We wondered who they were," said Sammor. "They have the quiet containment of Alta's own babes."

"That is quite a reaping of hillsides, Jenna," Amalda added.

Jenna nodded.

"Where are their mothers?" Amalda asked.

"Dead," Jenna said.

"All of them?"

Jenna said nothing.

"All." Skada spoke for the first time.

Amalda and Sammor turned and stared at her.

"But . . . but you are . . ."

Skada and Jenna both nodded and moved closer together so that their shoulders touched. Seen that way, their twinship could not be denied.

"I do not understand," Amalda said, coming over to stand before them, Sammor following. "You are at least a year away from your Night of Sisterhood. Surely the women at Nill's Hame had no time to set you before the glass. You had no training. You had never even *seen* the rites."

Jenna shrugged. "It just . . . just happened," she said.

Skada's shrug was more generous. "Need called to need," she said. "And I answered."

They were all silent for a long moment; then a four-year-old broke from the ring of children and came over to tug at Jenna's sleeve. "Anna," she whispered urgently, "we have heard the cough of a cat nearby. Some of the little ones are frightened."

"And you are not frightened?" asked Jenna, kneeling down beside her. Skada flanked her.

"No, Anna. You are here."

"Why does she call you Anna?" asked Sammor. "That is not your name."

"The Anna is . . ." Amalda began.

"I know what the Anna is," said Jenna, "but I no longer know who I am." She put her arm around the child on one side, and Skada did the same on the other. "Tell me again, sweetheart."

"We heard a cat in the woods. It coughed like this." The child gave a remarkably good imitation of a cat's rough voice.

"The tale will keep," said Sammor. "The cat will not. We will kill it for you, Amalda and I, and one of your babes will sleep in a skin warmer than her own tonight." Without another word, they slipped away from the group.

"Tell the others," Jenna said to the child. "We will wait here until they return. But no one is to worry further about the cat. At our Hame we say: A *cat who boasts once is a cat who boasts once too often.*"

"We say that, too, Anna," the child said, clapping her hands before she hurried back to the circle of children. Trotting around, she gave them all the message and they sat down in the grass to wait.

"That cat is not the problem," Jenna said to Skada.

"Nor is the telling of the tale," Skada added.

"Time is the problem," Pynt said from her cot. "Every minute we wait here is a piece of moon time lost."

"Moon time matters no longer," said Skada. "A-ma will help with the cot now. You will be able to travel by day, too, if you wish."

"If it were just Amalda, Pynt, and me, we would go both day and night. But the children are exhausted. Little food and less sleep is not a healthy rule."

"They are young. They will recover," said Skada.

Jenna looked over Skada's shoulder at the trees, dark and untidy in the moonlight. "I wish we were gone from this place. It is too close to bad memories."

"And a rough grave," added Pynt.

It was less than an hour, with the moon still climbing, when Amalda and Sammor returned, the cat's skin carried between them.

Jenna smiled thinly. "A small time," she said.

"A small cat," Amalda answered. "And only roughly skinned. It will stink, but we will clean it better once we are home. We worried about the time, you see."

"We worried, too," Pynt said.

They dropped the skin on top of Pynt's feet, and the children gathered around to touch it, jostling one another slightly to get a better look, their infant sisters forgotten for the moment in the high grass.

"One touch," warned Petra, "and that is all. Then we must go."

Silently and solemnly, the little girls touched the catskin; then they turned back to the grass where their sisters lay, and picked up their burdens before forming two straight lines.

Amalda and Sammor nodded toward the south. "That way is quickest. *And* it avoids a certain place."

"What place?" asked Jenna.

"A grave with a snarling dog's helm glowering over it from a broken cross," Sammor said.

"But I threw that helm into the grave," Jenna blurted out.

"And whoever uncovered the grave the first time gave him a proper burial according to their own rites," Amalda said.

"First?" Pynt asked, her voice thin.

"We uncovered it second," said Sammor. "We tracked the two of you with an ease that belittles our training. You trod a path in circles with frequent back-treading."

"There was a fog," Jenna said. If it was meant as an explanation, neither Amalda nor Sammor took it so.

"When we trailed you to that dirt-packed clearing and found the new grave, we feared the worst. But all we found in the grave was a big, ugly lump of a man," said Sammor.

"A man killed twice," added Amalda, "if we read his wounds right. Once in the thigh and once . . ."

Jenna made a small sighing sound.

"Please," Skada said, "Jenna has no stomach for such tellings. She scarcely had any stomach for the doing."

"I did what had to be done," said Jenna. "But I will not take joy in it, neither once nor again. The children are waiting. Can we go?"

* * *

They walked on and on, sharing out the last of the *brod* and fruit with the children, giving the infants drinks of water flavored with the honey that Amalda and Sammor had carried with them.

Along the road, first Pynt and then Skada recounted the horror of the Nill's Hame slaughter as starkly as they could, reciting just the facts so that Jenna's blanched face might find its color again. Amalda and Sammor knew better than to interrupt the telling and thus make it longer. And when it was done, they were all five silent, for there were no words for comfort after such a tale. They were careful, though, not to let the children overhear any of it, leaving them to Petra's gentle chivying.

At last the southern road turned into the woods, and Skada and Sammor disappeared, so that the cot had to be carried between Amalda and Jenna. They were silent far into the morning, when they led the children beneath a cliff into a great circling encampment with Pynt's cot at the center. They slept there, at the base of the Old Hanging Man, whose broad, rocky face watched over them until dusk.

The children were hungry and one or two even complained of it, despite Petra's warnings and the many songs she had them sing. The children were all were ragged from the long, steady, unending march, and finally Jenna and Amalda let several of the smallest take turns riding on their shoulders. Pynt cradled a few of the infants at a time in the cot by her breast and at her feet, freeing the older children from their heavy burdens. In this way the band of thirty-six straggled up to the gates of Selden Hame at dawn on the fifth day, flanked by two silent Hame guards who had not asked questions, fearing to delay them further.

The gates were opened at once, for the doors of a Hame were never shut to children, and the women of Selden boiled around them, lifting the children into much-welcomed embraces. Then they guided the ragtag crew into the kitchen for food.

Jenna knew that the Hame baths would be kept steaming long into the afternoon, and she could already feel the laving of the waters over her tired legs and back. She put her arm around Petra.

"Come, my good right hand, after we cram some hot stew down you and clean you up, you and I will have to go and speak to the Mother." She said it jauntily, though her own stomach knotted at the thought. When she looked down at Petra, to her surprise, the girl had tears in her eyes.

"Are we safe here, Anna?" Petra asked in a whisper.

"You are safe here, Petra," Jenna answered. "And the children, too, because of your good shepherding."

"The Goddess smiles," Petra said, her voice a small echo of the six-fingered priestess.

Jenna turned away slightly and under her breath, so that Petra could not hear, muttered, "The Goddess laughs, and I do not know if I like the sound."

"What did you say?" Petra asked.

Jenna did not answer, but guided her to a chair in the kitchen, where Donya set two steaming mugs of stew before them and a platter of thick bread slices slathered with melted butter and cloudberry jam.

Amalda had let no one question them while they were eating, then took Pynt to see the infirmarer. Kadreen checked Pynt's shoulder and back while she gulped down a second mug of stew.

"A good piece of work," Kadreen said, her mouth in its usual thin line. "You will not lose the use of the arm, which is often the case when a wound cuts across muscle. But you will have to exercise that arm as soon as you are able."

"When will that be?" Pynt asked.

"I will tell you," said Kadreen, "and it will be sooner than either you or your arm will want. We will work on it together, you and I."

Pynt nodded.

"There will be a nasty scar," Kadreen said.

Amalda smiled. "I will trace it for you myself, Marga. A warrior's scars are the face of memory, a map of her courage."

Pynt hesitated a moment, then looked up at her mother. "I am a warrior no longer, A-ma. I have seen enough death for twenty warriors, though my hand struck but one, and he only in the thigh. Yet was I a bringer of death, as surely as if I carried some contagion."

Amalda's face blanched. "But . . ."

"My mind is made up, A-ma. And it is not to shame you. But at my Night of Sisterhood, I will choose to tend the children, like Marna and Zo. I am good with them, and surely with so many new ones in our Hame, there will be need of me."

Amalda started to speak again, but Kadreen put her hand up. "Listen to her, Amalda. There are some scars that we cannot see and they heal slowly if at all. I know. I have such scars myself."

Amalda nodded and looked again at Pynt. "You are tired, child."

"I am tired, my mother, but that is not the reason I say what I do. If you had seen them in the end, all the beautiful, strong women of Nill's Hame: *sisters side by side.* Jenna pulled my cot into the kitchen and the hall that we might bid them farewell. She said—and I shall carry it with me always—that we must remember. For if we forget, then their death has no meaning. *Sisters side by side.*" She turned her face down and stared at the cot as if she could read some picture there, pushed the mug away, and wept.

Amalda sat down on the cot and ran her hand over Pynt's curly hair. "If that is your wish, heart of my heart. If that is your wish, child whom I carried beneath my breast. Then that is what shall be. You always were a stubborn little thing. Hush. Hush and sleep. You are safe here."

Pynt turned back and stared up at her, eyes still brimming with tears. "But, A-ma, you do not understand. I shall never ever feel safe again. That is the worst of it. Yet I shall dedicate my life to the safety of those little ones so that they do not have to feel as I do. Oh, A-ma . . ." She sat up suddenly and threw her arms around Amalda, without regard for the pain in her shoulder and back, and held on as if she would never let go.

THE BALLAD:

The Ballad of White Jenna

Out of the morning, into the night,
Thirty and three rode off to fight
To put the dreaded foe to flight,
Led by the hand of Jenna.

Thirty and three rode side by side,
And by the moonlight fortified.
"Fight on, my sisters," Jenna cried,
"Fight for the Great White Alta."

The blood flowed swift, like good red wine,
As sisters took the battle line.
"This kingdom I will claim for mine,
And for the heart of Alta!"

Thirty and three rode out that day
To hold the dreaded foe at bay,
But nevermore they passed this way,
Led by the hand of Jenna.

Yet still, some say, in darkest night
The sisters can be heard to fight,
And you will see a flash of white,
The long white braid of Jenna.

THE STORY:

The bath had been soothing and Jenna even fell asleep for a moment in the hot, scented water. Her white hair, free of the confining braid, fanned out around her like strands of bleached seaweed.

Petra picked at a single strand that had floated across her breast, silently waiting for Jenna to speak. At last, unable to wait longer, she asked, "What is your Mother Alta like? I shall be studying with her."

Jenna opened her eyes and stared at the wooden ribbing of the roof. She was a long time answering, and the silence stretched between them like a taut rope.

"Hard," she said finally. "Unbending. A rock."

"A Hame needs a solid rock upon which to build," Petra said slowly.

Jenna did not answer.

"But one can bruise oneself against unyielding stone," Petra said with a little sigh. "Our Mother always said that a priestess should not be rock but water. That there is an ebb and flow to a Hame. Our Mother Alta . . ."

". . . is dead," Jenna said very softly. "And the fault is mine."

Petra shook her head. "No, no, Jo-an-enna. There is no fault. *No blame, no shame*, Mother Alta always said. And she told me about the Anna. To study to be a priestess is to learn prophecy. If you are the Anna . . ."

"Am I?"

Petra tried to smile. "I believe you are."

"But do you *know*?"

"I will know a hundred years from now," said Petra. "I will know tomorrow."

"What kind of an answer is that?" Jenna asked disgustedly. "It is priestess talk, all words and no meaning." She slapped her hand against the water, splashing them both.

Petra rubbed the water from her eyes as she answered. "It is what Mother Alta said. She meant that we must act now for now, and leave the answers to those who come after. And so I believe."

Jenna stood and the water came up only to the sharp ridge of her hipbone. Her body, with its covering of fine white hair, seemed to glow in the darkened room. "I wish I could believe so simply. I wish I *knew* what to believe."

Petra stood next to her, the water past her waist. "Jenna, a prophecy only suggests, it does not tell. It can be read accurately only long after. We who live it must read it on the slant."

"Those were Mother Alta's words."

Petra shook her head. "Not just words, Jenna, but the heart of it. If you *are* the Anna, then there is much for you to do. If you are not, you must still do it, for events will happen whether you believe or not. The Hames must be warned." She put her hand on Jenna's arm. "And this Hame must be warned, too."

Jenna wrung her hair between strong hands, then quickly braided it up, tying a ribband around it, and flinging it over her shoulder. She smiled wryly. "I had hoped to put it off."

"Put what off?"

"Speaking to the rock."

"I will be there, Jenna. And I will be water over stone for you. You will see."

"Water over stone," Jenna mused. "I like that."

They slipped into clean clothes that had been left for them and, arm in arm, went into the hall. But the hot water had drained them both of any strength after the long nights of walking, and before they could be summoned to see Mother Alta, they had both fallen into a deep sleep across Jenna's bed. Jenna awoke only once all afternoon, when Amalda came to fetch them and instead tucked Petra into Pynt's old bed.

Amalda sat uneasily in the priestess' room waiting for Mother Alta to speak, wishing it were night and Sammor by her side. She had explained about the girls' exhaustion and had, in their stead, told Mother Alta the tale. Her recitation had been stark and uninterrupted. Though there were gaps in what she knew—and gaps in what she understood—she had told it without a warrior's usual flourishes, knowing that this was a time for truth and not balladry. Mother Alta listened with her eyes closed, a bad sign, nodding or shaking her head in unreadable glosses. Amalda could not tell if she was angry, sad, or pleased with the story. All that was certain was that she was making a judgment. Mother Alta always made private judgments, and the decisions she rendered afterward were as if written in stone. Amalda had never challenged those judgments aloud, though some, like Catrona, had often exchanged harsh words with the priestess.

Matching Mother Alta breath for breath, Amalda tried unsuccessfully to summon up a fragment of the chant to calm herself. But all that came to her mind were the words of the chorus of *Krack's Ride* and a vision of Pynt's agonized face.

"Amalda!" Mother Alta's voice, sharp and commanding, brought her back to the moment. "We shall hear all this tale tonight from the mouths of the three who lived it: Jo-an-enna, Marga, and this young Petra. We will listen for the truth and to discover what you may have—all inadvertently, I am sure—left out."

Amalda nodded miserably, trying to remember what she might have omitted in the telling, and could not recall a word of what she had said.

"The others, the infants and the children," Mother Alta continued, "shall go to bed and watch over one another while we speak. All shall know the horror and the shame of this. All."

Mother Alta's face seemed to have taken on a feral look, reminding Amalda of a fox on hens. It made her increasingly uncomfortable. She wanted to argue, but without Sammor to back her, she felt unequal to the task. So she said nothing and waited for some signal to indicate the priestess had finished speaking. After a moment of silence, Amalda stood.

Mother Alta made a dismissive motion with her hand and Amalda left the room, grateful to be away from the confines of those particular walls.

* * *

As soon as the door had closed after Amalda, Mother Alta stood. Smoothing down her long woolen skirt, she took a deep breath and turned toward the mirror. She snatched the covering from its face and stared at herself for a long moment. A familiar stranger stared back.

"Do I believe her?" she asked the mirror. "Why should she lie?" Shaking her head slowly, she considered the question. "No, Amalda does not lie. She has not the wits for it. She says only what Jenna has told her, a shameful tale. But what if there *is* a lie somewhere in the story? An untruth or a not-saying? The *Book* is clear, that *One falsehood can spoil a thousand truths.*" She waited, as if expecting the mirror to answer her, then reached out and touched the glass, palm to palm. The blue mark doubled itself before being covered, and around her hand the mirror fogged, making ghostly fingerprints.

"Oh, Great Alta, thou who dancest from star to star, I believe and I do not believe. I want to be the Mother of the Anna, but I fear the ending that comes with it. I have led a good life. I have been happy here. *It is a fool who longs for endings, a wise woman who longs for beginnings,* as you say in the *Book.*

"If I deny her, will I be wrong? She is but a girl. I have watched her grow. I have seen some strangeness there, true. But where is the crown of glory? Where are the voices crying, 'Holy, holy, holy'?

"To choose wrongly is to declare myself a fool. And like the fool in the tale who learns the game after all the players have gone home, I will be laughed at if I am wrong. Laughed at. By the women I command. Thou knowest, Great One, that I am no fool." She took her hand from the glass and watched as the moist prints slowly dried.

Staring at the ceiling, she cried, "I have waited fourteen years for an unambiguous sign from thee. Now, *now* is the hour. Give me that sign."

But it was a clear day and there was neither thunder nor rainbow, nor a voice from the sky. If the Goddess spoke to her, it was in whispers. Mother Alta put her hands over her eyes and tried to weep, but no tears came.

Up first, Petra brushed her long dark hair and braided it into a crown, which she pinned atop her head. Her dress was badly wrinkled, since she had slept in it, and there were creases on her right cheek still where the bed linen had marked her. Yet she seemed remarkably alert and cheerful nonetheless.

Jenna, on the other hand, felt as if someone had beaten her about the head and shoulders before flinging her onto the mattress. The bed looked as bad, the covers rucked up by the foot. She came awake slowly.

"Amalda was in, though you did not hear her," Petra said when Jenna began to move. "There is to be a meeting tonight at dinner and we are to tell the story then."

"Mother Alta will be there?"

"And Pynt. And all the women."

"And the children? I would not like to tell the story of Nill's Hame before them. They will know it soon enough, but not from my lips," Jenna said.

"They are to go to bed in one another's charge." Petra came over and sat beside Jenna on her bed. "But I am to be at the meeting. That way we can tell the sisters everything. *Everything*, Jenna."

Jenna looked down at her hands and wondered that she was twisting and winding them together.

"Do not be afraid of your destiny, Anna," Petra said, putting her hands over Jenna's.

"It is not destiny I am afraid of," Jenna said sharply, drawing her hands away.

"Then why are you angry?"

"I am not angry."

"Look at your covers," Petra said, pointing. "Look at your mouth."

Jenna stood and went over to the water basin and stared down into the still, silvered face. Her dark eyes seemed echoed by dark smudges on her cheeks. The cheeks themselves were hollowed. Her mouth was thin and sour. Touching her lips with her right hand, she suddenly felt as if her mouth had forgotten everything, even Carum's kiss. "I look like our Mother Alta," she said.

"Water over stone," Petra reminded her.

Jenna smiled at that and the face in the water basin smiled back. Turning, Jenna said to Petra, "I am ready. I think."

Petra held out her hand. "Sisters," she said, "side by side."

THE HISTORY:

Folktales and myths about women warriors, either avatars of their goddesses or female incarnations of the godhead, abound in all the religions of the world. The Greeks, according to Herodotus, knew of such women who—he claimed—lived on the northern coast of Asia Minor in the city of Themiscyra. The man-hating Indian princess Malayavati was another such unnature, commanding like-minded females. In Brazil, the Makurap of the Upper Guaporé River told of a village of women even farther afield who kept all men at bay. And so forth. (For an extensive monograph on the subject, see J. R. R. Russ' "The Amazon Explosion," Pasden University Monograph Series #347.)

So it was not unusual for the folk of the Upper and Lower Dales to have conjured up a White Goddess, an Anna (which in the old tongue means "white" or "the white one," according to Doyle), a female hero. But their Amazon warrior differs in several important respects from the classic mythos.

For example, the Altite Anna was not worshipped as a mare or in any other way associated with horses, as her Continental and Eastern counterparts were. In fact, in the few snippets of narrative which have been positively identified as part of the ancient Anna Cycle (see Dr. Temple's chapter on these stories in Alta-Natives: "Tongue-tied in the Dales"), the Anna is seen as afraid of horses or at the very least puzzled by them. In one battle she mistakes a horse for a monster (". . . the two-headed demon of the foggee . . ." is a line from a modern ballad that scholars agree is a remnant of the Cycle). In another she falls off a cross-grained gray mare into a puddle at the feet of her human lover. The modern Anna songs found today in the Dales are not heroic at all, but rather mock-heroic or even antiheroic. In some cases they are downright humorous. (Cf., "Krick's Horn," "The Battle of Anna and the Catte," and "How the Warrior Anna Knocked Heads.")

Also, the Altite Anna was in no way a man-hater. A number of the ballads are love songs that detail her rather lusty affairs with an amazing variety of men, most notably (and anachronistically) King Langbrow. There is one homeoerotic song, a rather wistful melody, about her best friend, Margaret, dying of love for her as the Anna strides off into battle once again.

It is safe to say, though, that the Anna of the Dales was not a historic personage but merely a popular mythic figure. That such a one as Anna or Jenna or Jo-hanna ever actually lived and fought pitched battles for the sake of her warrior sisters (as Magon in his sentimental essay "Anna of a Thousand Years," Nature and History, Vol. 41, would have it) is patent nonsense. It is true that the word history contains the word story, but every good scholar knows better than to confuse the two. We must, therefore, look deeper than the mere rota of events for the real meaning of the Anna of the Dales. We must probe into the very psyche of the Isles before we can begin to understand what needs brought forth a folk creature of such staying power as the Amazonian White Goddess during the time of the brutal and devastating Gender Wars.

THE STORY:

There was a tension throughout dinner that would not dissipate. Even the chatter of the children did nothing to dispel the dark mood. Everyone knew that Jenna, Pynt, and the girl Petra had much to tell. But the word from Mother Alta's room had been to wait. Wait until the meal was over and the children put to bed; wait until the moon rose to bring forth the dark sisters. They had heard tantalizing pieces of the story from the children themselves, and from Amalda.

Donya and her kitcheners had done their best. Slabs of venison made tender by beating, and early spring salads freshened with the sharp wines Donya had laid down from the year before, were at every place. But the meat and the crisp vegetables and the saucy wine did not perform their usual magic. The tension in the dining hall was as palpable as the mist around the Sea of Bells. And the women were as silent as if a Fog Demon had, indeed, stoppered their mouths.

Jenna and Petra sat at a small side table apart from the others. Jenna pushed the food around the plate the way a cat plays with its catch. Petra did not even bother trying, keeping her hands in her lap and silently watching Jenna's display of nerves.

At the three long tables where the rest of the women gathered, only the occasional *clink-clank* of foodsticks on platters marked the passage of time.

But at last the meal was over and Donya, disgusted at how little had been eaten, directed her girls to clear the places, muttering about the waste of food, saying, *"It is better to eat when the food is before you than to be hungry because the food is behind you,"* a piece of folk wisdom she had picked up from one of the men in the Dales. She used it all the time and no one paid her any mind.

Mother Alta had chosen to eat in her room, something she often did before a meeting. She knew how to use the tension to her own advantage; when to enter the dining hall and when to leave it. This time she timed her entrance so that the moon was just rising and the dark sisters slowly coming into view.

Standing in the doorway, side by side with her own dark twin, hair plaited with spring flowers, Mother Alta raised her hands in a blessing. Her sister did the same. The motion was sharp and commanding and all the women in the hall bowed their heads, save Jenna.

She stared into the priestess' face and was just opening her mouth to speak when Skada appeared by her side, the misty edges of her outline quickly brought into focus by the moon and the fluttering torches.

The look in Mother Alta's eyes was one of complete surprise. Jenna realized that Amalda—whatever else she had told Mother Alta—had left Skada out of her telling. Jenna smiled and her dark sister smiled, too.

The priestess' eyes slid away from Jenna's and she recited the blessing in a voice made wooden by surprise. "Great Alta, who holds us . . ."

The hall echoed with the response. "In thy care."

"Great Alta, who enfolds us . . ."

"In thy bounteous hair."

"Great Alta, who knows us . . ."

"As thy only kin."

"Great Alta, who shows us . . ." And for the first time the priestess' voice faltered.

But only Jenna seemed to notice, for the women countered immediately with the proper response: "How to call the twin."

Recovering, Mother Alta finished the blessing emphatically: "Great Alta, give us grace."

The answer resonated through the hall. "Great Alta, give us grace." Then the women looked up, anticipation shining in their faces.

Only a few of them noticed Skada at first, but soon the room was abuzz with it. Mother Alta moved in a slow, stately manner toward her great chair by the fire, as if the appearance of an unnamed sister were of no consequence. Her own sister enthroned herself in a slightly smaller chair by her side. They summoned the women from the tables to them with a slight wave of hands.

Pushing the benches away, the women of Selden gathered in

a semicircle by the hearth. Some sat on the floor. Others, like Marna and Zo, leaned against the fireplace stones. Jenna led Petra to a place directly opposite the priestess' chair, with Skada trailing slightly behind. They waited for Mother Alta to speak.

There was another slight flurry of excitement when Pynt came into the hall, escorted by Kadreen. She leaned heavily on the infirmarer's arm, but walked upright. When she saw Jenna and Skada, she winked at them. Then Kadreen led her to the fire and Amalda and Sammor brought over a chair with a deep cushion for her, which Pynt sank into gratefully.

For a moment after that the only sound was the crackling of the fire and a *thud-pop-pop-pop* as a half-consumed log slipped down into the blaze. Jenna strained to make out the sighing breaths around her. Looking about the half circle, at all the dear, familiar faces, she suddenly saw the features of the slaughtered sisters of Nill's Hame slip over them like masks. Like the hound's helm over the engorged face of the dead Kingsman. Reaching out, her hand found Skada's and she laced her fingers through her sister's. Only that touch kept her from tears.

Mother Alta began speaking in a low voice. "It has been two weeks since our young sisters, our four missioners, went forth. And in that time such events have transpired that will shake the foundations of our cozy Hame. But it is not my story to tell. It must be told by those who know it best: Jo-an-enna and Marga and Petra of Nill's Hame." She smiled her serpent smile, and though she looked as if she tried to put some warmth in it, Jenna saw none there.

So Jenna began the story, starting at the confluence of the two rivers where she and Selinda, Alna and Pynt, had said their good-byes. She spoke movingly of her feelings as she had walked away from them, and how the woods had seemed more beautiful because of their parting. When she got to the section of the story where Pynt had come after her, Pynt herself interrupted the account.

"I disobeyed the Mother's wishes," Pynt said. "I saw myself as dark sister to Jenna's light. You remember—I was always called her shadow. And so I became it in truth. I could not let her go on without me. I thought what Mother Alta had asked was too great a sacrifice. So I followed Jenna. If there is any fault in all of this, it is mine alone."

Mother Alta smiled broadly for the first time, and Jenna saw wolfish teeth.

By her left side, Petra muttered, *"No blame, no shame."*

As if Petra's comment spurred her on, Jenna took over the narrative again. She told them of the fog and the strange, low calling that had turned out to be the Hound hunting Carum. Deliberately, she did not describe Carum in any detail beyond the fact that he was a prince. If anyone noticed her omission, the sister did not say. But Pynt looked down at her lap during that part of the recitation, with a silly, knowing grin.

When Jenna got to the telling of Barnoo's death, she hesitated, and it was Pynt who entered the story again. Swiftly, as swiftly as a knife across a throat, and plainly she told it. Jenna stared up at the ceiling through that part, her hands remembering the feel of the sword and the awful sound it had made going into the man's neck. Then Pynt's voice got ragged and Jenna picked up the thread of story again at the burial of the Hound.

She introduced them to Armina and Darmina; she led them with the tale to the gates of Nill's Hame. As she spoke of the carvings, Petra interrupted.

"We were so proud of those gates," she said. "Oak and ash they were. And carved over a hundred years ago by . . . by . . ." She could not go on. Biting her lip, she folded her hands one around the other, the right gripping the left so tightly the knuckles went white.

Marna and Zo, who had been standing close by, their backs against the hearthstones, moved as one to her and enfolded her in their arms. It was the act of tenderness that undid Petra, and she began to cry in earnest. Her weeping made the warriors so uncomfortable, they did not know where to look. Though they did not speak to one another of it, most suddenly found themselves staring either at the high, ribbed ceiling or at the rushes on the floor. Mother Alta was still, unaccountably, smiling.

Jenna thought that if she continued the story, everyone would watch her and Petra might get control of her tears. So she quickly sketched out the buildings at Nill's Hame. Those who had visited the Hame on their own missioning nodded their heads at the memory. Then Jenna told them of the back stairs and described the six-fingered, blind priestess who ruled the Hame.

The rest of the tale tumbled out quickly: Pynt's wounding, the severed hand of the Ox, and the great leap into the Halla in which she and Carum almost drowned. She mentioned everything but Carum's kiss, though she brushed her fingers unthinkingly across her mouth when she told of their farewell before the walls of Bertram's Rest. Skada's hand, she noticed from the corner of her eye, seemed to linger on her own lips longer than was quite necessary.

And then she told them about her return to Nill's Hame and all she had found there. By the time she was done, even some of the warriors were weeping, and those who did not sat stone-faced or shook their heads slowly back and forth, as if by their denial they could make it not so.

Jenna stopped speaking at the moment in the story when she had brought the tiny Mother Alta, the last of them, down the stairs in her arms. A deep sigh ran around the room, but the priestess was not part of it. She leaned forward in her chair and her dark sister moved with her. "Tell me how you called your shadow forth, how one so young managed it. I understand this much: that you thought you had lost one shadow and needed another. But I need to know *how* you did it. For if you can do it, perhaps others can. It is a breach that must be repaired."

Jenna gasped. She had not thought of it that way—that having lost her dark Pynt, having lost Carum, she had needed a replacement. Was Skada only that? A poor substitute? But Skada's shoulder suddenly touched hers and she turned her head slightly, looking slantwise at her.

"Be careful," Skada whispered. "Or you will bruise yourself on that flinty heart."

Jenna nodded and Skada nodded back, a movement so slight no one could have noticed.

"I called and she answered," Jenna said to the priestess.

"I would have come sooner had she asked sooner," Skada added.

Then Jenna told of finding Pynt and the children in the hidden rooms and leading them away from the slaughterhouse, over the meadows, under the nose of the Old Hanging Man, and home.

Now dry-eyed, Petra spoke up. "Jo-an-enna has told you *what* has happened, but not *who* she is. My Mother Alta named her. Now your Mother must tell you the same."

Mother Alta turned her head by moving her entire body slowly, as if a mountain had turned. She stared angrily at the girl, but Petra stared back defiantly.

"What do you mean?" Donya asked Petra.

But Catrona turned to the priestess. "Tell us, Mother." There was a strange challenge in her voice.

"Tell us," the other women echoed.

Sensing she was losing control of them, Mother Alta leaned back slowly and held up her hands so that the blue goddess sign showed. Her sister followed suit, and their four palms flashed the powerful signal to quiet the room.

When she had their complete attention, she waited a beat longer, then began. "What young Petra means," she said, letting her voice linger on the word *young*, "is that there is a story about the Anna, the white avatar of the Goddess, that is still told in some of the more backward Hames."

Petra shook her head. "Nill's Hame was no backwater community. And the Anna is no story, Mother, as well you know. It is a prophecy." She took two steps into the semicircle, looked around at the women to gather in their attention, and began to recite the prophecy in that singsong voice priestesses affected for such things.

> *The babe as white as snow,*
> *A maiden tall shall grow,*
> *And ox and hound bow low,*
> *And bear and cat also.*
> *Holy, holy, holy.*

No one moved as Petra continued. "Was Jenna not a white babe now grown straight and tall? Have not both the Bull and the Hound already fallen to her?"

There was a low grunt of agreement from some of the women. Before they were fully quieted, Petra went on.

> *She shall bring forth the end,*
> *And sever friend from friend.*
> *The brothers all shall bend,*
> *And we begin again.*
> *Holy, holy, holy.*

"What is that verse?" Mother Alta asked. "I have never heard those five lines."

"Do you think I made them up?" asked Petra. "And me so young?"

The women's low mutterings began again.

Petra leaned toward the priestess and spoke as if to her alone, though her voice rang clearly in the room. "Never was there more of an ending than Nill's Hame, where sister from sister, mother from daughter, was severed. Surely Jenna was the harbinger of that end."

"I reject it!" Mother Alta roared above the women, who were now openly arguing. "I reject it utterly. I have asked for a sign from Great Alta and she has given me none. The heavens do not roar. The ground does not open up. All this was promised in the writings." She looked around the hall, her hands up, no longer signaling but pleading. "Did I not seek out the truth of it myself? It was I who, fourteen years ago, followed backward Selna and Marjo's trail. Yes, I, a priestess, who read the woodsign. In the town of Slipskin I found a farmer who spilled out his tale into my arms. This girl, this child you claim a wonder, was his, born from between his wife's dead thighs. Jo-an-enna killed her mother. Is that the act of an avatar of Alta? She killed the midwife as well. And she was the cause of her foster mother's death. Tell me, all you women who have born or fostered a child, is this the One you would follow?"

"Would you blame the infant for its mother's death? Would you shame the innocent? *No blame, no shame*—it is written in the *Book*," Petra said. But her voice, being still a child's, was weak compared with the full modulations of Mother Alta's.

The priestess stood, and her sister rose beside her. "Would I withhold from you such a miracle? Would I keep from you such a savior?" Seeing the women wavering, she pressed her advantage. "*Who is she?* I will tell you who she is. She is Jo-an-enna, a girl of this Hame. You watched when she spit pap from her baby mouth. You changed her soiled pants. You nursed her through rosy fever and dabbed at her dripping nose. She is your sister, your daughter, your friend, that is who she is. What more would you have her be?"

Jenna looked around slowly at the rolling sea of faces. She could not read what lay written there. Pulling into herself, she began the breathing chant and within a space of ten counts once again started to feel the strange lightening. Slipping the gross bonds of her body, she lifted above it to survey all who quarreled below. In that other state, all was silent and she could see each woman purely. Most clearly of all she could see herself. She wondered at the still, white center she found there. Her body was like the others, yet at the core there was a difference. Did that make her a savior, an avatar, the Anna? She did not know. But what seemed clear now was that Petra was right. Events would move forward whether she believed or not. She could be swept along, possibly drowned, like a child in the Halla. Or she could dig a channel to control the waters as the townsfolk of Selden had done with their flood. It was that simple.

She let herself slip back into her body and opened her eyes.

Moving into the center of the half circle, she raised her right hand. Skada did the same.

"Sisters," she began, her voice trembling, "Listen to me. *I am the Anna!* I am the Goddess' good right hand. I go to warn the Hames that the time of the endings, the time of the beginnings, is here. I am the Anna. Who goes with me?"

For a long moment there was silence and Jenna suddenly feared that the priestess had won and that she was cut off from all of them, now and forever.

Then Pynt said, "If I were fit, I would go with you, Anna. But my place is here, here helping with the children even as I heal."

"*I* will go with you, Anna," cried Petra, "for I know prophecy even though I do not know how to use a sword."

"And I," called out Catrona. "With my sister by my side." Her dark twin nodded.

"We will go, too," Amalda and Sammor said together.

Jenna looked at them and shook her head. "No, my fourth mothers. You must stay. Selden Hame needs to ready itself for what comes soon. The time of endings. Your arms are needed here. I will go with Petra and Catrona and, at the moon times, we shall have our dark sisters with us. We are messengers, after all, not a mob." Then she turned and spoke to the priestess. "We would go with your blessing, Mother, but we will go whether you give it or not."

Slumped against her chair, Mother Alta suddenly looked old. She waved her hand in a feeble sign that might have been a blessing. Her dark sister's motion was feebler still. Neither of them spoke.

"I know the way to most of the Hames," Catrona said. "And I know where there is a map."

"And I know all the words to be said," Petra added.

Jenna laughed. "What more can a savior want?"

"A sword would be helpful," Skada said. "And perhaps a sense of the absurd."

* * *

It took no more than an hour to arm and provision them, and Donya outdid herself with the parcels and packs. It was as if she were supplying an army, but they could not tell her no.

Skada whispered to Petra as they watched the food being packed, "Was it not strange that Mother Alta was unfamiliar with the second part of the prophecy?"

Petra smiled. "Not strange at all," she said. "I made it up. It is my one great trick. I was famous for reciting poems to order at Nill's Hame."

And then they were off on the road from the Hame into history, a road that glistened under the waning moon in a night lit by the flickering of a thousand thousand stars. As the five of them strode down the path, the women of Selden Hame cried out behind them in a long, wavering ululation that was part prayer, part dirge, and part farewell.

THE MYTH:

Then Great Alta set the queen of shadows and the queen of light onto the earth and commanded them to go forth.

"And you two shall wear my face," quoth Great Alta. "And you shall speak with my mouth. And you shall do my bidding for all time."

Where the one stepped, there sprang fire and the earth was scorched beneath her feet. Where the other stepped, there fell soothing rains and blossoms grew. So it was and so it will be. Blessed be.

Here Ends Book 1: *Sister Light, Sister Dark.*

THE MUSIC OF THE DALES

Prophecy

Lord Gorum

Plaintively

O where have you been all day, Go-rum, my son? The

bull, the bear___, the cat and the hound, (2.) I

Where have you been all day, my pret-ty one? And the

broth-ers have pull-ed me down.___

2. I've been far afoot, with my staff in my hand,
    The bull, the bear, the cat, and the hound,
    I have been out walking my dead father's land,
    And the brothers have pulled me down.

3. I looked in the mountains, I looked in the sea,
    The bull, the bear, the cat, and the hound,
    A-looking for someone a-looking for me,
    And the brothers have pulled me down.

4. What have ye for supper, Lord Gorum, my son?
    The bull, the bear, the cat, and the hound,
    What have ye for supper, my pretty young one?
    And the brothers have pulled me down.

5. I've nothing for supper and nothing to rise,
    The bull, the bear, the cat, and the hound,
    But fed on the look in my own true love's eyes,
    And the brothers have pulled me down.

6. What will ye leave to that true love, my son?
    The bull, the bear, the cat, and the hound.
    What will she leave you, my handsome young one?
    And the brothers have pulled me down.

7. My kingdom, my crown, my name, and my grave,
    The bull, the bear, the cat, and the hound,
    Her hair, her heart, her place in the cave,
    And the brothers have pulled me down.

Lullaby to the Cat's Babe

Liltingly

1. Hush, lit - tle moun - tain cat, Sleep in your den,
2. Sleep, lit - tle cat - kin, Per - chance you shall dream

I'll sing of your moth - er who cra - dled Fair Jen.
Of rab - bit and pheas - ant And trout in the stream.

I'll sing of your moth - er who cov - ered Jen's skin.
But Jen - na will dream of the dark and the light.

Flesh of your flesh did sweet Jen - na lie in.
Your moth - er will shel - ter her from the cold night.

The Ballad of White Jenna

With spirit

Out of the morn-ing, in-to the night, Thir-ty and three— rode off to the fight To put the dread-ed foe to flight Led by the hand of Jen-na.——

2. Thirty and three rode side by side,
   And by the moonlight fortified.
   "Fight on, my sisters," Jenna cried.
   "Fight for the Great White Alta."

3. The blood flowed swift, like good red wine,
   As sisters took the battle line.
   "This kingdom I will claim for mine
   And for the heart of Alta!"

4. Thirty and three rode out that day
   To hold the dreaded foe at bay,
   But never more they passed this way,
   Led by the hand of Jenna.

5. Yet still, some say, in darkest night,
   The sisters can be heard to fight
   And you will see a flash of white
   The long white braid of Jenna.

The Ballad of the Selden Babe

with great expression

Do not go down, ye maid - ens all who wear the gol - den gown, Do not go to the clear-ing___ at the edge of Sel - den town, For wick - ed are___ the men who wait to bring young maid - ens down.

rit. span, And a good and long life span.___

2. A maiden went to Seldentown,
   A maid no more was she,
   Her hair hung loose about her neck,
   Her gown about her knee,
   A babe was slung upon her back,
   A bonny babe was he.

3. She went into the clearing wild,
   She went too far from town,
   A man came up behind her
   And he cut her neck around,
   A man came up behind her
   And he pushed that fair maid down.

4. "And will ye have your way wi' me,
   Or will ye cut me dead,
   Or do ye hope to take from me
   My long-lost maidenhead?
   Why have ye brought me far from town
   Upon this grass-green bed?"

5. He never spoke a single word,
   Nor gave to her his name,
   Nor whence and where his parentage,
   Nor from which town he came,
   He only thought to bring her low
   And heap her high with shame.

6. But as he set about his plan,
   And went about his work,
   The babe upon the maiden's back
   Had touched her hidden dirk,
   And from its sheath had taken it
   All in the clearing's mirk.

7. And one and two, the tiny hands
   Did fell the evil man,
   Who all upon his mother had
   Commenced the wicked plan.
   God grant us all such bonny babes
   And a good and long life span.

Alta's Song

With great feeling

I am a babe, an on-ly babe, Fire___ and wa-ter and all___, Who in my moth-er's womb was made,

[1,2,4: take; 3,5: save]

Great Al - ta { take___ / save___ } my soul.___

2. But from that mother I was torn,
   Fire and water and all,
   And to a hillside I was borne,
   Great Alta take my soul.

3. And on that hillside was I laid,
   Fire and water and all,
   And taken up all by a maid,
   Great Alta save my soul.

4. And one and two and three we rode,
   Fire and water and all,
   Till others took the heavy load,
   Great Alta take my soul.

5. Let all good women hark to me,
   Fire and water and all,
   For fostering shall set thee free,
   Great Alta save my soul.

Come Ye Women

Jauntily

1. O come ye wom-en of the Isles, And lis-ten to my song,
2. But wom-en we be from our birth And will be till we die,

For if ye be but thir-teen years ye not be wom-en
Our count is made so dif-f'rent-ly To give the men that

long.— And if ye be—three score and ten, No long-er
lie.— O come, ye wom-en of the Isles, And lis-ten

wom-en be, Or so say all the mer-ry men Who
to my song, For we be wom-en all through life, Where

count so cru-el-ly, Who count so cru-el-ly.—
life and love are long, Where life and love are long.—